DARK TITAN UNIVERSE SAGA
SPIN-OFFS OMNIBUS
VOLUME 1

Dark Titan Universe Spin-Offs Omnibus: Volume 1 is a work of fiction. References to real people, events, establishments, organizations, or locales are intended only to provide the sense of authenticity and are use fictitiously. All other characters, all incidents, dialogue are drawn from the author's imagination and are not to be seen as real.

Copyright © 2018, 2020, 2021 by Ty'Ron W. C. Robinson II. All rights reserved.

In a Glass of Dawn: The Casebook of Travis Vail, Maveth: Bloodsport, The Curse of The Mutant-Thing, Trail of Vengeance, and War of The Thunder Gods are available in hardcover, paperback, and eBook.

Published by Dark Titan Publishing. A division of Dark Titan Entertainment.

Dark Titan Universe is a branch of Dark Titan Entertainment.

Paperback ISBN: 979-8-9856344-1-9
eBook ISBN: 979-8-9856344-2-6

darktitanentertainment.com

WORKS BY TY'RON W. C. ROBINSON II

BOOKS/SHORT STORIES

DARK TITAN UNIVERSE SAGA

MAIN SERIES
Dark Titan Knights
The Resistance Protocol
Tales of the Scattered
Tales of the Numinous
Day of Octagon Crossbreed
Heaven's Called
The Oranos Imperative
Underworld

SPIN-OFFS
In A Glass of Dawn: The Casebook of Travis Vail
Maveth: Bloodsport
The Curse of The Mutant-Thing
Trail of Vengeance
War of The Thunder Gods

ONE-SHOTS
Maveth, The Death-Bringer
Mystery of The Mutant-Thing
Shade & Switchblade
Retribution of Cain
The Mythologists
Ambush Bot
Kang-Zhu
Cheeseburger Man
Tessa Balthazar
Elite 5
Peacekeeper

COLLECTIONS
Dark Titan Omnibus: Volume 1
Dark Titan Omnibus: Volume 2
Dark Titan One-Shot Collection
Dark Titan One-Shot Collection II
Dark Titan Universe Saga Spin-offs Omnibus: Volume 1

THE HAUNTED CITY SAGA
The Legendary Warslinger: The Haunted City I
Battle of Astolat: A Haunted City Prequel (KOBO Exclusive)
Redemption of the Lost: The Haunted City II
Helper's Hand: A Haunted City One-Shot

SYMBOLUM VENATORES
Symbolum Venatores: The Gabriel Kane Collection
Hod: A Symbolum Venatores Book
Symbolum Venatores: War of The Two Kingdoms
Symbolum Venatores: Elrad's Chronicles

EVERWAR UNIVERSE
EverWar Universe: Knights & Lords

PRODIGIOUS WORLDS
Mark Porter of Argoron
Raiders of Vanok
Praxus of Lithonia

FRIGHTENED! SERIES
Frightened!: The Beginning

INSTINCTS SERIES
Lost in Shadows: Remastered
Instincts: Point Hope

DARK TITAN'S THE DEAD DAYS
Accounts of The Dead Days

OTHER BOOKS
The Book of The Elect
The Extended Age Omnibus
The Horde
The Eleventh Hour: A Chevah Mythos Story
The Supreme Pursuer: Darkness of the Hunt
Massacre in the Dusk
Venture into Horror: Tales of the Supernatural
The Universe of Realms Omnibus: Book 1
The Universe of Realms Omnibus: Book 2

THE DARK TITAN AUDIO EXPERIENCE
PODCAST *Season 1: Introductions*
Season 2: In a Glass of Dawn
Season 2.5: Accounts of The Dead Days
Season 3: Battle For Astolat
Season 4: Hallow Sword: Cursed

SPIN-OFFS OMNIBUS

DARK TITAN UNIVERSE SAGA

VOLUME 1

TY'RON W. C. ROBINSON II

CONTENTS

IN A GLASS OF DAWN: THE CASEBOOK OF TRAVIS VAIL
1

DARK TITAN UNIVERSE ONE-SHOT: MAVETH, THE DEATH-BRINGER
116

MAVETH: BLOODSPORT
126

DARK TITAN UNIVERSE ONE-SHOT: MYSTERY OF THE MUTANT-THING
163

THE CURSE OF THE MUTANT-THING
171

THE LONE OUTLAW: TARGETED
215

TRAIL OF VENGEANCE
219

THEUS: NOLDAR S TRICKERY
263

WAR OF THE THUNDER GODS
277

IN A GLASS OF DAWN: THE CASEBOOK OF TRAVIS VAIL

THE TALE OF THE HAUNTING

Occult Detective Travis Vail set out on his investigation to a mansion which is documented to be a very haunted location. Wearing his black coat with slacks, Vail arrives in the city of Hartford, Connecticut, where the mansion is located on the outskirts of the city. Vail gets to the mansion, known as the Rosebane Mansion. Outside of the mansion is its current owner, Lloyd Sharp. Sharp extends his hand as a greeting to Vail.

"Welcome to Rosebane Mansion, Mr. Vail." Sharp said.

Vail shook his hand in greet and allowed Sharp to invite him inside the mansion.

Within the mansion's interior is a beautiful structure for a century-year-old building. The walls are made of granite marble with historical paintings and picture frames across. The flooring was made of hardwood. Vail quickly examines the mansion's interior.

"What happened here that caused the haunting?" Vail said.

"The former residents were unaware of what was buried here centuries ago." Sharp said. "One day, their son was digging in the backyard and discovered a skeleton with Indian artifacts."

"An Indian burial ground, you say.' Vail said.

"Of course." Sharp said. "Once the parents discovered it, they had it taken away, which later became a regret to them as the poltergeist activities began to occur."

"Truly a mistake they made.' Vail said. "So, I've been brought here to investigate these haunting?"

Sharp brought Vail into the bedroom section of the mansion upper floors. Inside were a total of six rooms, the master bedroom belonged to the parents, another to their son, and four for guests. Vail walked through every bedroom, scavenging the entire location for anything resourceful. Sharp watched him as he went through every room like a focused individual. After Vail completed his search through the rooms. Walking through a corridor, Sharp took Vail out to the backyard. Once outside, Sharp pointed to the now buried sport of where the Indian burial was originally located. Vail walked over to the spot and rubbed the dirt on the ground. He raised his head, looking around the backyard. He turned to Sharp and thanked him for showing him the areas of the mansion,

"I take it you're ready to do your work.' Sharp said.

"Yes I am." Vail said.

Vail went to the nearest museum and did research on the mansion and the land. his hotel room and began setting up his equipment. From holy water to crosses to a book that is encrypted with proper ways to end curses or send spirits back into their world. After he left the room. He went back to the mansion to begin his investigation upon its encounters.

Later that night, Vail returned to the mansion, alone. He found the key to the front door underneath the movable block by the door. He entered the mansion and shut the door. No lights were on throughout the mansion, only the moonlight. Vail walked around the mansion, pulling out a book that contained previous reports and encounters inside the mansion.

"Very well." He said. "You have me here all alone. So, I would demand that you reveal yourself to me or at least give me a sign of your presence to start with."

The mansion is silent to the point where if a pen would fall onto the wooden floor, it would make a louder sound. Vail slowly walked through the corridor of the mansion, surrounded by frames of the previous owners of the mansion and the land of which it lies upon. He looked at the frames and walked over to one that resembled a English settler. Once he stopped to look, a banging sound was heard down the corridor. Vail paused.

"I see you're trying to get my attention."

He walked down to the end of the corridor. Once at the end, he sees nothing in sight. He heard another banging sound that came from the bedroom areas.

"I want to speak with the spirit of the burial ground." He said. "I know you're here inside this mansion with me."

Vail continued down the corridor as one of the picture frames instantly flew off the wall and down the other end of the corridor. Vail looked and ran after it. He reached the other end of the corridor and the frame was nowhere in sight. He turned back around walking upstairs toward the bedrooms. He heard a distant moan near the rooms.

"You're getting better at this."

The lamp on the side of the bed levitated and slammed itself against the wall. Vail walked into the bedroom, which was a guest room.

"Very violent I noticed."

"*Get Out.*"

The words caught Vail's attention as he heard the distinctive voice coming from the master bedroom nearby. He walked into the room and it was quiet, everything is the same as it was earlier in the day. Vail reached into his coat pocket and pulled out a cleansing artifact that he received during his research into Indian burial grounds.

"I suggest you prepare to see the other side."

Vail began blessing the entire mansion with the cleansing. As he walked through the mansion saying the blessing, more sounds of banging occurred along with moans and distant yelling. Vail ignored the sounds and decided to head into the backyard.

As Vail walked outside in the backyard, he noticed the wind beginning to blow. He continued the cleansing as he walked near the burial ground. Vail paused for a second as he seen what appeared to be fire coming from the burial ground. Vail kneeled in front of the burial and held the cleansing over it, blessing it once more. As he spoke louder while blessing, he looked up and seen an apparition of what appeared to be a Indian man, wearing Native American wardrobe. The Indian apparition stared at Vail, who did the same.

"I see you as you can see me." Vail said to the apparition. "It's time you leave this place and enter the afterlife."

The wind slowly calmed, and the fire vanished along with the apparition. Vail walked back into the mansion and he felt a sense of calmness. Vail walked through the mansion for a final time to double check. Every room he went into he felt a sense of calmness and peace.

Later in the morning, Sharp returned to the mansion as Vail began to leave. Vail walked up to Sharp as he wanted to know what he had encountered and experienced.

"What did you come across?"

"I came across a spirit that did not want to leave." Vail said. "However, he had no choice. He had his time in the world of the living, its time he entered the world of the dead."

"So, is the place safer to live in?"

Vail paused and looked back at the mansion.

"As long as they don't bother with the burial ground or bring in any type of spiritual items that may invoke a spirit, they should be just fine."

"Sharp extended his hand toward Vail.

"I thank you for coming and solving this problem." "Believe me, we really needed it."

"I just do what I must." Vail said.

Vail walked toward his vehicle that resembled a 1970s car. He drives away as the sun started to rise above the location of the mansion.

PRAYERS FOR THE DEAD

Occult detective and paranormal investigator Travis Vail has been called in to investigate a series of haunting events that have plagued an old-century church. The owners of the church have told Vail that it was once used as a place for satanic rituals by Satanists. Vail understands the power that Satanists tamper with and what they can release if not careful. Along with Vail on this investigation is Dr. Galen Donovan, a middle-aged African American who's well-practiced in the fields of exorcism and paranormal investigation.

Dr. Donovan arrived at the abandoned church to speak with the current priest. As they talked and discussed the series of haunting that have taken place, Vail entered the church, walking inside calmly while observing the interior. Dr. Donovan stood up from his seat and walked toward Vail.

"Detective Travis Vail, it's an honor to meet you." Donovan said.

"Same here, Doctor." Vail replied. "I hear you're going to be investigating the church with me."

"I am. I feel it's better to do mainly because of my history with exorcisms."

"Just in case I end up being partially possessed supposedly, you'll find a way to help me." Vail said.

"Exactly."

Vail nodded.

"Fair enough then."

Vail walked over to the priest, greeting one another as they shook hands. The priest escorted Vail and Donovan throughout the church.

Walking through the church, Vail noticed some distinctive red smears on the walls. He asked the priest about them. The priest had responded by saying those markings are the previous locations where pentagrams were once painted. The smears were done by wiping them off the walls. Donovan shook his head, rubbing his chin.

"They really chose a place like this to do their worshipping." Donovan questioned.

"Tell me, these folks have to be led by someone." Vail said. "Any idea as to where their leader could've gone?"

"Their leader hasn't been seen for some time." The priest responded. "We hope to find him.

"Surely you will."

The Priest continued to walk them through the church. Vail looked at the site and studied every room inside. Donovan thanked the Priest for showing them around and for allowing them to investigate the haunting. After saying thanks, Vail traveled to the nearest museum to do some extra research concerning Satanism and the Occult. Once he had studied the arts of both. He discovered that the cult's leader might be lurking around the surrounding land of the church.

Upon returning to the church, with Donovan at his side, the sun started to set as they enter the church. The Priest said a prayer for them before he left. Vail and Donovan looked around the silent church, walking through the chapel and passing through the pews. Donovan told Vail to be very careful and to watch his surroundings. Vail turned to him, looking prepared.

"I did some research of my own to prepare for this night."

"Hope you put it to good use."

"I will."

Vail looked ahead of him and seen something glowing underneath some of the pews. Vail looked closer, squinting his eyes and what he seen were two red eyes in the distance. He ran after it, Donovan startled and followed. Vail ran through the aisle between the pews, chasing the red eyes. Vail stopped at the podium, not seeing the eyes anywhere. Donovan caught up to him, looking around as well.

"What did you see?"

"Two red eyes." Vail said. "Very distinctive."

"They're here now."

Vail walked down the left hall of the chapel, passing through the other offices. As Donovan followed, he heard a distinct voice in the distance of the hall that sounded like a woman calling him.

"I just heard a voice."

"Did it sound like a woman or a child?"

"It was a woman's voice. She was calling to me."

"I'm sure you're aware not to follow that voice. Could be a demon mimicking a woman to lure you into a trap."

"Of course."

Vail heard the same female voice coming from the end of the hall. He is tempted to follow due to its high pitch sound. Spotting the two red eyes again with a laughing sound. He chases after it again. Donovan is quickly able to follow Vail this second time.

Entering another room that appears to be a lobby area, Vail stopped Donovan as they both saw the full apparition of a demonic entity. It appeared as a female, but Vail noticed the horns coming from its head, only to be seen by its shadow against the stone wall.

Donovan pulled out a cross at aimed it at the demon. It slowly backed up against the wall and started to laugh. Once, Donovan took a few steps back, the demon vanished. Vail turned to Donovan, noticing that the cross barely worked. Vail took out a bottle of holy water. He also took out his small notepad, re-reading what he had wrote down in the museum regarding demons.

They continued to walk through the church with only six hours left before sunrise. Getting no responses of any kind. They stumbled upon a red pentagram painted on the wooden floor. Vail glances more closely at the symbol and turned to Donovan.

"It's still wet and its blood."

Donovan kneeled, looking at the symbol. He told Vail that the blood is indeed what he feared, human blood. He took a sample of the blood for further testing. Vail put his hand over the symbol. He felt the sense of heat coming from it, intense heat.

"Whoever put this here knows what they were doing and have summoned up something."

"What could they have possibly summoned? More demons? More malevolent entities?"

Vail slowly looked around him and Donovan and glanced at the pentagram.

"One thing. You would think the person who placed this here would still be inside this church."

"Certainly."

They suddenly hear footsteps behind them in the distance. From the sound, they appear to be coming closer. Vail and Donovan slowly turned around as the steps became loud enough for the echoes to become silent. As they turn, they see a man wearing a black trench coat with all black clothing. The man has long wavy black hair.

"Who are you, fellow?" Vail asked.

"Vernon Lance."

Donovan looked at Lance and started to take a few steps toward him. Pointing at him with a question in mind.

"I get the sense that you're responsible for the pentagram on the floor."

"Indeed I am. I'm the cult's Priest."

"Using human blood! What kind of man does such a thing?"

"A greater kind. One needs the blood of a human to gain knowledge of the hidden power that surrounds us all."

"He's the one responsible for all of this. The demonic haunting, the previous pentagrams that covered the interior of this church."

"I understand that average people such as yourselves couldn't fully understand to have taken this course to bring about the next civilization."

Donovan stared.

"Quickly, Vail!"

Vail quickly pulled out his notepad, setting up to recite a ritual to Lance. Donovan took out a bottle of holy water, preparing to toss it at Lance. Lance looked unworried about his current circumstance.

"I don't know why you're preparing to attack me. I'm only human with demonic intellect."

"We're not going to attack you, we're condemning you." Vail said.

"You're ready?' Donovan said.

"I am."

Vail began to recite the pagan ritual as he stared into Lance's piercing green eyes with Donovan preparing to toss the holy water into Lance's face. Lance stood his ground with his arms standing upward, open for Vail and Donovan's attacks. Lance smiled at Vail and Donovan.

"It's really taking a while for you two to finish your condemning."

"Shut your mouth!" Vail said.

Donovan glanced at Vail, knowing Lance's distraction is causing Vail's ritual to cease working.

"Vail, his distraction is ceasing the ritual."

"That can't be possible." Vail remarked.

Lance grinned.

"Anything is possible in this universe to be maneuvered. Besides, I have to say it again, I am human with demonic intellect."

"What can we do now?" Vail said to Donovan.

Lance quickly raised his arm above his head, covering his face from the light coming through the window. Vail and Donovan notice Lance's strange behavior and turn around, seeing the sun rise and its light causing Lance to hide. Vail turned around and Lance has disappeared. Donovan notices burn marks on the ground where Lance was previously standing. The marks are still burning as if Lance was pulled into the ground by an unknown force of energy.

An hour later, the priest returned to the church, seeing Vail and Donovan standing and waiting in the chapel, sitting on the back pews. The priest walked up to them both, shaking their hands.

"Appears you two have had quite an investigation."

"We did."

Vail pulled out his notepad, revealing that he had wrote down Lance's name and description. He showed the priest as he told him about their investigation and how they later ran into Lance. Vail also tells the priest that Lance suddenly vanished as the sun rose and its light shined through into the room. The priest thanked them for their investigation of the church.

As they walked off, Donovan told the priest that they will have someone to come over and clean the pentagram off the floor and give a cleansing of the room to avoid any contact with demonic entities and to close to possible portal that may lie inside the room.

Vail walked to his car as Donovan approached him.

"It was a pleasure to work with you, Travis Vail."

"Likewise, here, Doctor. Hopefully we can work together again."

"I'm highly sure we will."

They shook hands as Vail gets into his car and drives off the location and down the road. Donovan looked around the surrounding areas of the church to find any further evidence of Lance's disappearance. Donovan discovers a track of burn marks within the grass. He followed the tracks as they lead him to an open field. Within the field, Donovan noticed a marking on the ground. The marking was an enlarged pentagram carved into the field that was large enough for a small home to fit in.

A LOST GIRL

In the suburbs of Chesterfield, New Hampshire, Cooper and Janice Lawrence have contacted Travis Vail to investigate mysterious behavior of their nine-year old daughter, Carrie Lawrence. According to the parents, Carrie had been participating in some unusual behavior, talking and playing with an imaginary friend whom she calls Leta. Within a few days, Carrie began to act a certain behavior that appeared to be abnormal to her parents, speaking in an unknown tongue and drawing art that seemed to have an infatuation with death and fire.

Vail arrived at the suburb home of the Lawrence family. He walked toward the door and knocked three times. Cooper opened the door and greeted Vail, allowing him to enter his home. When Vail walked inside the home, he immediately felt a negative presence. He looked around the home's first room, which was a living room, next to a kitchen. Sitting on the couch in the living room watching TV is Carrie.
"Carrie, meet Mr. Vail." Janice said.
Carrie turned and looked at Vail. She stared at him for quite a bit before turning back toward the TV. Vail turned to Cooper and Janice. He asked them about Carrie's behavior when she began to speak about an imaginary friend. Janice told him that it stared when Carrie went outside to play with some neighbors before she saw a young girl sitting by a tree, who she claimed to be Leta. Vail told them that he will investigate their home later that night to find evidence of Carrie's friend.
Vail returned to their home and began his investigation. Upon finding

no source that could trace to Carrie's imaginary friend. He started to doubt that he would find anything related to Leta. Though, Vail walked into the backyard to the site where Carrie came into contact with Leta. Vail noticed some form of objects buried in the dirt by the tree. What Vail found was a locket necklace. Inside the locket was a photo of a young girl with the name Leta under the photo. Vail took the locket and left the home, stating that more research had to be done.

The next day, Vail meets with Raynard Brown, a historian. Raynard greets Vail as he pulls out the locket and showed the picture. Raynard looked at the photo.

"I would like to see if you could tell me what century this photo was taken in?"

"Appears it dates to the late 19th century."

"The late 1800s you say."

"Indeed. Tell me, what about this picture intrigues you, Mr. Vail?"

"I'm currently on an investigation about a young girl's imaginary friend. This locket was buried by a tree where the girl first met the imaginary friend."

"So, I take it, you believe this young girl on the photo is the imaginary friend?"

"That's my current guess. Even though, when I walked into the home, I felt a negative presence that seemed beyond human."

"It is possible that a demon could have taken the form of this "*Leta*" and is using it to deceive and control the young girl."

Raynard handed the locket back to Vail, who placed it inside his coat pocket.

"I'm heading back over there immediately to do another form of test."

"Wish you luck on this one."

"Thanks, but I'm not an actual believer in luck."

Vail left the building, returning to the suburb home of the Lawrence Family.

Vail returned to the home, he sat with Cooper and Janice to speak with them about Carrie. Janice request for Carrie to sit in her room while they talk with Vail. Carrie walked into her room and closed the door.

Cooper turned to Vail.

"So, what have you discovered so far?"

"I found this buried in your backyard." Vail said, pulling out the locket from his coat pocket.

Vail handed the locket to them. Cooper opened it and seen the picture of a little girl. Janice placed her hand over her mouth as she saw the name "Leta" beneath the picture. Cooper pointed.

"That's the name which Carrie told us. That's the name of her friend."

"So, you're telling us this is who Carrie's been talking with?" asked Janice with fear in her voice.

"It's a possible theory. Not sure so far since I would like to speak with Carrie, if you don't mind."

"Sure."

Janice called out Carrie to sit with them. Carrie sat between her parents as she stared at Vail. Looking him in the eyes. Vail could feel the heavy presence from her.

"Carrie, I would like to ask you about your friend, Leta."

"She doesn't like you."

"How can you tell?"

"She told me that you're here to get rid of her. She says you won't be able to because we're friends."

"I know you're just a child, you shouldn't play around with things you can't comprehend."

"I understand enough, thanks to Leta."

Janice turned to Cooper, frightened at her daughter's words toward Vail. Cooper looked at his daughter, worried about her well-being.

"Honey, what has Leta told you?"

"Leta told me that we will be friends forever and no one can breakup our friendship. Not even this man here."

"Sweetie, this man is here to help you." Janice told her daughter.

"This man is here to ruin my friendship with Leta and I won't let him."

"Carrie, me and your mother have decided that you cannot be friends with Leta anymore."

"Leta is my friend and we will always be together. Whether any of you like it or not."

Vail looked into Carrie's eyes and noticed a slight change. Her eyes had shifted solid black for a quick second. He warned Cooper and Janice of this change and told them to stay guard of what could possibly happen.

"Carrie, where is Leta at this moment?"

"She's here with us."

Vail stood up and looked around the room, Cooper and Janice looked around, but saw nothing. They looked at their daughter with fear and confusion, not understanding what is happening to her.

"What is she doing?"

"She's plotting to kill you silly." Carrie said with a smile.

Carrie giggled as objects in the room began to levitate and throw themselves at Vail. He ducked the thrown objects that came his way. He yells to Cooper and Janice to take Carrie out of the house. They take Carrie and leave the home in a hurry. Vail is left inside the house by himself, seeing the objects in the room levitating and moving around with no natural explanation. Vail knew it was Leta's doings.

"Leta, I know it's you. If you wanted a fight, you have one with me."

The objects ceased moving and the room quickly turned silent. Vail slowly walked through the house, with a ritual notebook in his hands, equipped with a metal cross.

"Where are you, Leta? I know you're still inside this house."

Vail heard a set of footsteps coming from behind him. The footsteps become louder as Vail stood his guard. He turned to see what could be creating the footsteps and when he turned around, he sees Carrie's room and coming from the room is a young girl, the same girl from the photo. She is Leta.

"So, you're Leta."

"I am. Who are you supposed to be?"

"I'm Travis Vail, occult detective. My job is to find and solve cases that involve the paranormal, such as you."

"There's no reason for you to have ever come here. We were doing just fine before you came into our lives."

"First off, you don't have a life anymore. You're dead. Secondly, you're turning a young girl into a monster. Her parents are scared to death of their daughter because of your influence."

"Her parents are a thing of the past. Carrie is the future and I'm guiding her in the right direction."

"You're not guiding her in any direction but the paths of pain and death. You don't belong in this world anymore, Leta."

"What gives you the right to say so?"

"Because it's my purpose."

Vail took out the cross and held it toward Leta. She slowly backed away from Vail, her hands up, covering her face and screaming at him to drop the cross.

"I'm not dropping it." Vail stated.

Leta looked at Vail and smiled. She waived her hand toward the cross and it melted in Vail's hands. Turning into liquid ash. Vail stepped back, looking down at the remains of the cross.

"You know that stuff doesn't work on us." Leta smirked.

Vail had realized Leta isn't an ordinary ghost who's trapped on Earth. She is the negative energy that he felt, and he now knows she's a demonic entity posing as the young girl in the picture.

"What are you going to do, Spirit-Seeker?" Leta inquired. "Show me what you have to offer."

"It's time for you to go, little demon."

"You have no understanding. I'm not going anywhere!"

Leta raised her hand, causing a wave of energy to hit Vail. The wave was powerful enough to pick Vail off the ground and knocking him into a wall. He looked up and doesn't see Leta anywhere.

"This girl I tell you." Vail muttered to himself as he stood up.

Cooper and Janice walked back into the house with Carrie. Entering, they see the living room covered with shattered frames, vases, and other objects on the ground. Vail walked back into the room, seeing Cooper, Janice, and Carrie.

"Are you alright?" Janice said.

"I'm alright. Why did you come back inside?"

"We heard noises going on and we wanted to see what was happening." Cooper said.

"What did you find?" Janice asked.

"For starters, I seen your daughter's imaginary friend. She's a tough one to deal with."

"You're telling us that Carrie's friend isn't imaginary, but real."

"That's what I'm telling you. She wants the two of you to stay out of her way. She said she's influencing Carrie for the future."

"Influencing her? There's nothing wrong with our daughter."

"I thoroughly believe that your daughter is mildly possessed by Leta. That would explain the shifting eyes and her friend coming from her room"

"Why do we have to go through this." Janice stammered.

"Lot of people have these problems in a lot of different ways. I'm just here to help out."

Janice grabbed Vail's hand, looking him in the eyes with fear. Vail could feel her fear.

"You have to save our daughter. You must."

Vail nodded. Cocked his head with a nod and slight chuckle.

"I have one more solution that can be done."

"Name it."

"I'll have to exorcize your home and your daughter."

Later at nightfall, Carrie is sitting down on the couch in between her parents. Vail walked into the room with holy water. He dabs his thumb into the water and created an insignia onto Carrie's forehead. She screamed as the first touch of water burned her. Her parents held her tightly during the burning sensation that she felt.

"That confirmed she is mildly possessed." Vail said. "Thought you should know that. For the best."

"What are you going to do next?" Cooper asked.

"Read a ritual that will lift the essence of Leta from your daughter and send her to the other side."

Vail took out his book of rituals and began reciting the ritual of lifting Leta's essence. The home was quiet and there weren't any sounds to be heard.

"I, Travis Vail, read from the book of rituals, I hereby declare a cleansing of this home and its inhabitants."

Carrie started to shake, as if she was losing control of her body. Her parents held her down as Vail continued to do the ritual.

"I hereby command the spirit of Leta to leave this home and its inhabitants."

Vail looked at Carrie as she screamed in pain. Janice's face covered with tears as she held her daughter down. Cooper held in his emotions. Carrie looked at Vail with intense anger, now knowing that it isn't Carrie.

"You'll never take me away from here!" Carrie said with a changed voice. A deep-pitched voice.

"We'll see about that." Vail replied.

Vail continued reciting as black smoke started to emit from the house and from Carrie into the air. Vail ran over to the door and opened it as the black smoke swiftly flew out of the house. Carrie stopped screaming and fell unconscious. Janice called out to her for a response. The smoke left the home and Carrie. Vail shut the door and approached the parents.

"There's nothing to worry about. She's fine."

"Thank you." Cooper said.

"Thank you so much." Janice beamed.

Vail prepared himself to leave the home and was getting himself ready. Before he left, he was stopped by Janice, who hugged him for his help. Cooper stood behind Janice, smiling.

"Thank you again."

"It's my job to help."

"If I may ask, where did the spirit go?" Cooper inquired.

"Leta went to a place that she will feel comfortable, I hope. In truth, she was just a lost girl looking for a way out."

Vail left the neighborhood and Carrie awoke inside her room with her parents over here, smiling.

"What happened, mommy?"

"It's a long story."

LOCKED FOR ETERNITY

Travis Vail has decided to investigate a century year-old prison. The prison is called Desdemona Penitentiary. Its inner structure is surrounded with over thirteen cell blocks across acres of land. There have been notable deaths throughout the prison and through its existence. From murders, to raping, to riots, and suicides, there is no doubt that there are entities that reside within the prison walls.

Vail arrived at the prison, which is located on the east coast of London. Colton Levi, a close friend of Vail's comes to the prison's entrance. He joined Vail for the investigation as they are greeted by the owner of the prison and its land, Robert Leonard. A man in his middle age.
"You've finally made it here, Mr. Vail"
"I'm honored you've contacted me about this place. I've heard many stories throughout time."
"Who's the partner?"
"He's Colton Levi. One of my closest friends within the field."
"I take it he won't be afraid of what's inside."
"He shouldn't be. He's done this before in many places."
"Those places weren't Desdemona, my friend."
Leonard opened the gated entrance to the prison. They walked through the front yard, noticing gravestones that stand in a field on the side of the prison. Levi took out his camera, he began taking pictures of

the outer structure of the prison and the gravestones. Leonard pointed toward the gravestones.

"Those stones belong to some of the prisoners that died here."

"I notice there's no names on them." Vail mentioned. "Just only numbers."

"Their prison numbers. Didn't matter what their names were. They were called by their six-digit prison numbers."

"That's a terrible thing. I suspect they're not at rest." Levi said.

"They aren't' They're still here in these walls."

They entered the prison, looking at its intense inner structure. Vail looked around, seeing many cells toward them. Levi continues to take pictures. Leonard walked them over to three cells. He tells them that's where many soldiers from World War I were kept after the war was over. Levi took pictures of the interior of the cells. He looked at one and noticed a black smog hovering off the ground. Levi was shaking, but calm.

"Vail, I think I found something already."

Levi showed Vail the photo, seeing the black smog inside the second cell. Vail walked inside the cell, standing in the middle, quiet and calm. Leonard and Levi stood outside the door, watching Vail.

"Whoever decided to manifest themselves as a black smog, I suggest you tell us your name and place, now."

Getting no response, Leonard continued to take them around the prison. They walked through different halls of the prison.

"The first cell block was famously known for murders."

"How many murders exactly?" Vail asked.

"Estimated over six hundred. At least."

"That's a lot of death and anger." Levi said.

"That's right. The second cell block areas is known for the large amount of rapes that took place."

"You're saying male prisoners raped other male prisoners?" Vail said.

"There were female prisoners, visitors, and minor female officers. So, it's possible they were the targets."

"Of course."

Leonard walked by the last few cells and pointed down the halls.

"Suicides apparently dominated this entire area."

"It seems each cell block carries its own kind of death." Vail said. "If you wanted to be murdered, you have the first section. If you wanted to be raped, you had the second section. Now, if you wanted to kill yourself, you had the third section."

"Choose your own fate, basically." Leonard said.

"They chose it well I suppose." Levi said.

After seeing much of the prison. Vail traveled to the nearest library to read up on more history of the prison. Levi went on an errand to gather a pair of digital cameras, digital recorders, and EMP device to catch frequency energy signatures. Finding the library, Vail discovered the origin of the prison. It was founded by a well-known millionaire during the late 1800s.

The prison was first used as a correctional facility for juveniles and over the years became a penitentiary during the start of World War I. Both during and after World War I, many of the soldiers, from either side were kept within the prison. The prison continued to stand even after World War II and the Vietnam War. It was used briefly during the height of the Cold War. Vail read on how the prison was shut down in 2003 due to low funding.

Vail returned to the prison with Levi, who was carrying the bags of the digital supplies. Vail looked at Levi and took a glance at the bags. He smirked.

"You love your technology."

"How else are we able to capture images and video of spirits."

Leonard walked out of the prison towards Vail and Levi. They walk back inside the prison as Leonard closes the gate as the sun sets. Vail looked back at Leonard and nodded. Leonard nodded back in respect.

"Hope you find what you're looking for."

"Don't worry, we will."

Levi began to set up the digital cameras on tripods across the hallways of the cell blocks. Vail recited a ritual that is known to protect both himself and Levi from malevolent spirits that may reside inside the prison walls. Vail approached Levi, who's finished setting up the cameras and recorders.

"You're ready for this?" Vail asked.

"How can I not be ready for this."

Once the moon glinted across the prison windows, Vail and Levi started their investigation. They first decided to check the first six cell blocks. They stood inside of the circular shaped room, seeing all the entrances of the cell blocks, Levi looked around as he noticed something familiar about the circular room.

"This place is a smorgasbord of spirits."

"You know, Vail, this room reminds me of another prison in the states. I've seen it on one of the paranormal shows."

"I hope they did a good job."

"They did. One of the best paranormal shows on TV to date."

They slowly walk through the prison. Levi, with a digital camera in his hands, looks around through the LED screen as Vail uses his senses to track his location.

"You want to start the conversations?" Vail said.

"Sure."

Levi walked by the cells and stood in front of the fourth one. He pointed the camera towards the cell, looking inside, seeing the bed spring, sink, and toilet. Vail walked towards the other cells nearby.

"Is there anyone inside this cell?" Levi said. "We want to know if you're here or not."

"They're here, Levi. Just be careful."

Walking slowly and calm through the darkness of the cell block, they began to hear sounds of knocking coming from the cell blocks.

Levi looked around with his camera at the cells, seeing nothing in the lens. Vail entered a few of the cells.

"Are you in here? If you are, I demand you say or do something now."

The knocking increased as Levi spotted a shadow that walked by the cell where Vail was standing inside of. Levi ran over toward the cell, telling Vail what he captured on the camera and how it passed by the cell he was standing in. Vail left the cell and continued to investigate the other cells.

"So, more deaths took place in this cell block." Levi mentioned. "The other guys would've loved to see this."

"I'm sure they would. Over six-hundred murders in this location.

That's a lot of energy."

While walking toward the end of the cell block, Vail caught a shadow, which moved past the exit door. He looked back to see it, but nothing was there. Levi noticed Vail's behavior.

"What is it?" Levi asked.

"I saw a shadow. It walked past the exit."

"Let me try the digital recorder to capture their voice."

Levi pulled out the digital recorder. He talked into it, asking a series of questions to the spirits within the cell block. After a minute to a second, he received a response. Vail walked over and listened to the recorder. He hears the voice of an older man, threatening to kill them if they don't leave the cell block.

"It just threatened to kill us." Levi remarked.

"It can't kill us if it doesn't have enough energy to use. Don't lend them your energy. Block it all off. That includes the devices."

"I'll try."

"You will. There's no trying in here. We're in dangerous territory right now."

Upon getting no other signs of spirits within the cell block. They entered the second area of the cell block. While they walked in, they could hear disembodied screams coming from the cells. Levi looked around cautiously.

"You hear those screams, Vail?"

"They sound like women in pain."

"They're being raped!" Levi yelled.

"It could be just an irrelevant response. A sound that was once here repeating itself."

"We have to check to be sure."

"I am sure it's an irrelevant spirit."

Levi walked over to the cells, seeing no one inside. He looked through the camera to find anything. Seeing nothing, they walk further down the cell block. As they walked through the cell block, they heard a distant laugh coming from the left of them. Vail walked by the cells on the left, looking inside.

"Who's here with us?" Vail asked. "I demand you give us a response of your presence."

Across from Vail, a small rock is thrown toward him from the cell block. Levi scouted and found the small rock on the floor nearby Vail's area. He looked around, showing minor signs of fear while Vail was calm and quiet.

"You want to throw things at us now. I see you want to play rough. We can play rough."

"What are you talking about, Vail? They just threw a rock at you."

"I've went up against worse than a small pebble."

Vail walked around the cell block. They began hearing more screams and laughs. Levi started to shiver as he sweated and stood against a corner. Vail stood in the middle of the cell block, both arms at his side, with no expression on his face.

"They're playing with us, Colton. We're in their territory."

"They're playing kind of tough." Levi muttered.

The screams and laughs had silenced, leaving the cell block to become completely silent. Vail told Levi that they're going to the third and last section of the cell blocks. They entered the third section, feeling their energy being drained and feeling signs of dizziness. They started to feel depressed as they could hear crying within the cell block.

"What's going on?" Levi asked. "I starting to feel drained and dizzy."

"They're using our energy to fill themselves up. That crying might be the start of it."

The crying continued as they walk through the cell block. Still feeling drained and dizzy, they looked around, seeing shadowed, disembodied figures walking around them. Levi tried to hold the camera up to capture the shadow figures. As he captured them on the camera, the camera froze and completely shut down, signaling the sign of a low battery.

"I just charged this camera." Levi shouted.

"They're using its energy." Vail said. "They're gathering as much as they need."

"So, what do we do?"

"We use our instinct to see and to touch. Not all the spirits are intelligent or benevolent. I'm starting to sense a malevolent spirit in here and it doesn't belong in this cell block."

"They're jumping cell blocks now." Levi blurted.

Vail felt a presence surrounding him closely. He could feel something on his back, he knew they were hands. The presence of the hands shoved him violently against the wall. Levi looked and went to help him up. Vail scanned the cell block, still dizzy and drained from losing energy. He continued to walk through the cell block and stood upon staring at a black smog. Levi also saw the smog and he pointed toward it.

"That's what I saw earlier on the camera."

"That's not a benevolent spirit. Its malevolent and belongs in the murder cell block."

The black smog didn't move. It only stood still in the air. Vail and Levi continued to stare at it. Vail reached into his coat pocket, taking out the book of rituals. Levi looked over at the book seeing the variety of rituals inside.

"What are you about to do?"

"I'm about to send this spirit to the other side. Where it can be judged for its sins."

Vail recited the ritual, making a way to send the malevolent spirit to the other side. As he recited the ritual, the black smog slowly evaporated before vanishing into the thin air. Vail looked around, not seeing any more shadow figures. Levi rubbed his head.

"I'm not dizzy anymore." Levi said.

"Neither am I. The ritual must have sent them over."

Vail looked toward the window above them, seeing the sunlight peeking through the cracks into the cell block. He and Levi walked toward the entrance. Levi gathered the tripods and cameras that sat in the hallways. Leonard returned as the morning started and thanked them for their investigation.

"So, may I ask what you seen or heard?"

"We heard a lot and seen a lot." Levi said.

"There are many spirits that reside in this place. I would only believe that they're locked in for eternity because of the path they chose to go."

"I believe that very well. I guess they'll never find a way out of here."

"They'll find a way to leave and enter the other side. It will take some time of course for it to be done."

"Well, I want to thank you for coming over here and investigating this place. Not many would have done this."

"It's what we're here for."

Vail signaled to Levi to leave. Levi places the cameras and devices in the back of the car before getting in the passenger's set as Vail drives away from the prison.

CASE OF THE WHITE LADY

Travis Vail is set to investigate Huntly Castle where legends speak of a spirit known as The White Lady resides. Vail had read up on the history of the White Lady and how she is involved with Huntly Castle. After arriving in the country of Scotland, Vail traveled to *Aberdeenshire*, one of the thirty-two council areas within Scotland. Aberdeenshire is also a lieutenancy area. As Vail arrived in Aberdeenshire, he traveled straight for Huntly Castle. Once on Huntly Castle's land, he started at the castle, scanning its structure as a twelve-century castle.

A man walked from the castle, he greeted Vail as they stood outside the historic structure. The man is Barclay Iomhair, the current tour guide and owner of Huntly Castle's property. Vail speaks with Barclay about the castle and its history. Barclay tells him that the castle was built by Clan Gordon in the twelfth century as an L-Plan tower house. Vail began to ask about the castle's former inhabitants as Barclay tells him about how it was formally named *Strathbogie* and how it was granted to Sir Adam Gordon of Huntly in the fourteenth century.

He told Vail that the castle was once burned down and later rebuilt. They begin to walk through the interior of the castle, seeing all its ancient structure around them. Vail states that he can feel the emotions of the people that once lived in the castle. Barclay begins to tell him about the well-known folklore that travels around the castle. The folklore of the White Lady. Vail turned to Barclay, he showed a slight smirk.

"I'm curious about this folklore." Vail said. "What's the exact tale of this White Lady?"

"There are many tales of the White Lady to be exact according to my knowledge."

Barclay began to tell Vail about the case of a daughter of the Lyon Family. He tells him how she committed a folly that everyone else thought was heinous and how a male servant was involved in the folly. He tells Vail the daughter was banished to a bedchamber in the tower of the castle, which was believed to be over one hundred feet from the ground. He says she suffered from agony within her mind and later found relief from either jumping or pushed out of the tower's window and fell to her death. He continued saying the tale was passed from each generation that came afterwards. The room where she was banished to is now known as the Waterloo Room.

The second tale is the most well-known tale of the White Lady and how it's about the Countess of Strathmore who had entered her second ill marriage. Barclay tells Vail that the Countess has suffered greatly within the romance part of her life as she lived unhappy with the husbands who later turned another way. She wrote about her experiences as being wretched and her writing is still described today as the most damning indictment of a husband ever to be written by a wife in any age.

Barclay decided to tell Vail that the most-well known one is on the halfway of being the accurate story as he believes the Lyon daughter is the White Lady that haunts the castle. Vail tells Barclay he'll surely discover who the White Lady truly is during his investigation. Vail leaves Huntly Castle and heads toward a nearby library, where he will look up more of the castle's history and residents. He finds records of the castle being burned down and how King James IV of Scotland would come over and gave gifts to the stonemasons that worked on the castle. He also reads that in October of 1503, King James IV returned to play a shooting contest and later came the Huntly Castle every October after as part of an annual pilgrimage to the shrine of Saint Duthac of Tain, a royal bough and post town in the Highland area of Scotland.

Vail retuned to the castle grounds just before sunset as he spoke with Barclay. Knowing he couldn't be locked in for the whole night, he decided to stay on the castle grounds from sunset to sunrise. Barclay leaves the area as Vail stood and stared at Huntly Castle. He decided to walk around the area for a while until the sun had set. He examines the area twice as the sun starts to set. Smirking, while watching the sunset. He begins his investigation of Huntly Castle.

"The sun has set, and I am here on Huntly Castle ground. I am here to see the White Lady."

He walked through the ruined structure of the castle, calling out the legendary White Lady. Not receiving any sign of her in his presence, he continues his investigation. Upon walking through the ruined castle, he spotted a white mist moving from right to left in the darker parts of the castle. Vail takes out a flashlight and approaches the darker area.

"Who is here with me? I would like for you, whoever you are, to make some sort of contact with me, so that I know you're here."

Vail entered the dark area, not able to see anything in front of him without the flashlight. He begins to hear a distant cry coming from inside the dark area. Vail looked around the entire area, not able to see what the crying was coming from. He could still hear it while looking around the entire area. He does a double take around the area. Still seeing nothing, he decides to leave the area. As he approached the front of the castle, he sees a young boy dressed in a double-breasted sailing jacket. Vail approached the young boy slowly, staring into his eyes.

"What's your name, son?" Vail said. "You can tell me your name."

The boy gave no response to Vail. Vail continues to ask the boy about his name as the boy stayed quiet. After one last attempt to get a response from the boy, he walks away. Vail watched as the boy slowly faded away as he was walking away. Vail says to himself that he just seen a spirit, but it wasn't the legendary White Lady that locals and folklore speak of. The sun begins to rise as Vail takes one look back at Huntly Castle before leaving Aberdeenshire.

The next day, Vail traveled to *Longforgan*, Perth and Kinross in Scotland. He traveled through Longforgan to find a prison that's known as Castle Huntly. Sort of the sane title as the ruined castle in Aberdeenshire. While during research the day before, Vail discover documents containing information about a fifteen-century year old castle with Huntly as a name. Like the other castle, this Huntly is currently an HM prison. HM stands for His Majesty's Prison.

    Vail arrived at the prison castle, looking at its structure and seeing how it's been renovated and adapted to stay in modern times. Upon entering the prison, he discovers it's an open prison, with the capacity of two-hundred and eighty-five people. Not sure about how he could do an investigation throughout the prison, he decides to find a way. After speaking with officials within the prison and some of the prisoners themselves, he discovers that the White Lady has also been seen in the prison, including the same young boy that was seen at the ruined Huntly Castle.

    Later that night, Vail decides to do a minimal investigation throughout the prison. He decided to leave two hours after midnight to avoid the prisoners. Once his investigation started, he began to hear prisoners screaming across the hallways. He ran down the hallways to find the prisoners. Once at the end, he sees prisoners staring at a woman, who's floating in the air. She's only wearing white with white hair and clear glowing white eyes.
"It has to be her." Vail said.
    The prisoners run in opposite directions to avoid the lady. Vail walked up to the lady as she slowly turned toward him. They lock eyes as Vail has officially come face to face with the White Lady. Vail smirked as he stared at her. Her face showed no emotion as she continues to stare him down. Other prisoners look from across the hallways, staring at Vail and the White Lady.
    "So, you the legendary White Lady." Vail said. "After all this time, I've finally got the chance to meet you."
    The White Lady says nothing to respond to Vail. He continued to talk to her as the prisoners continued to hide across the hallways. Vail decided to reach into his pocket and take out his book of rituals. The White Lady glanced at the book, noticing its symbolic encryptions on the front and back. She vanished in seconds as Vail looked around, not seeing

her anywhere.

"Dammit."

Vail ran through the hallways searching for the White Lady. As he went through each hall, he continued to only see prisoners standing or sitting down. He stopped to take a breath and he started to hear what sounded like prisoners fighting each other down the hall he just past. Vail returned to that hall and seen the prisoners fighting each other as the White Lady went passed them in seconds. Vail followed the white trail of mist that was made by the White Lady.

He continued to search for the White Lady as it was only thirty minutes before he left the prison. He walked into a room that resembled a museum of the castle's history. As he walked slowly through the museum, he finds artifacts that date to the origin of the castle's existence. As he looked at the artifacts, he starts to notice the room's temperature lower. He pulled out a thermometer, which signified the room's temperature was below thirty degrees. He turned around, looking around the museum. Vail raised up his left sleeve and looked at his arm, noticing the hairs standing up completely straight.

"I know you're here." Vail uttered. "You can come on out, so we can discuss your place in the future."

Vail feels a swift breeze on the back of his neck. He turned and sees the White Lady. She's standing on the ground, facing Vail. Vail stared at her, looking unworried about his possible safety. He glanced at his watch, seeing he only had fifteen minutes before his investigation was over.

"I only have fifteen minutes to help you before I leave this place." Vail said. "So, I am here to help you move on to the other side."

The White Lady shakes her head, disagreeing with Vail's wishes. Vail slowly reached into his pocket for his book. The Lady moved an inch closer to Vail. He stopped moving his hand and stared.

"I am here to help you, miss. There's no reason for you to stay in this place. Especially in today's time."

"You can't help me." The White Lady said. "You can even help yourself."

"Please, let me read from this book and I can send you to a better place. A wholesome place."

The White Lady giggled at Vail. He glanced at his watch and noticed he only had about ten minutes left before the investigation was over. He pulled out the book and turned to the page he was previously on before. The White Lady looked at the book.

"I only have about ten minutes left before I leave. I am sending you to the other side at this moment."

Vail read the ritual from the book as the White Lady tried to leave the room. In front of Vail, a white light shines through the entire room. The light begins to pull the Lady towards it as she begins to be pulled inside the light. The light later consumes her and vanishes. Vail placed the book back into his pocket and looked at the watch, seeing only six minutes left before he was done.

"There's nothing else for me to do here." Vail said.

Two hours after midnight, Vail leaves the prison castle. After the sun rose, he went back to Huntly Castle to speak with Barclay. Barclay sits inside his car as Vail approached him.

"I hear you visited Castle Huntly prison." Barclay said.

"I did."

"How was it? Going inside that place by yourself?"

"It was a worrisome task, but, I managed to get through it."

"So, I take it you saw something at both Huntly Castles?"

"I saw a young boy here. He vanished before I could get anything in place. At the prison is where I've seen the White Lady. It took a while before I could send her over to the other side to be in peace. It seemed to be that both places have been covered with the folklore of the White Lady."

Barclay smiled as Vail walked to his car.

"This means your case on this is officially done?"

"The case of the White Lady has been solved in my opinion."

Vail gets into his car before Barclay walked over to the car door,

"Give me a little insight on your next case?"

"I feel my next case will be in the States. Mostly to involve the legend of Salem."

Vail drove away as Barclay watched on.

SALEM WITCH TRIALS

Occult Detective Travis Vail has entered Salem, Massachusetts to investigate the historic tales of witchcraft and the possibility of it be continued in today's time. Salem is the key location to many historical accounts and records of witchcraft. The Salem Witch Trials took place between February 1692 and May 1693. Throughout the history of the years, paranoia and fear overtook Salem as many believed that The Devil was watching their every move. Anyone they saw or talked to that resemble unusual behavior was considered a witch or warlock.

Vail looked through the town of Salem. Knowing that it was a great effort to gain permission to investigate Salem's dark history. After a town council event, Vail was granted access to all of Salem and its historical records. Speaking with many of the town's residents, Vail realizes that witches still reside in Salem in modern day. Knowing they no longer hide and look just like the average person today. Vail traveled to the downtown area, asking many residents if they have seen any witches or if they are a witch themselves. Vail approaches two women wearing black cloaks, covering themselves from the cold light rain.

"If I may ask you ladies. Are any of you witches of modern day?"

"Why would you like to know? You're investigating the trials, aren't you?"

"Yes ma'am."

The women looked at each other and smirked. They turned toward

Vail and shook their heads.

"I'll put to you this way, sir. Witches don't have a Jerusalem. They have Salem."

The women walked away, leaving Vail thinking about their last statement, saying how Salem is a witch's Jerusalem. Upon doing later research, Dr. Galen Donovan arrived in Salem and contacted Vail about his arrival. They later meet at the Lyceum restaurant, which sits on the land that once belonged to Bridget Bishop, the first woman who was hanged after being accused of practicing witchcraft.

"We're finally in Salem." Donovan said.

"It's been a long time coming. This one should be the one that's worth it."

"So, how was the town council meeting?"

"The meeting went great. Many residents agreed with what we're trying to do by discovering more evidence of their city's past and what truly happened."

"What's the current time that we head over to the Witch House?"

"Sometime this afternoon. I also plan to attend a play that resembles the trials exactly as the transcripts portray them. Once that's complete, we'll return to the house later tonight for the investigation."

Donovan nodded and looked down at his watch. Reading the time, he looked up toward Vail.

"Best we head over there at this moment."

"I agree."

Vail and Donovan arrived at the Salem Witch House. Looking at its old structure, Vail began to feel a chill coming from the house. Donovan noticed Vail's movement as if he's fighting something off.

"Is there something wrong, Vail?"

"I feel a presence of some kind. Not sure what it is, but it's coming from the house."

They approached the front door, being greeted by a woman named Fawn Verrucca. She greeted them as she allowed them inside the house. Once inside, they notice the historical artifacts the reside inside the rooms of the home.

"These are paintings that show the residents of this land. These are

Elizabeth Gibbs' children. She had a total of four children. One of the children had died a year before she married Mr. Judge Jonathon Corwin. Her daughter, Margaret has passed away the second year she decided to get married."

"So, are all of these paintings portrayals of women?"

"Not these two on the wall."

Fawn pointed toward the wall, where two paintings were set. Vail bent down and looked at the paintings. He turned and looked at Donovan before facing Fawn.

"So, these two are paintings of young boys?"

"Yes, it is. They were known as Little Henry and Little Robert."

"So, they wore dresses in the late 1600s."

"Mainly until they reach around six years old. At least that age we know of."

"Fascinating." Donovan said. "You learn something new every day."

"If you have an open mind." Vail said. "So, what else can you tell us about this place?"

"Mr. Jonathon Corwin and the jury in the court had presided over the courses of the trials. Condemning many who were considered guilty, were put to death. Corwin even lived in this home."

"Was there a way that they could confess the truth to the jury, so they would be set free?" Donovan said.

"Their integrity was too prideful as they would rather die in this life and keep their integrity in the next. Instead of being what's considered a coward and just giving in to the Judge and jury's demands."

"So, this Bridget Bishop was one of the first women to be considered a witch." Vail said.

"She was first to be brought in as potentially being a witch due to her being an easy target. All the men would flirt with her as all the women would hate her and many of them condemned her as practicing witchcraft."

"So, this home belonged to Judge Corwin during those times of the trials?"

"Yes, it did. He lived in this very home."

"So, there should be much energy in this home." Vail said. "Maybe that explains what I was feeling before I entered."

"Also, in a way to find out if the women were witches, they would take their urine and mix it with flour, baking it into a cake. They would feed the cake to a dog and watch the dog for any unusual behavior or movements to determine if the women were witches."

"They fed dogs cake with urine baked in it." Donovan said. "Utterly disgusting."

"Horrifying at the most." Vail said.

Vail and Donovan later visited a location where they're going to watch a reenactment of the trials taken directly from the transcripts. As they enter the school, watching the young girls portray the historical figures of the witch trials. Donovan watches uncertainly with fear as Vail appeared to be in a trance, studying the words and movement of how the young girls portrayed the figures. After watching the reenactment, they decided to head back over to the Lyceum restaurant as they speak with residents who are currently sitting inside the restaurant. Vail and Donovan question as many as possible about Bridget Bishop. A few residents show Vail photos of a wedding that took place inside a banquet hall where in the photo is an apparition of a woman who they believe to be Bridget Bishop. After speaking with the residents, Vail noticed the sun is starting to set. He tells Donovan that they must head back over to the witch house to begin their investigation.

Once they returned to the witch house, Fawn allowed them back as she locked them within the home. Donovan began taking out equipment as Vail began to say a prayer over himself and Donovan, protecting them from any malevolent spirits that may reside inside the home or on the land itself.

"Much of the equipment is ready and set." Donovan said.

"I'll start once you're ready."

"I'm ready."

While Vail and Donovan walked into the living room of the home, Vain began to feel a chill as the room's temperature suddenly dropped. Donovan sees his own breath coming from his mouth. He turned over towards Vail, who appeared to be fighting off something again.

"What's the problem?"

"I'm feeling someone else's emotions. I don't know who this is, but I am feeling a little sad for some reason and it's not my emotions."

"Are you going to be alright?"

"I'm not letting this get to me. But, I can't ignore what I'm feeling right now."

Donovan reached into his jacket pocket and pulled out an EMF Detector to find any EMF energy. Noting the major temperature drop, the EMF energy stops itself at the number "*666*".

"The energy is at "666"." Donovan said.

"What the hell is going on in here, Galen."

"We know there's something here with us right now."

Vail took out a digital recorder as Donovan walked around the home with the detector.

"Who's currently here with us? Mr. Donovan and I would like to know."

Donovan continued walking through the home with the detector.

"Find anything yet?" Vail said.

"Nothing yet. The temperature's back to normal."

Donovan suddenly felt hands on his back. He jumped up and turned toward Vail, who looked at him uncertainly.

"What's wrong?"

"I felt hands on my back."

"There's nothing behind you, Donovan. I'll check around this area to make sure what's around here."

Vail walked through the area of the room, using the digital recorder and asking questions towards the spirits. While asking the questions, he hears a disembodied female voice in the room he's currently inside. He turned quickly, scanning the room. Noticing Donovan inside the other room.

"Who's inside this room with me?"

He didn't get a response. A few hours later of not finding any signs of any spirit, Vail looked outside the window and seen the sun rising from behind the clouds. He turned to Donovan, who approached him with the other digital recorder and detector.

"The sun is rising." Vail said.

"Looks like this investigation is about over."

They packed up their gear and awaited Fawn to unlock the doors. Around 6:30 AM, Fawn arrived and unlocked the front doors, allowing Vail and Donovan to leave the house. Fawn, showing curiosity approached Vail as he began to enter his car.

"Did you discover anything?"

"Some uneasy feeling. Though, we must go through our recorders to make a perfect statement. Thank you for allowing us into this home."

Vail and Donovan leave the home as Fawn walked inside. She closed the door and through the window was an apparition of a female looking outside at Fawn as she left the house.

Within a few days, Vail and Donovan spent most of their time dissecting the recorders, searching for any signs of a spirit's voice. While scanning the recorders, Vail noticed a distinctive voice. He quickly paused and rewind the recorders, going back to the voice. Donovan approached him, looking at the screen.

"Find anything?"

"I believe I just did."

Vail played the audio, listening to himself asking the question of who was inside the room with him when he heard the disembodied female voice. After hearing himself ask the question, he caught a distant voice inside the audio. After enhancing it, he played the audio once again and caught the voice.

"Is that who I think it was." Donovan said.

"Bridget Bishop was in the home with us."

Vail and Donovan later appeared at a City Hall meeting in Salem with the city council and residents of the city. Vail and Donovan showed the audience all the information and evidence that they discovered inside the witch house. The audience was sort of stunned by the evidence. The last evidence that was shown was the voice of Bridget Bishop. Upon playing the audio for the audience and council, they were quietly appalled. Afterwards the gave applause to Vail and Donovan. Thanking them for their visit and their investigation.

Upon leaving Salem the following day, Donovan asked Vail what his next investigation would be if he already knew. Vail, sitting inside his car turned and faced Donovan. He gave a small smirk.

"From what I can guess, my next case will probably be out of the ordinary."

THE FOG FROM WITHIN

Many areas across the middle of The United States have reported sightings of a strange Fog that arrives in their cities and towns and causing a great disturbance throughout neighborhoods and counties. Many reports speak of strange anomalies inside the Fog itself. Some resemble human beings, others see animals, or other types of strange things that basically live inside The Fog.

Travis Vail has now been contacted by many of the cities and towns to investigate the mysterious Fog. As Vail prepares himself to investigate the sightings, he begins to think to himself what he can back up on the mysterious Fog. The first city that Vail investigates is Boulder, Colorado. As Vail enters Boulder, he meets with a few of the residents that reside in Boulder that reported The Fog's appearance.

While speaking with the residents and listening to their view of The Fog's appearance for over several hours, Vail noticed many of the residents had particularly seen the anomalies moving inside The Fog. Upon further research about the mysterious Fog, Vail discovers that the Fog was seen centuries ago after the genocide of many soldiers and innocent people.

Vail contacted his fellow Historian, Raynard Brown to investigate the history of the mysterious Fog. Raynard suggests that the Fog was created by way of witchcraft, possibly due to Pagan rituals and celebrations. Vail takes those suggestions into his mind and keeps them there for further references later throughout his investigations. Vail continued to speak with many other residents who've seen the Fog in front of their homes. Vail declares to Boulder's Mayor that he will begin an investigation throughout the neighborhood that night, which the Mayor allowed with no problems.

The following night, Vail walked throughout the neighborhood, awaiting the possible appearance of The Fog. He doesn't feel anything unusual nor see anything that resembles paranormal. Though, Vail noticed the wind began to pick up slowly as the trees slowly moved along with the cold breeze. Vail walked through the empty streets in the neighborhood, following the breeze's whereabouts. As he walked closer to the breeze, he hears a sudden whistle. Vail turned and seen no one behind him.
"If anyone is out here, please state your name and purpose."
No individual makes themselves known before Vail as he continued to walk down the street. He continued to follow the breeze.

The following day, Vail continued to study on the Fog and its ghostly inhabitants. Raynard contacts him once again and they discuss the Fog and its possibilities of being conjured by a Pagan cult through Witchcraft or a possible supernatural entity that only appears during the Winter season of the year. Vail continued to take those suggestions to his mind and began focusing on the Pagan root of the Fog. Vail later set a return date to Boulder after he visit's the other cities that have been reporting The Fog.

Vail arrived in Topeka, Kansas, where The Fog had reportedly attacked individuals in the streets during a Christmas festival event. Vail speaks with Topeka's Mayor and the residents who were present during the Christmas festival. Upon listening to the residents and even the Mayor's own account of The Fog, Vail tells the Mayor that he will have an investigation of the location later that night. The Mayor allowed him to have his investigation and commanded police to close the whole area just for Vail to have complete clearance to proceed with his investigation.

Later that night, police gather around the entire area of where The Fog attacked the festival. Vail walked throughout the area, seeing its damaged Christmas lights and stands on the ground. Vail began to call out The Fog by yelling out names of Pagan gods and goddesses. Though, Vail had seen no signs of The Fog or anything that was related to Paganism or the paranormal.

The next day, Vail thanked the Mayor for his time in Topeka, yet having not seen The Fog himself, Vail continued his investigations across the other cities. Vail decides to head over to Tulsa, Oklahoma to discuss The Fog's appearance within their city. Upon entering Tulsa, Vail is highly greeted by the residents of Tulsa and their Mayor. Vail talked with all of them during an assembly as the residents each stood up and took their chance at telling Vail what they seen about The Fog.

Vail investigated Tulsa that night and begins to feel something unusual in the air. He looked around himself and turned toward the streets in front of him. Vail sees what looked to be three anomalies approaching him. As Vail decided to walk toward the anomalies, he sees a giant white mist behind them, which he cannot see through.

"There's the Fog." Vail said.

Vail stared at The Fog as it approached him. Through its path it knocked down street signs, destroyed windows on buildings and nearby cars and even made the ground itself tremble as if a miniature earthquake erupted in Tulsa. Vail did not run from The Fog as it approached him even closer. Vail stood his ground as The Fog ran right through him. As Vail was inside The Fog, he seen many spirits walking through The Fog. Vail quickly stared and studied the spirits that walked past him, noticing their outfits resemble the mid-1800s. Vail sees soldiers that appeared to have died during the Civil War and even sees innocent civilians walking through The Fog. Inside the Fog feels like a giant fan is blowing directly in front of you. Vail continued to stand his ground as the wind began to pick up as The Fog was coming to an end.

While the Fog was coming to its end, Vail noticed six druids walking slowly at the end of The Fog. Wearing black and red cloak with their hoods on. They were silent and didn't even glance at Vail as they walked right past him. Vail turned and watched the druids leave as The Fog ended. The druids and spirits disappeared in the air along with The Fog.

"That was something I've never encountered."

The next day, Vail told Tulsa's Mayor about The Fog and said that he has no idea what could conjure it up, though it may have already been finished. Afterwards, Vail returned to Topeka, where he tells the Mayor and residents that he seen The Fog back in Tulsa and said that it might not return. Vail last returned to Boulder, where he has a conversation with the Mayor. After their conversation, Vail began to leave Boulder as the Mayor approached him.

"It's a good thing that you came in time before Christmas." The Mayor said.

"Hope the residents are happy with their Christmas."

"Do you celebrate Christmas, Mr. Vail? It's just a question because you seem like a man who doesn't have time for holidays."

"I celebrate certain days. Not Christmas."

"Why is that?"

"I'm not Pagan."

Vail walked away, getting into his car, driving away.

THE REVENANCY VOYAGE

The ship that's known as *The Revenancy* was one of the most graceful and respected ships that has ever sailed across the Atlantic Ocean. Its service ran for over three decades until its untimely demise after it was attacked and raided by pirates of the European Union. Now, the ship sits on a dock near the Atlantic Ocean where it is presented as a historical relic and used for tourism.

The ship is also known for its large amount of haunting after its demise. Many people who have went into the ship have reported paranormal disturbances throughout the entire ship. Some have reported footsteps, voices, moans, and even screams. One reported that a lamp was thrown toward them. Due to the increase of reports, the current owner of the ship has contacted Travis Vail to investigate the ship's haunting.

Within a few days, Vail arrived in Charleston, North Carolina to the dock where the ship is currently residing. Along with Vail is Colton Levi, his longtime assistance in the paranormal. They approach the owner of the ship, Clay Haskett. He approaches them as they greet each other. Haskett allows them into his office.

"It's a great honor to finally meet you, Mr. Vail."

"No worries, Mr. Haskett." Vail said. "So, what have you with these reports of the ship?"

"We've received many, if not dozens more of reports that contain paranormal incidents within the ship."

"What kind of incidents, if I may ask." Colton said.

"Voices, footsteps, moans and groans." Haskett said. "One report contained a lamp being thrown."

"Seems to me that these are spirits that do not want to be disturbed or have a darker history that what we were told by the officials." Vail said.

"What's your current plan, Mr. Vail?"

"Colton and I will walk through the ship and I will head over to your museum to do more research on the ship's history."

Haskett stood up from his desk and walked towards the door. He opened it and stood by, allowing Vail and Colton to approach the ship.

"May we enter the ship?" Vail said.

"Of course." Haskett said. "Just don't try to startle the tourists, please."

"Sure. No problem."

Vail and Colton enter the ship. Passing by tourists who are laughing and taking photos with each other.

"Try not to get distracted, Colton."

"No worries."

They entered the lounge area of the ship, noticing many tourists inside taking photos. Colton tells Vail to search another area of the ship before the lounge, due to the number of tourists within the lounge. Vail agrees with Colton as they approach the other rooms of the ship. After a left turn down a hall, they notice rooms that appear to be hotel rooms.

"This was used as a hotel facility?" Colton said.

"Appears to be so." Vail said. "This is new to me and I wonder what else will present itself."

They scanned the hotel rooms, searching for evidence. Upon approaching the other rooms, Colton heard a distant moan from deeper within the hall. Vail looked up and down the hall, seeing no one in sight.

"You heard it too." Colton said.

"I did." Vail said. "I suggest we take a look before we head out."

Vail and Colton walk down the hall, taking slow and quick looks in the rooms nearby searching for whatever the moan came from. They reach the end of the hall and find nothing that relates to the moan. Vail turned to Colton, suggesting they head to the museum for further research. As they walk back down the hall, a book is thrown at the wall in front of Vail. He stops walking and turns to his left, looking in a room where the book flew from.

"It seems these spirits are not too friendly." Vail said. "We better get moving and we'll return later tonight for our investigation."

They exit out the ship, seeing Haskett approaching them nervously.

"Did you find anything as of this moment?"

"There's something inside this ship and we'll find it tonight when we return." Vail said. "Nothing to worry about, Mr. Haskett. We will solve the problem."

Vail and Colton leave the dock of *The Revenancy* as Haskett looks at the ship with a little sign of fear.

At the Charleston Museum, Vail and Colton gather books containing historical records of *The Revenancy* and its historical tragic voyage. After reading through a few books and scanning their notes, Vail realizes that the ship was used in a cruise line and even in military use. He even finds a record that contains information of the crew being murdered by pirates near the European Union.

"This ship has some very dark history." Vail said. "Being used for military warfare as well as a cruise ship."

"What shall we focus on during the investigation tonight?" Colton said.

"We'll focus on the spirits that reside in the ship." Vail said. "Try to find a way for them to cross over."

Vail closed the books, placing them on their shelves before leaving the museum.

Near nightfall, they return to the ship where Haskett waits for them. He sees them and approaches them.

"You two sure you're ready for this?"

"We've done far much worse than this, Mr. Haskett." Vail said. "There won't be any problems tonight.:

Vail and Colton enter *The Revenancy* as Haskett leaves the dock. Once inside the ship, the silence air slowly brings up a chill to Colton.

"It's deeply quiet in here."

"Don't run off on this one, Colton." Vail said. "You've been inside a prison where hell basically took place. Don't let a ship scare you near death."

They approached the lounge. Now, it's not crowded by the tourists from earlier in the day. Vail looked around the lounge for any clues. Colton searches the other side of the lounge.

"See anything?" Vail said.

"Nothing yet." Colton said. "Sure, something will make itself present."

"It will make itself present." Vail said. "Maybe sooner than we're expecting it to present."

While searching the lounge, they hear a distant yell coming from the dwells of the ship. Colton turned to Vail, who tells him to walk down the hall near the yell's whereabouts. Colton slowly walked down the hall, somewhat a little startled.

"Is anyone here with me?" Colton said. "I'm just asking to be a little perspective."

A bucket had suddenly fell from a shelf in front of Colton. He stopped and looked at the bucket. Vail walked behind him and approached the bucket.

"You're not afraid of a water bucket, are you?" Vail asked. "Because it seemed to startle you."

"I'm doing just fine, Vail." Colton said. "No problems at all."

Vail continued to walk down the hall, passing by rooms that resembled a dining hall where many of the passenger had dinner and occasional parties. Colton looked in the room seeing the tables and banners which were inside the ship. Through a few turns down the right hall, Vail discovers a room that is packed with medical equipment.

"This must be the medical room." Vail said. "It's highly possible that many people died inside this room."

"It's sure able to have a pack of spiritual energy in here." Colton said.

"The energy is here, Colton, and it's getting stronger as we're in here."

Vail looked around the room. He told Colton to take out the digital recorder and place it on the table. Vail stood by the recorder on the table.

"I am Travis Vail, and this is Colton Levi. We are here to speak with any spirits who reside in this *Revenancy* ship. We're here to discover your existence and to send you over into the afterlife."

A sound creaked from the medical room's door. Colton turned and stared as Vail continued to talk by the digital recorder.

"Vail, looks like something is in here with us."

"I hear it Colton. Whoever has entered this room, please speak into this recorder device on this table next to me to respond to my questions."

Colton stood by the door, looking out down the hall as Vail began asking questions toward the spirits. Vail asked if the spirits worked on the ship during its military run or its cruise line run. They caught a voice that said military, which Vail believes it's a military Navy officer that must have died on the ship in the line of duty. Colton looked further down the hall and saw what appeared to be a silhouette of a man wearing a casual Ship Captain uniform walking into the dining room.

"Vail, I just saw an apparition down the hall. It walked into the dining room."

"I suggest you go and look. If you, please."

Colton walked down the hall and entered the dining room. Seeing no one inside the room, he turned back to the exit. Once he turned, he was staring a Ship Captain right in the eyes. Colton yelled and ran back towards the medical room. Vail paused and ran out of the room towards Colton.

"What's wrong?" Vail asked.

"It was standing in my face!" Colton said. "Right in my face!"

"What did you see?"

"I saw the ship captain staring me right in the eyes. A complete stare. I thought it lasted for eternity, yet it was a few seconds."

Vail looked out the window and saw the sun beginning to rise, signaling the end of their investigation. He turned toward Colton and looked down the hall.

"Seems our investigation is done." Vail said.

Vail grabbed the recorder as they left the ship.

The following day, Vail speaks with Haskett about the investigation and tells him about the Navy soldier that spoke about the military as well as Colton's sighting of the ship's captain. Vail says the spirits have claimed the ship their home. Haskett thanked Vail and Colton for their service. They leave the dock and Colton turned to Vail.

"This ship freaked me our more than the prison we've once visited."

"*The Revenancy* will continue to scare people towards the point of death."

"May I ask what's next on the horizon of the paranormal?"

"Whatever comes my way."

THE FOREST OF THE VANISHING

Within the outskirts of Seattle, Washington is a mysterious forest that many decide not to enter due to its intensive history of people vanishing without a trace. Animals walk through the area calmly and are not disturb. Only human beings are the ones that walk through with fear and paranoia who are later vanished. News reports have scattered across the nation with concerns of the forest being burned down to avoid any more people going missing. The debate is currently ongoing amongst the Washington State Governor and the US Government.

The occult detective known as Travis Vail arrived in Seattle as he prepared to do an investigation by himself inside the forest. While walking through downtown Seattle, Vail decided to meet with Seattle's Mayor to discuss his investigation into the forest. As Vail walked down the streets, he spotted the Mayor delivering a speech outside in the open with over a dozen residents standing and listening. Vail stood in the back of the crowd as he watched the Mayor talk about their city's future.

After the mayor finished his speech and the residents began to leave the area, Vail approached the Mayor. As he introduced himself, the Mayor instantly recognized who Vail was and they entered a small office inside a nearby building. While inside the office, Vail discussed to the Mayor of investigating the Vanishing Forest. After about an hour through the conversation, the Mayor gives Vail his blessing and Vail leaves the office building, heading towards the forest itself.

Vail entered the outskirts of Seattle and stands not too far from the highway. He began walking toward the tree and noticed a medium-sized sign sitting on his left side of the field, saying *"Do Not Enter! Forbidden Area."*. Vail smirked and started walking into the forest. As he proceeded through the quiet and smelly forest, he noticed ahead of him was a small shrine. As Vail inched closer to the shrine, he spotted it was built upon with bones of what appeared to be a buffalo.

"What is this." Vail said.

Vail began to step into the middle of the shrine, though being cautious. As Vail turned around, looking at the surrounds, he realized that there was more than one shrine. There was a total of thirteen shrines. The shrines were decorated with crosses, candles, bones, skulls of various animals and some even human, meaning there were possible animal and human sacrifices within the forest at some point. As Vail approaches each of the shrines, he knows that this is a site of a pagan ritual and burial ground. To his mind, he sees that as being a possible reason why many people have disappeared while inside the forest. Vail also spotted a few obelisks standing inside the forest as well that stood near twelve feet in height.

"Why would they choose a place such as this?" Vail said.

Vail continued to examine the surrounding shrines within the forest. As he studied each shrine and what it was built upon. While he was aware of the location of which he was standing in, he began to move very slowly. The forest began to grow a fog in the air, surrounding the shrines that Vail was studying. He began to write down every shrine that stood in the forest and the description of the shrines. While writing, Vail heard a distant sound coming from his left inside the forest. He stopped writing and walked over to the noise. Hearing a slowly dripping sound, he walked near the noise. Going through the fog that's growing larger and thicker. Vail stopped and looked down as he saw what appeared to be blood dripping from a tree nearby. As Vail looked up toward the tree, he finds an array of decorated skulls sitting and hanging on the tree.

"What did they do in this place?"

Vail backed away from the tree and decided to continue writing down the other shrines before leaving. As he wrote down the last shrine, he felt the wind blowing behind his neck, he turned as it began to pick up with the fog slowly evaporating into the air. Vail noticed that something was going on inside the forest. As The wind continued to blow, Vail spotted what appeared to be shoes laying on the ground. He ran over toward them and picked one up. Upon looking at it, the shoe belonged to a young boy. Vail looked around the spot for any other trace. Only finding the two shoes, he took them with him as he decided to leave the forest. As Vail walked through the forest, finding his way back. He begins to feel nauseous and drained. He placed his hand on his head, shaking it so he can focus.

"I don't know what you are. Now leave me be."

Vail regained his focus as he left the forest and returned to Seattle to show the Mayor the shoes and the shrines inside the forest.

Later that afternoon, Vail spoke with the Mayor about the shoes and the shrines that laid inside the forest. The Mayor began to call on a police force to head into the forest to search for the missing boy. Vail declined the force as the Mayor was running out of ideas as of who to send inside the forest. Vail looked at the Mayor and stated that he was returning to the forest that night to do a full complete investigation of the forest and the shrines. Believing that something might be going on during the night rather than the day. The Mayor paused as he returned to his desk and nodded. Giving Vail his answer to go into the forest after dawn. Vail left the Mayor's Office and headed toward Seattle's Museum of History and Industry to study more on the forest and its disappeared victims.

As the sun began to set and many of Seattle's residents were awaiting Vail's word of entering the forest, Vail approached the forest from the same direction as before, only this time, Vail carried a bottle of holy water and even his ritual book as he entered, which would only mean that something more was going on inside the forest with the shrines. Vail nodded to himself as he returned into the forest. Now, walking through the forest in pitch darkness and only hearing the echoes of animals, insects, and the sticks and branches breaking and cracking underneath his feet as he walked, Vail focused on the shrines and the feeling of being drained earlier before he left.

A distant flutter approached Vail from his right side. He quickly turned, looking through the darkness of the forest. Not seeing anything unusual, he continued walking through. Knowing he felt uneasy inside the forest, he continued walking as he approached the area of the shrines. Vail stood in the middle of the location, where all the shrines were facing. He rubbed some of the holy water on his forehead and held his ritual book close to his heart.

"I know you're here. I know you're all here."

Vail held his arms out as he turned around, making a full circle, while holding the book in his hand.

"Whatever you are. Whatever you've done to these people. I declare that you stop your terrorizing and return to the other side where you belong."

Not seeing or hearing anything, Vail continued to call out whatever was lurking inside the forest, which is responsible for the dozens of disappearances throughout the years. As Vail continued, he felt that something was watching him inside the forest. He stopped talking and looked around.

"I can feel you watching me. So, why don't you come on out, so I can see you."

Vail stood still as the wind picked up once again. Vail could smell the evaporation inside the forest. As he looked around, he began to hear moans coming from each of the shrines. He looked at them as he seen druids from all over approach him. Vail noticed that the druids are all in different pairs, each pair is arriving from one shrine. Each pair was covered with six druids. Vail stared at the pairs as he realized it was seventy-eight druids that were approaching him. The druids slowly surrounded him in a circle with the leaders of the pairs approaching Vail inside the circle. The druids wore all black cloaks with hoods covering their faces.

"I demand that you tell me who you are and who you worship." Vail said.

The druids stopped and only faced Vail. None of the druids speak or make any sudden noises as Vail stared at them.

"I suggest you say something about the missing people."

The druids stood silently as Vail walked around them. He glanced at the druids that circled him as well as the leading druids. As Vail walked around, he glanced toward one of the druids that stood on the outside. Looking at its height and size, Vail realized that druid had to be a child. He ran over toward the druid as the others approaching him and shoved him back into the circle. Vail looked at the leading druids and glanced back at the child druid.

"Who is that child? Answer me! Who's the child?!"

One of the leading druids approached Vail and raised his head, facing Vail. Vail stood his ground as he took an extra step toward the druid.

"I will ask again. Who's the child druid?"

"The druid you speak of is the child that the common people consider a missing person."

"You're saying to me that the child is the one that I'm looking for?"

"Indeed. That child is one of us now."

Vail rubbed his head as he looked at the other druids that surrounded him. He turned back to the leading druid as he pointed out the surrounding druids.

"So, who are the other druids circling me? Are they the other missing or vanished people?"

"Yes. They are the vanished ones. They came into our forest, stepped onto our sacred land and decided to disobey the oath that stood on this land for centuries."

"You can't keep these people here. They need to return to their homes and families."

"Their families wouldn't accept them the way they are today. They have changed greatly and with a cost they can't turn away from."

"What are you saying exactly?"

"The people you see around you on this day are not the same people that vanished throughout the centuries. If they were to return to their previous grounds, they would only destroy not only the ones they loved and cared for, but also the land they lived upon."

Vail nodded as he raised his book and held it in the face of the druid.

"I'm sending you and these people back."

"If you know the words of which to say."

"I do."

Vail began reading from the book as the wind picked up again. The druids began to back away from Vail as he continued reading. The surrounding druids had disappeared and only the leading druids remained. Vail continued as each druid disappeared one at a time. As he read from the book, the druid he was speaking withstood still and watched Vail read from the book. Vail looked up toward the druid with energy flowing through him.

"Time for you to go."

"I will leave this time. But, listen carefully Mr. Vail, there will come the time that I shall not leave, and neither will you."

The druid slowly backed away and disappeared through the wind. The wind had stopped as Vail finished reading from the book. He exhales as he placed the book back into his coat pocket and proceeded to leave the forest.

The following day, Vail spoke with the Mayor and the residents of Seattle about the forest and what he had seen the previous night. Mainly frightening the residents, he told them about the druids and how they were all the people who reportedly went missing or vanished without a trace. Vail said they were in a better place and that no one should ever enter the forest again. The residents applauded Vail for his bravery as he and the Mayor left the stage. The Mayor thanked him for visiting Seattle and hoped he would return. Vail turned and nodded.

"I will make my return when the time is accurate to do so."

Vail entered his black 1970 impala and drove down the highway, leaving the city of Seattle.

THE ABANDONED HOTEL

During the early fall season and with heavy snowfall, Travis Vail traveled past Vancouver, Canada, heading towards an abandoned hotel named The Black Raven. The hotel is known for its prestigious setting as well as its number of floors. The floors of the hotel are a total of thirteen floors and all of them have a large majority of haunting that witnesses have suspected to be spiritual and demonic occurrences, some have even been attacked by the unseen forces.

Vail arrived at the Black Raven Hotel and found no one there but himself. While walking closer to the front entrance of the abandoned hotel, he heard a vehicle approaching him from behind. He took a turn around to see the vehicle and its driver. The vehicle parked next to his and the driver exited.

"I do not know who you are or where you come from, but you cannot enter this place." The driver said.

"Why shouldn't I enter?" Vail said. "Is it because of the spirits?"

"Yes sir. I'm giving you a fair warning here. I heard that some guy was going to go inside the place and try to contact those things in there. You make a mistake. You could release them out here."

"Judging by the way you speak, you do not understand the spiritual realm nor its duties." Vail said. "You are speaking with the Spirit-Seeker and there aren't many as I in this field. So, please do me a favor and return to your home in peace and leave the spirits to me."

Vail turned away from the driver and approached the hotel entrance doors. The driver, filled with emotions, ran over toward Vail and snatched him by his right arm, trying to pull him away from the doors.

"You need to leave this place, sir!" The driver said. "It is not safe to be here at this particular time and season!"

"Unhand me or I will suggest placing you inside this hotel and you can deal with those who are unseen to the human eyes."

"You wouldn't do that to me. I'm just an ordinary guy. I have a job, I have a wife, children, a home, a car. I have a life. I'm just trying to get you to understand that you must save yours before you make a mistake."

Vail stared at the driver and smiled.

"As always. Men like you aren't truly built for what awaits you after this life you're currently living in. Men like you will never fully awaken to understand what lies behind the scales that cover your sight. You and people like you are blinded to the truth and you never seek to find it nor the ones who hide it. Therefore, you are wasting your time trying to change my ways because I've already chosen my path as it presented itself before me."

"You must not enter this place! You cannot! Its suicide!"

"Suicide is what you do when you've given up your belief and strength in things beyond your comprehension."

Vail snatched his arm back from the driver and approached the hotel doors. He placed his hand on the door handles and pulled them back toward him. The hotel doors swung open as if a gust of wind had blown out of the hotel and into the open area. The driver panicked and ran to his car, screaming for his life.

"You've opened the doors! You've released the spirits!"

The driver pulled back and drove away as Vail watched him leave and gave a slight smirk.

"Now, let us see who's waiting for me in here."

Vail walked into the hotel and looked at its interior lobby area. Vail took a few more steps into the lobby area, the two entrance doors shut as if someone had closed them from the inside. Vail looked back and circled the lobby.

"I fully understand that there are thirteen floors in this place and I intend to search them all before the night is fully over. I hope those of you in this place can and will understand that."

Vail walked by an elevator, knowing there was no electricity operating inside the hotel since its abandonment. Vail walked past the elevator and as he approached the end of the hallway toward the staircase, a small bell rang behind him. Vail turned back and sees the elevator light blinking.

"Interesting and intriguing."

Vail walked back toward the elevator and the doors opened as if it was set up for him to enter. Vail nodded and entered the elevator. The door shut and the elevator operations as if it was still in use. The elevator goes up and stopped at the second floor, the door opened, and Vail exited the elevator.

"I take it that someone is on my side in this place."

Vail found himself in the hallway of the second floor and all that surrounded him are the rooms and the equipment which was left behind before its closing. He walked through most of the hotel searching for any signs of spirits. Not finding anything related to the spirits in the rooms on the second floor, Vail went toward the staircase door and the elevator dinged again. Vail turned toward the elevator and its door opened once more. Vail chuckled as he entered.

"Third floor I take it."

The elevator moved up and stopped. Its door opened, allowing Vail to step onto the third floor of the hotel. Vail stepped out and felt a gust of wind move past him. Vail quickly turned to his right and saw a shroud of mist hovering through the hallway, entering a room without the door being opened.

"Here we go."

Vail ran toward the room door and opened it. He gazed around and doesn't spot the mist which flew into the room, although he can hear what appeared to be people talking amongst themselves in the hallway, which doesn't startle him, but raised his awareness of his surroundings.

"There's more of you on this floor I take it. Proves very interesting."

Vail stepped out into the hallway and could still hear the voices speaking to each other as if they were having a conversation to themselves. Vail reached into his coat pocket and pulled out the book of rituals. He raised the book up above his head and circled in his steps.

"You see this book I hold above me, spirits? This book will send you into the Other Side, where you all will be judged for your actions here on earth and will prove your eternal place."

A form of wind began to pick up from inside the hallway, Vail continued to speak toward the voices and held the book above his head. Vail continued as he saw shady forms of humans, all appeared to be yelling at him in anger and hatred. Vail knew these kinds of spirits and raised his voice as he spoke to them.

"I will not repeat myself to you spirits of the demonic darkness!" Vail said loudly. "You will respond to me and you will enter the Other Side and be judged for your earthly account."

The spirits screamed toward Vail as each of them began to fly toward him and entered the wall behind him. Vail never flinched when the spirits flew pass him. He continued to speak to them and held the book continuously above his head.

Vail understood a few of the spirits had indeed went over to the Other Side while the remaining ones had decided to remain in the hotel to attack Vail in any shape they could.

"I know you've traveled to the upper levels of this hotel, spirits. I intend greatly to seek you out and to release you from this place you currently call your home."

Vail walked toward the elevator and it no longer worked. Vail shrugged his shoulders, taking the stairs up to the fourth floor. Upon arriving on the fourth floor, Vail didn't receive any communication or sound from a spirit of any kind. He searched every room on the floor to make sure there wasn't a spirit hiding amongst his presence.

"Fourth floor appears to be clean." Vail said as he checked the last room.

He went up into the fifth floor and all he could see around him was trash and left-over furniture sitting out in the hallway. The hallway had an odor resembling a dumpster, which would be sitting out back or on the side of the hotel, though there were no dumpsters near the hotel. Vail searched every room on the fifth floor, jumping over rugged and molded furniture to get into some rooms. Some of the rooms had a damp feeling and they possessed the smell of damp air after a rainfall.

"Fifth floor is clean. Spiritually clean I might add."

Vail arrived on the sixth floor and as soon as he took a step forward, a mist of cold air blew past him. He could feel the presence of a spirit, whether it be human or demonic. Vail smirked as he walked slowly down the hallway, which was much cleaner than the fifth floor.

"Finally, one of you has started to present yourself toward me and of all the floors you decide to pick the sixth floor. Guess six is your lucky number."

"We do not like your trespassing, hunter." A disembodied voice said from the hallway.

"I heard that very clearly and I would like for you to speak to me again, so I can get a sense of your character and afterwards send you to the Other Side." Vail said.

"We demand you leave our home." The disembodied voice commanded.

"I'm not leaving this hotel until all of you are gone from it and it becomes nothing more than an old building waiting to be crumbled down."

A loud scream shrieked through the hallway, Vail covered his ears quickly to avoid minor damage to his ears. The shriek had immediately stopped. Vail removed his hands from his ears and the entire hallway was dead silent.

"Whatever you are and where ever you've come from, I am here to send you to another place where you will never escape your fate."

After searching the entire sixth floor, Vail continued to make his way upward toward the remaining floors, seven through thirteen. On the seventh floor, during Vail's searching of the rooms, he found a note which was left behind by someone who was either staying or working in the hotel. Vail read the note as it had implied there was some otherworldly force that dwelled before he hotel closed. Vail placed the note in his coat pocket.

"Seems you've been here a while." Vail said.

The eighth floor possessed neither anything related to the supernatural nor were any spirits contacted by Vail throughout the entire floor. The ninth floor possessed very little furniture and a shortage of rooms, whereas the first eight floors were settled with a total of twenty rooms where the ninth floor had a total of ten rooms. Vail kept his patience in check as he noticed there were no spirits being found within the upper floors.

"I know you're here and you are waiting on me to find you, yes?" Vail said. "I will find you and we will have our confrontation."

Vail stepped foot onto the tenth floor and spotted a difference in the air. A change of sorts which could only be caused by a weather effect, though it was continuing to snow on the outside, whereas the interior of the tenth floor felt a mixture of cold and heat. Vail had placed into his mind that he was dealing with a spirit or spirits that were unlike any he has encountered in his previous investigations.

"If you are on this floor with me, make yourselves known unto me." Vail said. "I heard one of you speak to me on the sixth floor and I demand that you speak to me now before I reach the thirteen floor and end this for good."

"Why have you come here, Travis Vail, the Spirit-Seeker." A voice said from the other end of the hallway. "You seem to be determined to eliminate us from our dwelling place and yet here we are."

Vail couldn't see the figure from the other end due to a dark mist covering its presence. Vail pulled out a flare and threw it toward the middle of the hallway. The flare lit up most of the hallway and all Vail could gather by his sight was a figure and on its hands were long sharpened nails and its eyes were like the cold sky to him.

"Come. Come Travis Vail. Follow me up to the thirteen-floor and you will receive what you've come for." The voice said as it disappeared.

Vail ran toward the other end of the hall, fanning away the dark mist that covered the end. Vail saw nothing and ran up toward the thirteen-floor, surpassing the eleventh and twelfth floors. Vail ran unto he reached the door that would lead him to the thirteen-floor. Vail kicked the door opened and looked around, realizing that the floor was a place where people would stay. The thirteen-floor appeared to be an office of some kind, apparently a secret office.

"What kind of place is this?" Vail questioned.

"This is our dwelling place, Spirit-Seeker." The voice said. "As is mine."

The voice appeared closer toward Vail as the entity revealed itself to him. The entity appeared to be a hybrid of both man and demon. Vail took a step back as he stared at the creature, never seeing a living being of that kind before in his lifetime.

"What in the hell are you?"

"I am known throughout the ages as Kamagrauto, servant of Dagor, the Soul Eater."

"Dagor? Soul Eater? What in the hell are you speaking about, demon beast?!"

"It seems you've never studied in the occult as deep as you thought. We're always hearing about what your work has done for many in the world. From your little stop at a mansion to that forest of druids. We know of you, Spirit-Seeker."

Vail stared at Kamagrauto, scanning the room for any others that might appear before him on the thirteen-floor.

"How have you been watching me? Why have you been watching me and for what purpose?"

"You are one of our enemies, Travis Vail." Kamagrauto said. "You and countless others all share the same goal of eliminating our kind from this earth to leave only the righteous alive to subdue it."

"There aren't others like me, demon. If there were, I would've already made myself known to them."

"The intriguing part of this meeting here is all of you mostly have encountered one another in the past at some point in time. Whether it was a small crossover or a passing by on the road. You've all met at some point in time and you all will meet each other again in the coming future, but that will be the moment where all of you get agree to join sides to face us."

"This isn't making any sense. I'm about to send you over."

Vail pulled out his book and raised it over his head. Kamagrauto laughed at Vail for doing the task. He even started clapping his hands and rubbing his sharp nails together to sidetrack Vail's focus.

"That little book isn't going to work on me, Vail. I am beyond an ordinary spirit. I was created by my master Dagor and only through him may I be put away."

"I won't let you leave this place alive and intact, demon." Vail said. "You must leave this place and take the remaining spirits with you."

"Why do you think I'm here?" Kamagrauto said. "I'm here on orders from Dagor to collect as many souls as possible and bring them back to him for observation."

"What is he observing them for?"

"Why to consume them of course and go gain as much strength as he needs to succeed in his plans."

"I will not allow such destruction to be cause in my presence!" Vail said as he ran toward Kamagrauto.

"You small pest."

Kamagrauto lifted Vail up off the ground and threw him against the wall as a frame that was hanging on the wall fell onto his head, cutting his forehead open.

"Very well, I will be leaving now, Travis Vail and we will indeed come across paths once again. But, that day will most certainly be your final investigation."

Kamagrauto vanished in a puff of smoke as Vail ran after it. Seeing nothing but an empty room, Vail leaves the thirteen floor and travels back down to the first floor. The sun began to shine down on Vail as he walked outside and sealed the hotel doors shut. He entered his car and drove away. Though, in his mind was Kamagrauto's words of what would come concerning Dagor and others whose work was similar to Vail's own.

TRAVIS VAIL, SPIRIT-SEEKER: FIRST SINS

I

WHAT CAME BEFORE

Reading through his past investigations and encounters with the otherworldly, Travis Vail, known in the occult circles as the Spirit-Seeker, is researching more of his past encounter with Kamagrauto, the demon who opened his mind to the larger world. After the visitation from Kamagrauto at the Black Raven Hotel and in finding the Mutant-Thing, Vail is curious about the world he's about to enter. A world where the supernatural comes into conflict with the rising heroes. A mixture that will only end in chaos.

Still studying, Vail's phone rang, and he answered with slight haste and ease of movement. His instincts were still kicking. His mind on Kamagrauto's words and his encounter with Abraham and The Swordman.

"Vail speaking."

"Trav, good to hear your voice."

"Ah. Dr. Galen Donovan." Vail said with a smirk. "Same here. Why have you called?"

"I have a case for you. If you're interested."

"What kind of case if I may ask humbly?"

"From what I've learned, it concerns the first sins?"

"First sins? As in the first sins committed after the Fall?"

"Correct."

Vail nodded. "I'm on board. Send me the details and I'll follow suit."

"Will do." Donovan said. "You'll have the information shortly."

Vail hung up and within several minutes, the information was sent to Vail through his email. Reading the files, Vail learned the first sins were moving through the world in slow form. Unusual to his previous encounters in past cases, there was a map attached to the files which detailed the past locations of the sins' movements. Vail packed his gear, what was needed, grabbed his black trench coat and left his lair.

Following the map's layout, Vail went across most of the United Kingdom into France and into Germany. Vail has spoken with several witnesses to the sightings and they explained the sins appeared as one. Embodied to moving around single filed. Whatever it was, it had no motives other than to terrorize and to instill fear into the humans it came across. After each movement it made, the more aggressive it became. From startling humans to torturing them if came close.

"This is something else." Vail noted. "Something far more powerful is at work here than just some series of haunting."

Vail continued his investigations and interviews for the next several days. During those days, Vail began to come across what looked to be plague doctors. Crouched in the shadows to walking past him in crowds. Vail took nothing from it until he managed to see one staring at him from the distance. The plague doctor dressed in an all-black robe. Covered from head to toe with its doctor's mask sticking out of its hood. Vail smirked.

"You think that frightens me, lad? Tell you what, take off that beak and we'll settle this like men."

The plague doctor stood still. Vail waited, yet, nothing came from the doctor.

"Figures." Vail said. "I'm going on about my business. Don't try to follow or you'll end up somewhere you won't like."

Vail contacted Donovan concerning the case and the uprising of plague doctors. Donovan stated the doctors are probably the result of the sins' travels. The doctors are following the path of the sins.

"They may be, but, there's something more to all of this. Something sinister at work."

"Why don't we meet up and discuss our ideas on this case?"

"Sure. Where are you right now?"

"In Italy."

"Let me guess, Venice."

"I'm having a word with Ms. Belinda Grazio. You remember her I presume?"

"I can't forget a face like hers. Anyhow, I'm leaving Germany. I'll be there as fast as possible."

"Take your time. Belinda is patient of your coming."

"She would be."

II

WHAT CAME AFTER

Vail entered the city of Venice near nightfall. Vail had walked through Venice reaching the hotel. When Vail came closer, he could see Donovan standing outside of a door.

"There he is." Vail said walking.

Vail made his way toward Donovan and the two hugged.

"You came quicker than I expected."

"I was on the move right after our conversation."

"Good timing."

"Not my best, but I try."

Vail investigated the hotel room. He saw no one inside. He gazed his eyes toward Donovan while pointing into the room. Donovan looked back into the room and turned to Vail.

"Looking for something?"

"I thought you said Belinda was here?"

"She's at her home." Donovan said. "She will meet with us in the morning. In the meantime, you and I need to discuss this case."

"Sure thing."

Vail entered the hotel room and Donovan followed. Inside, they sat at the coffee table. Atop the table were files Donovan had brought with him. The same documents he emailed to Vail to begin with. Donovan had passed Vail a bottle of beer and Vail drank.

"Plague doctors?" Donovan asked with confusion.

"I saw them at every location the sins had come across. They just stood there. Staring. I taunted one."

"Sounds like something you'll do."

"What would you do if you had a plague doctor staring down at you from across the area?"

"Where did the doctor go?"

"Not sure. I walked away afterwards. Warned it if it followed me it would end up in a far worse place."

"What is your conclusion so far?"

"These areas are connected. The sins aren't traveling by themselves. It's as if they're merged into one. Like they've become an entity."

"You believe the sins have become a living entity? Your presumption I'm assuming?"

"It would explain this more clearly. Besides, the only way for the sins to have merged into an entity, it would need to be brought together by someone of a darker power."

"What of that demon you encountered at Black Raven Hotel? Could he be responsible for this?"

"Wouldn't surprise me. However, he was keen on something else. Regarding others like myself in the field."

"How would it know of your future to start with? Demons aren't that intelligent when it comes to one's future. The past they're aware of."

"That demon was more powerful than our usual demons. This one claimed to be a lieutenant demon who worked for somebody called Dagor The Soul Eater."

"The Soul Eater?" Donovan jumped. "He hasn't been seen since the Middle Ages."

"Well, if his lieutenant is bumping around the world, he mustn't be hidden anymore."

"Your words are true." Donovan nodded. "Well, once we meet Belinda tomorrow, she'll tag along with us on this case."

"No offense, but, why is she interested in this case? I'm sure she has plenty of cases in this city."

"She wanted this case to work with you again. Though, not as I expect it to be. We're not going to Poveglia this time."

"Noted." Vail stood up from the table. "I'm going to get myself a room in this place. I'll speak to you in the morning."

"Sure thing, Travis. Good night."

"Same to you." Vail left Donovan's hotel room.

While Vail had obtained his own room, he walked down the hallway toward the room. Before he could put the key in, Vail spotted another plague doctor standing at the end of the hall. Cloaked in darkness. Yet, its' beak was glowing. Vail sighed.

"You choose to do this now?" Vail asked. "I would like some kind of answer here."

The doctor kept still. Vail shook his head and rubbed his hands together.

'Guess I'll have to make you."

Vail moved with haste toward the doctor and once he reached him, the doctor had vanished into a thin dark mist. Vail searched the surroundings and found nothing.

"This nonsense is something else."

Vail returned to his room and unlocked the door. He entered and went to sleep.

III

WHAT CAME BETWEEN

The following morning, Travis Vain and Galen Donovan entered a café and inside sitting was Belinda Grazio. They noticed, and Vail only sighed as they approached the table and sat down.

"I know." Belinda said. "You're thrilled to see me again."

"I know why you're here." Vail said. "Besides, that's not why I'm here."

"She's here to assist us on this case."

"I'm aware. So, let's get to it shall we."

"Fair enough." Donovan said. "We need your skills to help us solve this case around the first sins."

"The first sins? That's your case?"

"Can you help us is the question." Vail pointed out. "Can you?"

"I can help. Only if I can come along with the two of you."

"She would do this." Vail said.

"You can."

"*Prego*." Belinda said. "Glad we can work together again."

"I'm sure you are." Vail said. "Now, can we discuss this case?"

"Yeah. What do you mean by the 'first sins'?" Belinda asked.

"Travis can give you the details. It is his case after all."

"Sure thing. I've come across a number of plague doctors recently and all pf them have some sort of connection to the first sins."

"Like all of them?"

"Yes."

"And you want to find out where these doctors are going and who could be leading them?"

"Precisely. Which is why Galen decided to speak to you. Believing you could be of service to solving this obscure case."

"Well, I can be of service."

"Excellent. Help us and you can go on your way." Vail said.

"What is the plan for today?"

"Since I was visited by a plague doctor last night, I figured we make a trip back to the hotel and search the area. Perhaps, the quiet doctor left something for us to find."

"Well then, I will gather my things and meet you there."

Vail nodded as Belinda hugged Donovan and left the café. Vail turned to Galen, shaking his head.

"Is it always going to be like this with the two of you?" Donovan asked.

"As long as she focuses on the mission, everything will run smoothly."

"And if not?"

"Then, we will have problems. Delays. Something this job doesn't require us to have."

Vail and Donovan left the café and as they walked down the sidewalk, they stumbled across a pair of street preachers. Dressed in bright colors with the menorah and the Star of David on their clothing. They carried with them signs and a chart, detailing locations of the earth. Vail approached them, glancing at the chart.

"And what is this?"

"What do you think, Esau." The preacher said.

"Heh, Esau now." Vail uttered. "Is that what you just called me?"

"Esau is the white man. You are the Devil!" The Preacher yelled.

"Me the Devil? Look here, fellow, the only one of us who's truly the Devil is you and your gang of deceivers."

"Deceivers?! Read the Word, Esau!"

The Preacher looked, seeing Donovan approaching them next to Vail. The Preacher's eyes glanced back and forth between Vail and Galen.

"My brother, you can't be hanging around with the enemy."

"The enemy? This man is my friend."

"You can't be friends with Esau, my brother. Look at this chart right here."

Donovan looked at the chart and nodded. Facing the preacher and his brothers-in-arms.

"I have a solution to the problem. Mind if I speak it to you?"

"Yes sir."

"If the white man is truly Esau, then he is your brother."

"What do you mean by that?"

"Esau was born from Isaac's loins. Thereby, Esau is in fact a Hebrew."

"That's not what we're discussing, my brother. The white man is the Devil and the white man is Esau."

"Then, if Esau is the white man and the white man is the Devil, you should get busy at casting the Devil out of him. Free him from the demonic troubles."

The preacher stepped back, grabbing a hold of the Bible in hand. He shook his head.

"We can't help those who's minds have been wiped by the white man. We can't. You're a lost cause, my brother. I am deeply sorry. But, I hope **Yahawashi** has mercy on you and grants you entrance when he returns."

"As do I." Donovan said.

"Heh." Vail chuckled. "Hmm."

The two walked away as the preacher continued his preaching. They turned, entering an alleyway. Vail laughed, and Donovan shook his head.

"Didn't think they would be here." Vail said.

"They're growing. Besides, it's part of the endgame."

"As are many things happening today."

From there, smoke arose from the ground, startling the two. A thick black smoke.

"What is this?" Donovan asked.

"I know who it is."

From the smoke came Kamagrauto, the lieutenant demon. Cloaked in its robe and hood. Its eyes visible from the shadow and its horns spiked out. Kamagrauto levitated over the smoke. His legs could not be seen.

"Travis Vail. Galen Donovan. How intriguing it is to find you both here."

"Is that the demon you talked about?" Donovan asked.

"Yeah. That's him."

Kamagrauto glanced at Vail and Donovan. Its hands held together with his long, sharp, and dirty claws.

"Alright, what do you want?" Vail asked.

"To warn you of your current mission. You will not succeed."

"Is that so?"

"Your future depends on this case and I already know, you will fail. The first sins alone are far too vast for Travis Vail to solve on his own. You need guidance. Guidance from the other side and I can provide such."

"I understand your nobility. But, me and Galen have this under control."

"Oh, you do?" Kamagrauto gestured. "Then, I will be watching your every move and when you desire my aid and you will, I will make myself known unto you and those who will be at your side when the moment comes."

"What moment?" Vail asked.

"You will know. You will know."

Kamagrauto vanished into the smoke by falling. The darkness cleared from the alleyway and there was nothing remaining.

"That demon is noble?" Donovan asked.

"He has honor. I know. Strange for a demon to possess such a moral trait."

"Well, there are things not even we can comprehend."

"True. But, someday, I hope we can. Right now, we need to go and meet Belinda."

Making their return to the hotel, Belinda waited for them. She saw the looks on their faces.

"What happened?"

"We came across a demon." Donovan said.

"Or the demon came to us." Vail added.

"What kind of demon?"

"The lieutenant kind."

"That's not making any sense, Travis."

"I'm afraid it is true, Belinda. It's the same demon Travis met at the Black raven Hotel some time ago."

"Kamagrauto? Here?"

"Oh, you know his name." Vail chuckled.

"I thought you were only seeing things. I didn't expect him to exist."

"Well, lass, he exists and trust me, he's not one you would like to meet. Ask Galen of the encounter."

Donovan looked to Belinda and shook his head.

"Kamagrauto is not the typical demons we face. He is something far more ancient and we could feel his power."

"But, do not fret. He offered to help us."

"I hope you refused."

"Not the slightest. He told me whenever I needed his help involving this case, which he is aware of. So, I assume there are others in the spirit world who are familiar with this and aren't giving us any help. Kamagrauto told me to call on him if I needed his aid."

"But, you won't. we'll solve the first sins together."

"True. But, then again, stranger things have happened in this line of work."

Vail walked to the hotel room door.

"I'm going to return to my room and get ready for the work we have to do. I won't be long."

Vail left the room. Belinda turned to Donovan with uncertainty expressing from her face. Galen knew it and sat down.

"What's with him?"

"What do you mean? That's the way he works. Travis is a very different kind of occult detective."

"Yeah. Not one I would assume to have help from a demon. An ancient one at that."

"Why don't you go and talk to him. See what he tells you."

"He already doesn't want me here."

"And that is more reason for you to talk to him. Get through to him. I know it's possible."

"How so?"

"Because I am the one who trained him in this field. His mentor in a way. Anyway, go and speak with him. It'll give us enough time to prepare to find these plague doctors."

Belinda approached Vail's hotel room door and immediately the door opened. Vail stared at Belinda and she did the same. No words.

"What do you want?" Vail asked.

"Can we talk? For just a second."

Vail sighed as he allowed Belinda into his room. Shutting the door behind, Belinda stood, and Vail walked over to the table and sat down. He gestured his hand toward the other seat. Belinda sat with him.

"What?"

"What's with you?"

"How do you mean?"

"I mean your demeanor, your attitude. What's the problem?"

"There's plague doctors roaming around with the first sins on their back. I have to find out who's causing this and way."

"That's not what I'm talking about."

"Then I'm confused."

Belinda sighed.

"Why couldn't it have worked between us, Travis? Why didn't you bother to give it a chance?"

"You are not seriously asking me about relationship details right now."

"I am."

"Women always want to talk."

"Only if the men would listen to our words."

"I'm not trying to build up bitterness in my heart, lass. Besides that, I've told you before. A relationship with me won't work."

"Why not?"

"Because when I was young, I was visited by an angel. The angel warned me not to get married. Otherwise, tragedy would follow. Now, I see what the angel meant. Me traveling on this road of life. Dealing with the supernatural daily. Heh, if I did have a wife, she would've most likely divorced me or been killed in the process."

"But, there's always a way."

"Even though you're in this line of work, tragedy still strikes. The fact of Kamagrauto confronting me, proves the angel's point."

"Well, did this angel have a name?"

"He did."

"What was it?"

"Hmm. Michael."

"As in Michael the Archangel."

"Correct. Funny enough, he's been overseeing my activities since I was a little boy. No worries. However, I am keen on the fact he hasn't intervened with my confrontations with Kamagrauto. Maybe time will tell this course."

Vail sighed. Standing up from the chair, he grabbed his coat from the back of the chair, putting it on.

"Now, let's continue this case of ours."

IV

WHAT CAME WITHIN

Vail and Belinda met with Galen, who found the two of them together somewhat odd, but never the case. They moved forward with the case and after studying the trail of the plague doctor that Vail saw, a clue was given. A name connected to a series of plague doctor sightings. Belinda had the name.

"What is it?" Vail asked.

"Here's the name of the recent plague doctor sightings. All from witnesses who've seen the doctors and later a man would come and visit them. Asking about the doctors before they ever went public with a concern."

"The man's name." Donovan said. "What was it?"

"Timothy Ellis."

"Timothy Ellis. I've never heard of him before."

"I have." Vail said. "It's familiar to my ears."

"What do you know of this man, Travis?"

"He's deeply into the spiritual arts. Mystic stuff as well. But, in the occult circles, he doesn't go by that name. he is known and referred to as Balthazar."

"Is this the mage Balthazar a few have talked about?"

"It is. Balthazar is a mage. A powerful one. Took the name from the biblical magi. Cloaked in his dark-orange hood and robe, he gained power from a deep malevolent force. One of which I am unknown to. But, in time I will find out."

"So, where is Balthazar?" Belinda asked.

"New York City." Vail said. "Which means we have some traveling to do and in little time."

"Yeah, but how long before he finds out we're on to him?"

Vail turned and noticed a shadow hovering in the distance. He stared, and it revealed its eyes.

"Not long." Vail said, staring at the shadow.

"What is it?" Belinda said, turning to also see the shadow.

"What is that?" Donovan asked.

"Balthazar sent him." Vail said. "He already knows."

Vail ran after the shadow without haste.

"Where are you going?!" Belinda yelled.

"I'm going to see what this spirit knows!" Vail answered. "Don't follow me!"

Belinda went to follow, and Donovan held her back.

"Travis can handle himself."

"That's not what I'm worried about."

Vail chased the shadow, leaving Belinda and Donovan behind. The shadow brought Vail to a spot which was filthy, and the ground was covered in feces and vomit.

"Smells like shit." Vail uttered.

From its appearance, Vail knew it was a spot for homeless people.

"Show yourself, spirit!" Vail yelled.

"In front of him, the shadow appeared. Yet, no fear within it as it morphed into physical form. It resembled a young man, yet he was covered in blood, and chewed on swine's flesh. Vail smirked.

"The hell have we got here. A sin entity."

"Balthazar will have your soul." The entity uttered.

"I think not."

Vail tossed a handful of salt on the entity, startling it. There, Vail began to recite a chant, commanding for the entity to be loosed from Balthazar's hold and to return into the void. The entity was powerful enough to break Vail's chant, forcefully shoving him to the brick wall behind him. Vail fell to the ground and quickly, Kamagrauto arose from the pavement, snatching the entity by the throat and biting it, ripping off its astral head as the body returned to shadow form and fell. Evaporating into thin air.

"I'm not understanding any of this." Vail said.

"You have a higher calling, Travis Vail and I will not allow anyone to turn you away from your cause."

"You know about Balthazar? And how he's behind these plague doctors scaring folks."

"Balthazar has risen up the first sins. Yes. But, there is another spirit lurking the world. One far more powerful than Balthazar and is on the run from another soul as we speak."

"I wish that particular soul the best in his endeavors. Could use the bit of the help every now and then. How come you didn't tell me all this before I went further?"

"I know many things. Things even the smartest man would tremble at the sound."

"Good thing, I'm not the smartest man. I'm just an exorcist."

"One with a higher purpose."

"Then, why don't you just travel onto New York City and stop Balthazar for me? That way, I can focus more on this 'higher purpose'."

'Because it is not my duty to finish your work. You started this case, you must finish it."

Vail chuckled.

"I'll be. You know your kind are some slick sons of bitches."

"Do not compare me to the common demons you've slain."

"I'm not." Vail asked. "But, you really are a strange demon, lad."

"I am not like those demons. I am Kamagrauto. Kamagrauto."

Kamagrauto vanished into the black smoke as before. Vail shrugged himself and scoffed.

V

WHAT CAME ABOUT

Vail returned to Belinda and Galen, who saw his tiredness and often slackly behavior after things have arisen. They approached him with concern and he only smiled.

"What happened to the shadow?" Donovan asked.

"It was taken care of."

"How?" Belinda wondered.

"Kamagrauto killed it."

"The demon Kamagrauto?"

"Yes, Galen. The same demon we met in the alleyway. I confronted the damn thing. By the way, the shadow was a sin entity."

"That can't be so?" Donovan said. "there hasn't been one of them since the World Wars."

"And yet, here it is and not out of curiously either. Balthazar conjured it up."

"What happened to the spirit, Travis?" Belinda asked.

"I nearly came close to casting it away, but it possessed a power that outweigh my voice and tossed me against the wall. After that, Kamagrauto appeared and decapitated the spirit. Good for me."

"The demon helped you?" Donovan asked. "It killed the spirit right in front of your eyes?"

"Yes. Afterwards we spoke, and he revealed to me he's been aware of this whole case the entire time. I scoffed and wondered how come he couldn't do the work for us. Said it wasn't in his purpose. However, Balthazar is the one behind all of this and there's another sin spirit roaming the earth. But, Kamagrauto confirmed to me that another individual is chasing that spirit right now. So, hopefully we won't have too much work on our hands."

"So, what is our current objective?" Belinda asked.

"Galen, call Colton, tell him to meet us in New York. We need to confront Balthazar now and fast before more of his little ideas manifest into reality."

Vail, Belinda, and Donovan made their travels and arrived in New York City. Prepared to meet Balthazar. Wherever he may reside.

VI

WHAT CAME TO BE

Vail, Belinda, and Donovan stood in Times Square. Seeing the crowds go by, walking about their business. Galen shook his head in shame.

"They're just coming and going."

"It's their nature, Galen. Besides, it proves we're not the ones trapped in Pop Culture and materialism."

"Now, where will Colton be?" Belinda asked.

"He should be around here somewhere."

Vail looked out, not seeing his ally. Later, he turned his head and from there, he managed to get a glance at Colton. He pointed.

"He's coming this way."

Colton Levi approached them and shook hands. Standing in the middle of Times Square mind you amid the roaming crowds.

"Good to see you." Vail said. "Now, why did you want us to meet you out here?"

"Because, the guy you're looking for oftentimes roams through here."

"Are you sure?"

"Plague doctors are seen continually here. It's looked at as just a cosplay show."

"Point us in the direction." Vail said.

They followed Colton through the Square, moving past the crowds.

There, Vail and Galen noticed a group of street preachers, yelling at all the white men in the crowds. Vail scoffed as the argument escalated to a brawl.

"They're everywhere."

"It's part of the times, Travis." Donovan said.

"True one."

Colton had led them into a spot where they set shops. He pointed toward the spot which had a crescent moon carved on the door.

"Is this the spot?" Belinda asked.

"It certainly is." Vail confirmed. "Let's see what's inside."

They entered the shop and quickly, surrounded by plague doctors. They raised up their guards as the doctors stood quirt and still.

"Oh, this is the place." Vail said.

The doctors approached them and suddenly, took steps back. Moving in a fashioned line on each side, leading them further into the shop down a hallway. They walked down the hallway and they reached a room. In the room were images of occult symbols, sacrifices, and spells. A pentagram was carved into the wooden floor. Vail stepped forward, seeing a hooded man crouched down at the fire.

"Stand up, you're embarrassing yourself here." Vail said.

The hooded man stood up, removing his hood. Revealing himself to be Balthazar. Vail smiled. Pointing.

"You son of a bitch!" Vail laughed.

"Travis Vail. The Spirit-Seeker."

"In the flesh."

"I figured you would come."

"Had not choice, lad. I've come to stop your doings. Raising up plague doctors and spirits. The shit has to stop."

"It will not cease until my work is complete."

"Your work is done. Just let it all go. Quit working for the enemy and just retire."

Balthazar raised his hands, shoving Belinda, Galen, and Colton to the floor. Holding them in place with a sort of spiritual bind. Only he and Vail remained standing.

"Why are you doing this?"

"Because I have a master to praise. One who granted me these gifts. I must serve him with all my might."

"Then, your master has to deal with me. And others out there."

"My master's coming was already thwarted by someone. I will not allow the Cryptic Zone to remain shut. He will rise."

"No, he won't."

"And what will you do when he rises and comes for you?"

"Don't all malevolent forces come for me? It's my job to piss your kind off."

"How about a deal."

"A what now?"

"A deal. You leave me to my work and I let your friends live."

"Um, deal declined. However, I can offer you a deal."

"Like so?"

"Let my friends go or find yourself entering Hell a little early than you expected."

"You cannot kill me." Balthazar declared. "No man can murder me!"

"I'm not going to murder you. I'm simply going to offer you a trip. Besides, best you deal with me and not Kamagrauto."

Balthazar froze. His eyes went wider.

"Kamagrauto?" Balthazar asked.

"Yes. You know, lieutenant demon. Works for Dagor the Soul Eater. That kind of guy. He knows of your work by the way. Told me of it. Raising the first sins and all. Plague doctors and such. He knows. And if he knows, who's the say the others know as well."

Balthazar shook, dropping the hold on Belinda, Galen, and Colton. Vail smirked.

"They will not have me." Balthazar said. "My master will protect me!"

"Then, let's see him protect you from this."

Vail raised up his hand, shoving Balthazar down. He began to chant and before he could start, a whirlwind of blue flames surrounded Balthazar. Taking him away. The room was silent. Galen approached the spot. Belinda and Colton were confused.

"The hell just happened?" Colton asked.

"His master took him." Vail said.

"What of the first sins?" Belinda asked. "What of the doctors?"

"We'll see if they still stand." Donovan said.

They returned to the entrance, discovering the doctors are gone. Vail knew Balthazar's fear had driven the doctors and the first sins away. He smirked as they left the shop. The case was done. Yet, Balthazar was somewhere in the world. Possibly in other realms of existence. Vail knew he would see him again down the road.

With everyone returning to their proper places, Vail sat inside his own domain, researching more on the sin entity Kamagrauto mentioned in their conversation. There, Vail discovered there's an ancient power had risen, which is the cause for the sin entity's presence.

"In my line of work, things happen for the worst. Usually the better."

He knew the power was far too great for himself to face. By that standard, Vail went to visit a friend. A friend in Washington D.C.

HEAVEN HAS CALLED: ALL CALLED FROM ABOVE

I

AFTERLIFE VISITOR

Gabriel Abraham turned around in his office, staring at the door. Where Travis Vail, the Spirit-Seeker stood. Vail had his hands in his coat pocket with a stern look on his face. Abraham was confused to Vail's unknown and sudden visit.

"Too soon." Vail said grinning.

"Why are you here?"

"Something's happening, and I can't handle it on my own."

"What do you mean?"

"Something huge. There's a powerful force that's rising beneath the earth. Preparing to make an entrance into our world. One that will certainly end all on this world."

"Demonic force?"

"Stronger."

"Good to see you two here." A voice said, coming from the lobby area of Abraham's Revelation Center.

Vail and Abraham left the office to find the stranger, standing in the lobby. He was of African descent and was dressed modestly. Brown slacks, shoes, with a long-sleeve shirt and vest. He also wore a black fedora. Vail and Abraham have never seen the man before in the fields.

"Who are you?" Vail asked.

"How did you get in?" Abraham questioned.

"Front door was open. Figured I would make myself in and on serious purpose."

"Your name, lad?" Vail said.

"Name stays with me. But, those in our field of work call me Papa Afterlife."

"Papa Afterlife?" Abraham said. "What kind of name is that?"

"Afterlife? As in the magician Papa Afterlife?"

"That would be me."

"Hmm." Vail said. "Funny, you're different that I thought."

"You know this man?"

"No. but, I've heard of his work across the Atlantic. Done some things in Africa, India, places as such."

"Good. Then, you have an idea as to why I'm here."

"Something of the sort."

"Now, what is this thing of serious purpose?"

"There's a dark force coming. Almost near the physical plane of this existence. I was planning on paying you both a visit at your residence. But, given the tow of you here now, makes the message all easier."

"And the message is?"

"This force is ancient. Very ancient. You came across the sin entity during your mission overseas, Vail. You've already sensed the power. Plus, there's a stronger entity roaming around called the Sin Phantom. The Phantom was already chased down by the Death Chaser and is still on the loose."

"Death Chaser?" Abraham said. "There's no such thing as one of them."

"You haven't been studying much have you." Afterlife uttered. "The

Death Chaser has been around for ages. You'll need his help in stopping this coming threat."

"You're here to tell us to form a team?" Vail smirked. "Like the heroes over after the Retropolis incident."

"Something along those lines. Because, this threat cannot be stopped with just the two of you. You'll need a unit. One made up of detectives like yourselves, and other forces at work. Spiritual assassins, cryptids, anything you can get to muster up enough power to send this force back into the prison where it belongs."

"And will you be a part of this team?" Abraham asked.

"I'll be watching. An overseer if you so ask."

"Great." Vail said. "Watching from the sidelines."

"I can do more when I'm invisible to the enemy. Soon, you may find that out."

"One can only dream, sunshine."

Afterlife turned away, approaching the door. He stopped, turning back toward Vail and Abraham.

"Unify your members. You do not have much time."

Afterlife exited the Center. Vail turned to Abraham, who was confused about the entire scenario.

"You think Cinderella will be of use to us?"

"We'll have to ask her." Vail said. "Right now, we need to gather some information on possible recruits. If what Afterlife is saying is true, we will need all the help we can get."

II

CALLING THOSE THAT ARE ABOVE

Vail and Abraham set out on their journey to recruit the members possible for their unit. After doing some digging, Vail came up with a list of names. Through much research and sightings across the world, the names he chose were the ones felt closest to the possible unit.

"Where are we headed first?" Abraham asked.

"Chicago. There's a man out there who calls himself the Spiritual Assassin. Figured giving him a look will determine much more."

"His name?"

"John Terror." Vail said. "Supposedly, he's a nubreed."

"One of them. I see."

"Plus, he was in Retropolis during their incident. Means he's in good company with the rising heroes. Maybe he knows more than we do."

Vail and Abraham traveled from D.C. to Chicago. There, they came across a place in the outskirts of the city. Away from the public. They looked around, it's quiet and still.

"He's here?" Abraham asked.

"Said to be. Might as well knock on the door."

Abraham knocked, the door opened. They didn't see Terror, but they saw his ally.

"Who are you guys?"

"We're detectives." Vail said. "Looking for John Terror. Heard he resides at this place."

"And how would you know that?"

"Like I said, lad, we're detectives."

"Then, you're pretty sloppy." A voice said from behind Vail and Abraham.

"Shit." Abraham said.

They turned around to see terror himself standing behind them with two guns pointed at their heads. Vail smirked while Abraham was unsure of what to do. Terror looked at the young man standing at the door.

"Carl, go inside. You two, follow him."

"Sure thing." Vail said.

They followed Carl into the hideout of Terror. They were placed at the chairs near the working table. Terror approached them, removing his black trench coat and sunglasses. He sat in front of them, measuring them from their size to potential skill set.

"I know what you're doing." Vail uttered.

"Good." Terror replied. "Now, tell me, why are two strange detectives suddenly at my door?"

"We're not ordinary detectives." Abraham said. "We're occult detectives."

"Occult detectives?"

"Yes." Vail said. "He is Gabriel Abraham. Known as the Devilhunter of Washington D.C. You've heard of the Revelation Center, haven't you?"

"Once or twice. And you are?"

"Travis Vail, the Spirit-Seeker. I travel much."

"Ok, so why are you here? Why come to me? And what for?"

"We are recruiting possible members for a team. There's a supernatural threat coming, and it could very well-"

"Not this shit again."

"What?" Vail asked. "What shit?"

"I've done my team shares with those heroes."

"The Retropolis Incident? We know all about it. That tells us, you aligned yourself with those major heroes. Swordman and the like. I have to ask, was this before or after The Swordman confronted the Mutant-thing in the woods?"

"How should I know?"

"Then, how did the two of you meet?"

"We had some similar business. Taking down the same crime lords. We had an early scuffle, but, we're on good terms now."

"Splendid to hear. Then, you don't mind joining yourself with us."

"I'm not a team player. I did what I had to do in Retropolis for those who couldn't defend themselves."

"I get that." Vail said. "But, I have to ask, if the opportunity arose once more, would you take it?"

"Instead of just a city, it's the world." Abraham said. "Much larger than what you're accustomed to."

"How large of a threat are we talking?"

"One that could wipe out all life on this earth and perhaps breach the spiritual planes."

"That bad, huh?"

"It is." Abraham said. "So, what do you say?"

Terror nodded.

"When the time comes, I'll be there."

"How can we be sure of that?" Abraham asked.

"Lend some trust my way. You'll see I'm telling the truth."

"Fair enough." Vail said. "May we leave now?"

"By all means."

Vail and Abraham left Terror's hideout. Returning to Vail's vehicle. They sat inside as Vail looked over the other names. Vail circled Terror's name.

"Who's next?" Abraham asked.

"A friend in London. Figured she would help us out."

"Off to London. Again."

Traveling to London, they waited near the Big Ben once again at night. Abraham looked around for her as he did before.

"She's not here yet?"

"I gave her a phone call." Vail said. "She knows we're here."

Sliding down the walls of Big Ben was Cinderella. She landed, standing in front of the two occult detectives. They hugged each other with smiles. A rare thing to see in their fields.

"I got the call." Cinderella said. "What is it this time?"

"We need your help. Again. Only this time, it involves a more powerful force."

"How powerful?"

"Strong enough to wipe out all life and enter the spiritual dimensions."

"Well, this all sounds like a lot to handle. I'm still in an ongoing investigation."

"If this force rises, you won't have any investigations to cover. Cindy, please, you have to align with us and take out."

"That bad?" Cinderella asked.

"It is."

"Confronting the Mutant-Thing was fun. I guess I can add in the spare time."

"Great." Vail said. "Now, we wait."

"For what?" Abraham asked.

"Cindy wasn't the only one I contacted."

"Who else is in London besides me?"

"An old soul."

From the ground erupted a white mist. Surrounding Vail, Abraham, and Cinderella. The mist turned, morphing into itself, forming an astral body. The body formed and stood before them. Wearing clothing from the Victorian era. The body was of a man. Vail applauded the entrance.

"Abraham, Cindy, meet Robert Shaw. Or as the folktales call him, the Ghost of England."

"The Ghost of England?" Cinderella said. "I thought that was only a story."

"It's more than a story, lass. See, you're looking at him."

"Travis Vail, Spirit-Seeker." Shaw said. "Gabriel Abraham, the Devilhunter. Cindy Lawson, known as Cinderella. I stand before the three of you this night to declare my allegiance to your cause."

"That was easy." Abraham said.

"I figured you may know this we don't." Vail said. "Is there anything we don't know?"

"Best for you to meet with the Unholy Knight called Creed and the Death Chaser, a Soul of Retribution."

"Creed and the Death Chaser?" Cinderella asked.

"Me and Abraham were already told about meeting the Chaser. Trust me, that is soon to come. But, about this Creed fellow, where can we find him?"

"I will guide you to him. But, beware of his aggression. For he is keen to discovering the rising force that threats this world."

"Duly noted." Vail said. "Then, let's get going."

III

THE UNHOLY KNIGHT AND THE SOUL OF RETRIBUTION

Returning to the States, Vail, Abraham, and Cinderella are guided by the Ghost of England toward an old church in the Northwest counties. Reaching near the city of Hartford, Connecticut. The Ghost of England signaled a peculiar church building. One with a large black cross standing atop the structure.

"I've been there before." Vail said.

"What for?" Cinderella asked.

"Exorcism of a old man. However, Connecticut is filled with much paranormal and demonic activity. I know from experience."

"And is this where we find this Creed?" Abraham asked Shaw.

"Yes. He will be here soon. Trust my words."

"How soon?" Vail uttered. "I'm just curious is all."

"Soon."

"Tonight? Tomorrow morning? Next week? When? You must have a particular clue."

"You'll see."

"I guess I will."

The Ghost turned to face the group and his eyes shined upon the cross. Yet, he caught movement atop the structure. Vail caught his glimpse and gazed up himself.

"What is it, Trav?" Cinderella asked.

"We've found him. Or, he's found us."

The moving object lunged down toward them, landing on its feet in front of them. They stepped back as the dark blue cloak edged itself back to reveal Creed himself. Creed raised up from his bent position of the landing. Standing tall, facing the unit. His golden eyes gazed at them. His cloak echoing the sound of a chilling wind.

"Who are you?" Creed asked.

"We're detectives." Vail said. "Besides the Ghost here."

"We have no intention of bothering you." Abraham declared. "But, we need your assistance with a dire cause."

"The world is full of causes. Mine aren't sealed in the natural realm."

"Which is why we're here." Vail said. "There's a powerful force rising from beneath the earth. If we don't stop it soon, it will wipe out all life. Everything. Humans. Animals. Plant life. All of it."

"Where is the origin of this threat?"

"I… I don't know."

"Then you are wasting your time."

"Please, listen to us." Vail said, grabbing a hold of Creed's arm.

"Best you remove your hand before you have it no longer."

Vail pulled back his hand from Creed. Smirking.

"You must have some knowledge of a powerful force. Something."

"You speak not of the cryptic Zone."

"Don't think so. I thought that place was sealed."

"It is sealed." Creed said. "I and a fellow angel closed its portals from opening across the world."

"Then, it can't be someone from the Cryptic Zone." Abraham said. "Vail, what do you think it could be?"

"I'm working on it."

From behind them, a spiraling flame emitted from thin air. Causing them to turn around, startling them without haste. Creed stood in front of them, his cloak flowing roughly, his claws sharpened and his gaze keen.

"The hell is that?" Cinderella asked.

"I've seen such a thing before." Vail said.

"Where?" Abraham wondered.

"It's the entrance of the Death Chaser."

The Death Chaser walked out of the spiraling flame and shut its door behind him. He stood face to face with Creed. Two opposing forces of the supernatural realm.

"The Unholy Knight." The Death Chaser said.

"A Soul of Retribution." Creed remarked.

"What's going on here?" Vail asked.

"I should ask you the same, Travis Vail." The Death Chaser said. "I have been tracking all your movements since you were visited by Papa Afterlife."

"Seriously?" Abraham asked.

"Don't feel too bad. It's his job."

"Death Chaser." The Ghost of England said. "Tell us of your purpose here. What do you know of this rising power?"

"More than all of you combined."

"That's good to know." Vail uttered.

"The rising force is a malevolent entity known as Demonticronto. My sworn adversary. Me and my liege were dealing with a soldier of his. A sin phantom."

"Sin Phantom?" Abraham asked. "The hell."

"Don't be too shocked. I know what he's speaking of. I came across this sin phantom during my investigation in Italy. It's a powerful foe. But, a lieutenant demon protected me from its wrath."

"What demon?" The Death Chaser asked.

"Kamagrauto. Heard of him?"

"I have."

"Who is Kamagrauto?" Abraham asked with confusion. "What is going on here?"

"We can explain later, Abraham. For right now, we need to focus on how to stop this Demonticronto demon from rising."

"Creed, Death Chaser." Shaw said. "Align yourselves this day with them. Aid them in stopping Demonticronto and the Sin Phantom."

"I will aid you." Death Chaser said. "Only to stop Demonticronto from causing much harm to this reality."

"As will I." Creed said.

"Excellent." Vail said. "Now, all we need is some guidance on finding a place where Demonticronto's power is growing."

A great flash of white light pierced through he air. Causing a rift between realms. Everyone covered their eyes from the great shine except for Creed and Death Chaser, who are immune to such power. From the rift appeared a man dressed in black with an midnight blue cloak, white gloves and a hat. His long white hair stood out amongst his white facial hair and shining eyes. His pupils could not be seen.

"Who are you supposed to be?" Vail asked.

"I am the Visitant Outlander and I have come to guide you all in this quest you have taken upon yourselves.

IV

THE BROTHERLESS ONE AND THE WRATH OF *YAH*

"Visitant Outlander?" Vail asked. "My, I thought you were just a myth. Hidden away by the ancestors of old."

"I am very real as I stand here before your very eyes."

"I can see that. Which means the other guy exists as well."

"He does."

Vail nodded.

"This is great."

"I don't get what's happening here?" Cinderella asked. "Why have you come to help us? We have Creed and the Death Chaser for that."

"All of you combined together cannot stop Demonticronto's grown power and with the Sin Phantom at his side. I have come to grant an offering to you."

"What kind of offering, lad?"

"To lock away Demonticronto."

"Lock him up?" Abraham asked. "What on earth for?"

"There is no prison that can keep the sin fire from burning Demonticronto." The Death Chaser said. "I will kill him when it comes."

"You shouldn't" Outlander said. "For Demonticronto's existence serves a much greater cause."

"I thought the greater cause was to take him out." Vail said. "Eliminate the evil. Put away the evil. Not imprison it so it can break out."

"Killing such a powerful force will only cause more tragedy than peace."

"And how would you be aware of such causes?" Creed asked. "What happened in the past to alter someone's mind such as yours of a simple cause?"

"I've been around for ages. Much longer than this physical realm. I know what happens when the greater plan is thwarted or tapped."

"Now, I get it." Vail uttered.

"Get what?" Cinderella asked.

"Why the other guy doesn't like Outlander here. He's too into the whole justice motif."

"What other guy?" Abraham wondered.

"He's here." Vail grinned, looking up.

Like a falling cloud, he came down from the night sky. Cloaked in a dark violet cloak and hood. Only his red eyes were visible unto the shining of his presence caused his face to appear. Brighter than Outlander's light. His amulet glowed like the sun. he approached Outlander, standing toe to toe with him.

"Dark Manhunter." Outlander said. "The walking embodiment of the Wrath of Yah."

"Visitant Outlander." Manhunter said. "The Brotherless One. Looking for a way to assist all humanity in its endeavors."

"This is good to hear." Vail said. "Now, we don't need a scuffle between two cosmic forces. Not yet anyway. Manhunter, may I get your view on all of this?"

"Demonticronto must be killed. Execute him before more damage is done."

"Killing him will only bring more harm into this world." Outlander said. "You're speaking tragedy upon their lives."

"Their lives will only find peace when those like Demonticronto and the Sin Phantom are eliminated from existence. Permanently."

"Then, it's settled." Vail said. "We take down Demonticronto."

"As we should." Chaser said. "I will give the final blow."

"Oh, will you and Outlander be joining us on this journey?"

"We will be around." Manhunter said. "Right on time."

"I'll take your word for it."

Manhunter and Outlander vanished from their sight. Vail looked around, seeing everyone else still standing by. He nodded. Impressed.

"Now, all we need is one more member."

"And who is that going to be?" Cinderella wondered.

"A fellow friend from Retropolis."

"Come on." Cinderella said. "He's not going to stop what he's doing just to help us out."

"I'm not talking about him. I'm speaking of the other guy."

Cinderella thought for the moment. Abraham sighed and Vail grinned.

"Oh. Him."

V

THE MUTANT-THING RISES

The unit traveled to the city of Retropolis. Upon arriving, they noticed the city was under a minor form of martial law. Streets were still and quiet. There was hardly anybody along the sidewalks or outside.

"What's been happening here?" Vail wondered.

"I guess he's cleaning the city faster than I would expect." Cinderella said.

"Hmm." Vail replied.

"Whatever happened to John Terror joining us?" Abraham asked.

"Fumy you mention that. I called him as we were headed this direction. He said he would meet us in the wilderness."

"Meet us there? Why not here?"

"Out in the open I guess."

"We must reach this forest soon." Shaw said. "I can sense Demonticronto's power surging from below our feet."

"Understood." Vail said.

Entering the dark forest near Retropolis, they traced their steps from before, coming across a large crater-sized hole in the ground.

"This was the spot." Abraham said.

"I remember." Vail replied.

"How do you plan to conjure him?" Cinderella asked.

In the distance, motorcycle sounds entered the forest. They turn back, seeing Terror getting off his bike, walking toward their direction. Vail waved his hands for Terror to see.

"Good thing he's here." Abraham said.

"We'll see for sure."

"I told you I would come on my time."

"Yeah. Right after I called you."

"Seemed like the right moment." Terror grinned. "Now, why are you all out here in the woods? At night?"

"Here to find an old friend." Vail said.

"I wouldn't call him a friend." Abraham gestured.

"Then what is he?"

"A monster." Cinderella said. "One of cryptid origins."

"Nice to know."

Death Chaser started to move around the area. His eyes gazed on the surroundings. As he turned, facing the city. He pointed with great intension. The unit wasn't sure to what he was seeing.

"The Phantom." Chaser said. "He's in the city."

"Are you sure?" Vail asked.

"I know."

"Well, I have an idea." Cinderella said. "Why don't we split up."

"How so?" Abraham questioned.

"Me, Shaw, and the Chaser go find this Sin Phantom while you, Vail, Terror, and Creed summon up the big creature."

"I'm not for this, Cindy." Vail said. "But, since what Chaser said is true, best be going, lass."

Cinderella nodded as she, Shaw, and the Chaser went back into Retropolis. Vail sighed, turning back to the crater in the ground. He stepped into it. Stomping the soil, twisting his foot.

"What are you doing?" Terror asked.

"Waking the big fellow up."

"And he's just going to pop up out of that hole?"

"I hope so. Otherwise, I'm dirtying up my shoes." Vail smirked.

Cinderella, Shaw, and the Chaser walked on he road within Retropolis. Still no one outside. The Chaser moved faster than the two, walking near an alleyway. Cinderella and Shaw followed him. Discovering him coming to a stop, where they saw the Sin Phantom himself.

"You've found me." The Phantom said.

"I'm sending you away." The Chaser said.

"You're not supposed to be here." Cinderella gestured.

"Then, where can I go?"

"To the pit!" Chaser yelled.

Chaser emitted sin fire from his hands and threw it at the Phantom, who dodged the flames. Cinderella ran toward him, trying to grab him by his throat. The Phantom morphed his body into a transparent form, causing Cinderella to slip as he snatched her by the coat and tossed her against the Chaser. Shaw levitated toward the Phantom. Both entities staring down.

"You have violated the natural law." Shaw said.

"And you are going to lecture me on law? I know your history, Robert Shaw. Don't assume yourself as one of the helpless."

"My past is dead. Just as your soul!"

Shaw went to touch the Phantom, but the Phantom grabbed him by his head and his hand glowed like a blue flame above Shaw. He shook himself, trying to get free and as he reached for the Phantom's arm, he was let go.

"Shaw?" Cinderella yelled.

"He's currently occupied right now." Phantom said. "You will have to wake him up."

Shaw's ghostly body arose from the ground, facing Cinderella and the Chaser. The Chaser stepped forward, sensing something odd with Shaw.

"Stand behind me, Cinderella."

"What's wrong?"

"The Phantom, he's done something to Shaw."

"Like mind control?"

"No. he's awoken the once living nature when his being. Sin has crawled back into his soul. Wickedness is consuming him."

"What can we do?"

"We can beat it out of him. He's only a spirit. Not living flesh."

"Do well with such." The Phantom said. "I must be going. See you all soon when my master arrives!"

The Phantom vanished. Shaw's sin-filled spirit rushed toward the Chaser, grabbing him by the throat and holding him close. Cinderella attended to punch Shaw, but him as a spirit, she was powerless.

"Poor girl." Shaw said. "You're no help once more."

"You leave the woman out of this." The Chaser said. "I will cleanse your spirit of the sin that has entered you!"

"Why? I've never felt more alive."

"You're not alive. You're dead."

Vail, Abraham, Terror, and Creed stood around the crater. Vail reached into his pocket, pulling out his ritual book. Terror was confused, standing amongst a group of men he's never met. He gazed toward Creed, looking at his flowing cloak.

"How does that work?"

"It works with my mind." Creed said.

"Is that so." Terror replied. "I guess it works wonders."

"When it needs be."

"I'm going to read this ritual in Latin." Vail said. "It should summon the big fellow."

"Why Latin?" Terror questioned.

"It works for circumstances like this."

"What of Hebrew, Greek, Arabic, or Persian?"

"I've dabbled in it before. Best be careful with those if you ask me."

Terror nodded. "I see."

"Are you sure this will work properly?" Abraham asked.

"You were with us last time, remember?"

"This isn't like last time. He knows who we are."

"He doesn't know Creed or Johnny boy. We'll be fine."

Abraham shook his head and Vail grinned. Opening the book, turning the pages. He stopped and looked at the three around him.

"Ready?"

"Sure." Abraham said.

"Proceed." Creed said.

"Go for it." Terror gestured. "I'm curious."

Vail stood steady, gazing into the crater. His eyes focused on the page within the book. One hand stretched outward over the crater.

"*Voco super te, qui habitas in terra ejus qui creavit elementa. Ergo surge, et sta in conspectu nostro.*"

The crater began to glow a bright green. They stepped back as the dirt flew into the air, falling upon them like heavy rain. After the dirt had fell and settled, their eyes were focused on who was standing in the middle of the crater. Vail smiled.

"You rose!"

Vail approached the Mutant-Thing. Standing in the center of the crater. His appearance hadn't' changed since their last encounter. Mutant-Thing looked around, seeing Abraham, Terror, and Creed. He looked down toward Vail.

"Travis Vail." The Mutant-Thing said.

"Listen, bog fellow. We're here on important notice. Not like last time."

"Why have you truly come? Why disturb my slumber?"

"Because there's a powerful force preparing to rise from beneath the earth. If it does, it has the potential to destroy everything."

"What is the destroyer's name?"

"Demonticronto apparently."

"Hmm." Mutant-Thing uttered. "His power is great. He was defeated ages ago by those such as yourselves. But, I see you're missing several warriors"

"They're currently busy finding a sin phantom. Working for Demonticronto it seems."

"And you require my aid in taking Demonticronto down?"

"Yes." Vail said. "That is why we're truly here. Honestly."

Mutant-Thing turned, seeing Creed. He pointed toward him, letting the others look and see.

"He is unholy. Made of malevolent origins. How can he be trusted in such a time?"

"I rebelled against the one who formed me in such manner."

"I smell the stench of the Cryptic Zone on you."

"I was chosen as an apprentice to Adrambadon, Lord of the Cryptic Zone. His demands were dire. But, over time, I broke from his grasp and chosen to make a better change with this curse he has bestowed upon me."

"No matter. He has power over you as long as you're connected to the source."

"Not to cut off this contact." Vail said. "But, we're going to need Creed in order to stop Demonticronto and his little sin lad roaming on about."

"As you say. I will give my aid to this cause. Only to help the earth remain in its current stead."

"Understood." Vail said. "How will this work now? When we find the phantom and Demonticronto, how will you help us? Am I to summon you once more?"

"When the time comes, you will know of my help."

"That's it?" Vail questioned. "A tight, but small riddle."

"Take it for what it's worth, Spirit-Seeker. Now, leave this forest. I must return to my slumber."

"Fair enough."

The Mutant-Thing burrowed himself into the crater as the dirt covered him completely.

"Now what?" Terror asked.

"We find the others. Tell them it's time we come up with a plan."

"Hopefully, they've captured the Sin Phantom first." Abraham said. "Save us all some time."

"Let's find out."

The Chaser and Shaw fought one another with Cinderella giving slight aid to the Chaser. A ring of sinfire had surrounded the sin-corrupted Shaw. Cinderella moved over, standing next to the Chaser.

"You must be purged once more." The Chaser commanded.

"You can't take away such a feeling. I can feel pleasure again. Lust. Greed. I can sense them all."

"That is why I must do this. Only for the purity of your soul."

The Chaser balled up his fist and quickly, the sin fire had rose from the ground, consuming Shaw. The others arrived as they saw Shaw within the flames and chaser with Cinderella standing back.

"The hell's going on?!" Vail yelled.

"The Sin Phantom planted a seed within Shaw's mind. He became consumed with sin. I am purging it from his spirit form."

"Is he still in there?" Abraham asked.

"Yes." Cinderella said. "Chaser is burning the sin seed out of him."

Shaw continued to burn, and the Chaser opened his hand, ceasing the spiral sin fire as it returned to the ground, only leaving Shaw's spirit remaining. They ran over toward him. Chaser placed his hand upon Shaw's head.

"How is he?" Cinderella asked.

"He's still in there. The sin is gone."

"Just like that, you burned it out of him?" Terror asked.

"Yes. This is my line of work."

"Would be nice to have all humans enter this treatment."

"It would kill them." The Chaser said. "They're still in their mortal forms. The human body cannot handle such pain from sinfire."

Shaw's eyes opened as he arose from the ground, looking at his body.

"You purged it from me."

"As I only could."

"Now, since that's out of the way, we need to make a plan and quickly." Vail said. "I fear Demonticronto's is not as far away as we assume."

"He isn't." The Chaser said.

"And how are you aware of his whereabouts?" Abraham asked.

"I can sense him. He's walking upon the earth right now and he isn't far from our location."

"Then, you can track him."

"I can."

"Then, let's get going." Vail uttered.

VI

THEY HAVE BEEN CALLED

The unit followed the Chaser out of Retropolis and have stumbled upon a cemetery near the United States border. The cemetery was calm, quiet, and still. Vail shrugged his shoulders walking past the headstones on the ground.

"What is it now?" Cinderella asked Chaser.

"He's here." Chaser said. "He is here."

"Where?" Vail wondered. "Is he under the ground or standing in front of us? Just invisible?"

Dirt kicked up from a grave as the Sin Phantom made himself known once more. The unit stood their ground toward the Phantom, who did not move past the gravesite.

"You've come." The Phantom said.

"No shit, lad." Vail replied. "You know why we're here."

"I do, and he is proud to have you here. To bear witness to his uprising."

"Then, where is the bastard?"

"Where's Demonti?!" The Chaser yelled.

"He's right here."

He grave turned into molten lava within seconds and created an opening in the ground, a deep pit. The Phantom moved from the grave as lava flew up in the air, yet, not falling back toward the ground.

"You see what I'm seeing?" Vail asked Cinderella.

"Yeah. I do."

Within the lava, the unit could see something moving. Hovering within the lava. As the lava settled its pouring, the figure could be seen. His red-skin, torn tunic, and long fiery hair. He landed on his feet beside the Phantom.

"There you are!" The Chaser said.

"Yes. I am here."

"Demonticronto I presume." Abraham gestured.

"In the flesh as they say."

"You've come to the wrong place, fellow."

"Oh, have I?"

"We're sending you back into your prison." Abraham said.

"I give you the opportunity to try."

The Chaser grunted, running toward Demonticronto with his arms covered in sin fire. The Chaser went for an attack but speared to the ground by the Phantom with a quickening force.

"You and I have a score to settle, Retributor."

"You've forgotten me." Shaw said, tackling the Phantom.

The unit began their battle with Demonticronto. Creed went for the aerial attack as Demonti's height was near thirteen feet tall. Demonti's strength from his arms, knocked Creed from the air, as well as his dragon-like tail, swiping Vail, Abraham, and Cinderella off their feet.

"This is depressionaly easy." Demonti grinned.

"*Depressionaly*?" Cinderella said. "Is that a word?"

"Doesn't matter." Vail said. "We're not here to learn new words."

Vail chanted out a binding spell, causing the air around Demonti to constrict him. Holding him steady while Creed attacked him from his head to his torso. Abraham also chanted a spell to keep Demonticronto still. Meanwhile, the Chaser and Sin Phantom battled it out through the cemetery. Chaser snatched Phantom by his neck and tossed him against a headstone. Phantom dodged an incoming punch from Chaser with sinfire dripping from his fist. Shaw went for an attack of his own yet tripped by the Phantom.

"This is sad for your kind." Demonticronto said. "I assumed humanity had learned the means of working with such magic feats."

Demonti increased his strength, breaking the spiritual bonds around him, knocking down Vail, Cinderella, and Abraham. He grabbed Creed's cloak and slammed him into the ground. Terror ran up, firing shots with his pistols. Demonti grabbed the pistols, slapping Terror with them and stomping on his back. Demonticronto savored the moment.

"You're no match for me. I am above such primitive feats."

"I've heard that before." Cinderella said.

"Haven't we all."

The sky quickly opened above the cemetery and from there, Visitant Outlander and Dark Manhunter appeared before them. Standing in front of Demonticronto. He moved from the downed team and stepped forward to Outlander and Manhunter.

"The two of you, working as one? Impressive."

"Don't take this lightly, demon." Manhunter said.

"You have trespassed upon a realm you have no authority."

"Spare the reasoning, Eidolon. I have come for my purpose only."

"And your purpose shall be?"

"To rule over Man. As the others should have done eons ago."

"That is where you're wrong." Manhunter said, raising his hand.

"You cannot end me." Demonti said. "I am still needed. I know the end of all this. I am not a fool."

"Yet, you know the end and continue to act as such." Outlander said. "No, we will send you back to your realm until the opportune time arises according to the Word. However, this team of outcasts have revealed they're just as a match for you when the time comes."

"Look at them! They're not a match for me!"

"So, you truly do not know the end of all things." Manhunter said. "Go home, demon."

Manhunter conjured up a portal beneath Demonti's feet and he fell into the deep lighted pit. The Phantom also was pulled from the Chaser's grasp and dragged into the pit. Once they were inside, the pit closed at the command of Manhunter. Then, the area was still once more. The unit returned to their feet, approaching the embodiments of justice and vengeance.

"I'm confused." Vail said. "What's happened here?"

"Demonti knows of his end." Outlander said. "This day was not such."

"The end?" The Chaser uttered. "I know his end for I have seen it."

"You have, Soul of Retribution." Manhunter said. "But, this is not the day."

"Hold on." Vail said. "When is this end you're speaking of?"

"Soon." Outlander said. "Sooner than the world will know. For the end is near and it is right at the door."

"As in the days of Noah and such like?"

"You know the details, Spirit-Seeker." Manhunter said. "For a dark force will return to this world and claim it as his own. Many will fall at his feet in opposition and will rise once more. For now, continue as such and you will succeed."

"Fair enough."

"Best you all go your own ways." Outlander said. "Demonti will not return quickly as you will imagine. For there are other threats that pose damage to this world and the realms. When the time comes, you all will be united once more. For you all are *Heaven's Called*."

"Yet, you will not know the day, the time, nor the hour." Manhunter said. "We bid your farewell. For now."

Outlander and Manhunter disappeared from their sights. Vail looked back at everyone and chuckled.

"Well, shit."

Afterwards, they each returned to their domains. Creed and Death Chaser continued their spiritual work, Cinderella and Shaw returned to London, Abraham made it back to the Revelation Center in D.C. and Vail continued his work across the world. Yet, somewhere secretly, a stash of grimoires had been taken by an unknown group. A group led by a priest who has a past with Vail.

DARK TITAN ONE-SHOT
MAVETH, THE DEATH-BRINGER

"Your first mission is given, Maveth. See you do it well."

"I will, and I will receive payment as promised."

"Yes. Your payment will come in full."

The phone hanged up. Standing in his armory, Danton Thomas prepared himself for the mission. An assassination contract. Danton grabbed his weapons of choice and last, he grabbed his sword. One used casually during his missions. Danton was set and placed his helmet on, giving him the appearance of a Black Ops grim reaper. His demeanor and presence is what gave him the name: Maveth, the Death-Bringer.

First order of business is meeting with one of the heads of Glasco, Inc. Danton traveled to their headquarters in Germany. There, he met the woman dressed in green and black. Marion Von Eldric. A woman's whose confidence matches the men around the organization. Sometimes, overcoming them in precision and ethic.

"Great you've made it in time."

"Likewise." Danton said. "I was told Ezekiel McKnight would be speaking with me. Not you of all people."

"McKnight is currently occupied with another meeting. You will speak with me and you will listen."

"Will I now?"

"If you want your payment delivered to you in full."

"Fair enough, Lady Von Eldric." Danton nodded.

"Follow me, Mr. Thomas."

Danton walked with Marion into the headquarters. Inside were many employees, dressed in scientific apparel with others pertaining to military services. Danton is impressed with the number of people working within the headquarters.

"I wonder how you've managed to acquire such a number of employees under your wings."

"We have our methods of persuasion."

"Didn't use any of them on me, did you?" Danton said smirking.

"You're a natural charmer when it comes to it." Marion said. "No reason for us to try and please you."

"There are other ways to please me." Danton said, staring hard into Marion's eyes.

"Don't try it." She demanded. "Not here at least."

Entering her primary office of the headquarters, Danton looked up at the board on the wall, seeing several headshot photos of various individuals. He approached the board, staring at the photos while Marion sat behind her desk, pulling out a file from the drawer.

"Who are these people?"

"Traitors to Glasco." Marion said. "Traitors to be found and put to death."

"And that's why you contacted me? To eliminate these traitors of yours?"

"Not all of them. Just one. For now."

"Which of these is the one you want me to kill? The fellow man or the lovely woman?"

Marion opened the file, pulling out another photo, sliding it toward Danton. He grabbed the photo from the desk.

"And who might this be?"

"His name is Austin Harris. He was one of us before he went rogue and aligned himself with T.I.T.A.N."

"Oh. I see it now." Danton said. "He went to work for the competition."

"I wouldn't call it competition."

"So, what would you call it? Because from my point of view, it's always a competition. Which organization can retrieve new information on these rising heroes of the world?"

"You know of them? These figures rising up all over the world?"

"I may keep to myself, but I am fully aware of what's going on in the world. I've heard stories of these kinds of heroes. Coming out of the blue and saving the innocent. There's all kinds of them."

"And you don't find it strange how they're suddenly showing up at once. As if it was destined to happen like this?"

"I believe every moment has its purpose. The purpose of these heroes is yet to be revealed and I know for certain that my future will have a part in their purpose."

"Like what? You're going to join them and save the world?"

"No. I'm going to eliminate them one by one. If there are heroes, then someone must be the villain. All in the balance."

Marion nodded. Sensing Danton was speaking the truth concerning himself and the heroes. She understood him well and knew him well enough to determine where he'll end up in the future and she was happy of it.

"Now, where is the present location of this Austin Harris?" Danton asked calmly.

"We're been receiving Intel concerning his whereabouts." Marion said, handing Danton a map. He gazed at the map for several seconds.

"I've heard of this city."

"That's good. So, you know where it is and how to get there."

"Of course. I've done a few missions there. Dealing with their criminal underworld."

"How soon can you get there?"

"By any means." Danton declared with confidence emitting from his voice.

Marion nodded, standing up behind her desk. She extended her hand toward Danton. He looked and stared.

"Then, you know what to do."

"Yes, ma'am." Danton said, shaking her hand. "I do."

Danton walked toward the exit and stopped, turning back toward Marion.

"Since Retropolis is far from here. I will stay at a local place tonight and leave in the morning."

"Do what you must." Marion said. "As long as everything goes according to plan. That's what I care about."

"I see." Danton said, leaving the office.

Danton went to a local place of residence, purchased by him some time ago during one of his earlier missions. The place was of a small home in the wilderness. The wilderness and the quietness of the land pleased Danton and he enjoyed it. Later in the night as Danton was preparing for his rest, a knock came from the door. Danton wasn't sure who could know where he'll be, grabbed his sword as he approached the door. He opened it and saw Marion.

"You are prepared everywhere you go." She said, staring at the sword in his hand.

"I have to be." Danton said. "It keeps me focused."

Marion's presence confused Danton. He looked around in case the premises were crowded with Glasco soldiers or those involved with V.A.U.L.T. he was certain her presence wasn't no accident or test to prove his loyalty.

"I have to ask, why are you here?"

"May I come in?"

"Why?"

"I'll tell you why I'm here if you would let me in."

Danton thought to himself. He nodded and allowed Marion to enter. Shutting the door, Marion looked around the home. It is a casual home. Nothing out of the ordinary except for the complete layout of weapons on the floor next to the bed.

"Was all of this here already or did you bring it with you?"

"Little bit of both."

"Very well." Marion said. "We chose well to contact you."

"Don't concern yourself with this Austin Harris. Once I reach Retropolis, I will find him and eliminate him. Problem will be solved."

Danton walked up to Marion, drinking a glass of whiskey. His presence intimidated Marion. She was out of her element and there were no Glasco soldiers to protect her. She knew it and Danton knew.

"Now that you're inside, why are you here?" Danton asked.

"I came for another reason."

"What is this reason you've chosen to come?"

"I wouldn't call it another briefing. More like an intact deal between you and I."

"What kind of deal were you thinking?"

Marion kissed Danton. She backed away as Danton processed the kiss and the intent of Marion's presence. He nodded slowly. Taking in a breath.

"This was your kind of deal?"

"You could say that."

Danton smiled and grabbed Marion roughly by her waist. Kissing her. Danton tossed her atop his bed, kissing her more and more. They ripped off each other's clothing. Now, fully naked and on top of the bed. Danton pleasured Marion as she moaned and screamed in enjoyment. Danton treated Marion's body as if it was his own and Marion had done the same.

After their rough intercourse, Danton prepared himself to leave as the sun was starting to rise. Marion watched him dress in his armor and gear. It turned her own watching him sharpen his swords and load his guns. She smiled as he did every act.

"How can you carry all of it?"

"Because there's no other way to keep it close." Danton said.

Danton was prepared and ready. Marion dressed herself and left the residence. Kissing Danton as she left. Danton was set and headed out, traveling toward the airport. He walked toward his plane, codenamed *04191*. Danton entered the plane as the pilot was informed by Marion earlier. The plane, a dark gray in nature took off from the airport. Making its way to Retropolis.

The morning of Retropolis is somewhat bright and gloomy. Civilians move about on their daily routine. Danton stood atop a roof, overlooking a site dedicated to the faithful leaders of the city. Danton held his binoculars and scoped the area. Searching, Danton spotted Austin. He nodded.

"There's the man."

Danton placed his finger on the earpiece while watching Austin stand with men wearing black with the T.I.T.A.N. emblem on their uniforms. On the other end of the earpiece speaking to Danton is Marion.

"I've found him."

"Can you get the shot?" Marion asked.

"Not from this angle." Danton said. "There are too many T.I.T.A.N. agents standing near him. As if they're aware."

"Aware of what?"

"As if they know someone has been sent to assassinate their prize."

"They can't possibly know that. Unless we have more traitors in our camp."

"That is a job for yourself and your associates." Danton declared. "Leave Austin to me and only to me."

"Can I be sure of this?"

"After that night we shared and the fact that I'm standing on a rooftop in Retropolis, overlooking the man whom you want dead, yes, you can be sure of it. Austin Harris will be dead by the day's end."

"See that it is."

Danton could hear the silent on the other end of the earpiece. Marion had hung up. Danton smirked faintly as he gazed over, watching Austin standing around the surrounding agents.

Danton continued to follow Austin throughout the city as he made movements. Austin led Danton to a warehouse outside of the city limits. Danton scouted the warehouse, noticing the location was owned by someone within Retropolis or Mass City, its sister city. Danton watched while Austin entered the warehouse with the T.I.T.A.N. agents.

"Come nightfall, I will be prepared."

Danton suited up in his gear and uniform, last equipping his masked helmet and sheathing his sword. Danton has become Maveth. Running down toward the warehouse from the nearby cliff, Maveth scouted the warehouse's landscape. He moved near one of the shattered windows, peeking through. Inside, Maveth could see Austin and the T.I.T.A.N. agents. Standing around a table with a laptop and several suitcases.

"Packages must be important." Maveth remarked. "Wonder what they could be hiding."

Maveth moved throughout the area, finding a way into the warehouse from prying eyes. As he made his way in, he noticed several T.I.T.A.N. agents were heading outside with rifles. Intrigued and relieved, he knew what they were setting up. A perimeter.

"Good timing. I made it in."

Maveth hid behind several crates, all stamped with the T.I.T.A.N. emblem as a few moved over into another room of the warehouse with the Glasco, Inc. stamp and the V.A.U.L.T. emblem. Maveth was on point and at the precise location.

"I should take him out." Maveth said. "But, before that is done, I must rid his surroundings of these agents. Keep the area clear for my kill."

Maveth watched, counting five T.I.T.A.N. agents standing around Austin at the table. Maveth counted closely and planned his move of attack. His plan has worked before and he was confident it would work well again. Maveth nodded.

"Time to make my move."

Maveth tossed a smoke grenade near the agents. The grenade bounced with a tipping sound of metal hitting concrete. The grenade rolled toward the agents. The agents heard the sound and they spot the grenade. Stopping its rolling. The grenade sounded off a clicking beep and exploded. Covering the area in thick grey smoke. Through the smoke, Maveth moved swiftly, killing the agents one by one with his sword. Austin ducked down underneath the table. Austin glinted through the smoke and saw the agents falling dead. The smoke cleared and only Maveth was standing in the room amongst the dead agents. Austin bolted from the table, running toward the door. Maveth threw a blade, hitting Austin in his calf. Austin fell, yelling in pain and gaining the attention of the sniper agents.

"Better if you kept your agony down." Maveth said.

"Who are you?!"

"I'm here to kill you."

"For what reason?"

"You're a traitor to Glasco, Inc. They sent me here to make sure you didn't deliver any details to T.I.T.A.N. and by the look of this place, you have done so."

"Only for good reason did I betray them!"

"It's not my call and it's not my problem."

Austin begged Maveth to spare his life. Maveth nodded and shot Austin clear in the head. Maveth placed his gun into its holster and sighed.

"Mission accomplished." Maveth said.

Outside, he could hear the sirens coming toward the warehouse. Maveth moved out as the Retropolis Police rammed through the doors. Running in were Detectives Justine Copeland and Cash Hankinson. Behind them entered Commissioner James Austin. They saw the bodies of the agents with Austin lying on the floor. The used grenade sitting amongst them.

"What the hell happened here?" Commissioner Austin asked.

"We'll find out soon." Justine said. "Give us a little time, boss."

While more officers entered the warehouse, Maveth was standing atop the cliff from which he came. He nodded once more, removing his mask helmet. He took a moment to breathe and contacted Marion through the earpiece.

"Report Maveth."

"Mission has been fulfilled. Austin Harris is dead."

"No traces back to Glasco?"

"None. Everything is secure. As planned."

"Excellent." Marion said with gladness in her voice. "Return to base and you will have your payment."

"Wonderful." Danton responded, hanging up the call.

Danton turned around to leave the area and felt a disturbing presence within nearby. Danton slowly decided to turn back to the warehouse and when he did, he saw someone. Standing across from him on the other end of the high round. He saw the figure with a cloak and hood. Its eyes glowed through the night sky and the figure wielded a sword. Danton and the figure stared down one another for several seconds. Danton smirked, realizing the figure's identity. Putting on his masked helmet, Maveth raised his sword, pointing it at the figure.

"Soon." Maveth declared, leaving the area. "I will return to this city. For a bigger prize."

MAVETH: BLOODSPORT

I

TAKE THE CALL

On a bright clear day, Danton Thomas fired some rounds from his M4 on his private range. After taking several more shots, blowing the head of the dummy clear off, his cell phone rang. Lowering the firearm and gazing down at the table behind him, seeing the phone blinking.

"Danton."

"It's Marion. You know why I've called."

"I do. What's the mission?"

"Come by the headquarters as per usual for briefing and I'll tell you everything as scheduled. Get yourself ready."

"I'm on my way."

Danton left the range and entered his weaponry. Glancing at the arsenal around him before approaching the closet and opening it, revealing his tactical suit of Kevlar. Known as the *Death-Bringer* armor. He put on the armor and grabbed his weapons of choice before grabbing his sword last. He left the armory and his homestead.

Sometime later, he arrived at the Glasco, Inc. Headquarters in Germany. The same location as his previous briefings for missions. Upon entering the building, he was approached by Marion von Eldric. She greeted Danton with a smile, yet not a friendly one at that.

"Good of you to arrive."

"I'm here for business. Now, what is the mission?"

"This way."

Unlike Danton's last encounter with the place, there were more military personnel than before. Danton's sense of awareness increased as they walked down the hallway toward the office. They entered Marion's office and she shut the door, walking behind her desk. Danton sat down, removing his helmet and placing it on the desk, waiting.

"The mission, Marion."

"Don't rush me."

Marion reached over to the bookshelf, raising up a folder, sliding it toward Danton. He grabbed the folder and saw what was inside, reading carefully.

"A Don?" Danton questioned.

"Yes. One we've been looking for, for quite a while."

"And you finally found him. How so?"

"We have connections."

"I'm not buying the proposed fact that some organization tipped this guy off to you and your militia pals. This type of mission had to have been done by someone on their own. Someone in higher authority."

Marion nodded.

"There was someone who told us. Plainly simple."

"Where was this Don sighted?"

"Enigma City."

Danton chuckled.

"Enigma City? I have a feeling who might've told you now."

"Who do you have in mind?"

Danton paused. Shaking his head and closing the folder.

"Doesn't matter. I'll find this Don and report back to you as planned."

Maveth went and left from Marion's office. Taking the trip similar to the previous ones, Maveth grabbed his gear and hopped into the plane. While in the air, Danton took the moment to think on the matter at hand. Another mission. More pay. More solitude. Elsewhere, Marion was on the phone speaking to an individual who's searching for a mercenary to hire. Marion responded to the caller by stating she's knows one and more than the one.

Maveth arrived in Enigma City during the midday. Scouting the city, seeing it's much cleaner and slick than Retropolis. The scenery bothered Maveth to the point where he entered the building to avoid looking out at the glistening cityscape. The cleanliness irked him.

"This city is no place for me."

Reading up on the files, he learned the Don was kept at a homestead near the outskirts of the city. Danton made his travels to the outskirts by way of a vehicle which was provided to him by V.A.U.L.T. Driving out of the city, he saw what appeared to be a flying blue and white streak past ahead of him in the sky.

"He's around these parts. Figures much."

Making it to the outskirts, Danton spotted the homestead, guarded by a dozen armed guards. Four of which stood in watchtowers around the wooden home. Danton prepared himself, putting on his helmeted mask. He stepped out of the car from a distance. His sword were set and his firearms loaded. He snuck into the region, immediately taking out the four watchmen by slashing their throats. He moved from tower to tower by the cable lines connecting them to the home. After the watchmen were taken out, he moved to the ground and began running through the armed guards with his sword. Others he shot with his silencer pistol. Maveth moved with speed to take out the guard and he was finished. He approached the front door of the home, kicking it down to see there was no one inside.

"The hell is this guy?"

Maveth entered and from behind him stood someone else. Another mercenary who through Maveth's mind off the mission for a split second. Standing before him, the mercenary wore complete armor and Kevlar of white and silver. His face covered with a helmeted mask of their own. Maveth knew them and he knew them well.

"Gunbaine." Maveth said. "What are you doing here?"

"I could ask you the same thing."

"Skipping A.B.'s orders for her Enforcement?"

"She knows why I'm here and the purpose of it."

"Perhaps, you should focus on those matters and leave the mercenary duties to me."

"And why would I do that? Leave all the fancy jobs to you and I deal with the scraps."

"This is my mission. My duty."

"I don't see it that way. Neither does V.A.U.L.T."

"What do you know of them? Has A.B. spoken with you about this?"

"Marion informed her of the plans. The Enforcement was planned to be a part of this. However, the members saw opportunities which didn't sit well with A.B.'s orders. She's talked with a lot of us about V.A.U.L.T. The two of us are just a few who are informed of their secrets."

"What of the Don?"

"A ploy. To get you to realize you're not the only mercenary around. Besides, it was a test."

"A test for what cause? To see my loyalty?"

"To see if you were ready for the reveal."

"Where's Marion?"

"I was just going to meet us. I'm sure you'll want to come."

Maveth walked past Gunbaine swiftly. Gunbaine scoffed under his breath, placing his pistol in the holster as Maveth walked away.

"Do you know where to go?" Gunbaine wondered.

"I'll see you there, Smalls."

II

INTRODUCING THE CHALLENGERS

Marion contacted Danton, Gunbaine, and the others, signaling them to arrive at the V.A.U.L.T. headquarters. Upon Danton's arrival, he saw more soldiers around the facility, and they were shook. Their firearms up and ready to fire. Inside, Danton saw Marion standing in the midst of other mercenaries.

"What is all of this?" Danton asked.

"I see you've made it." Marion replied. "Good. Now, I can tell you all everything you must know."

Danton took a look at the others inside the facility. Some he knew. Others he didn't. The mercenaries inside the facility besides Maveth and Gunbaine were Tessa Balthazar the Treasure Huntress, the Exchange Force, Cartavious Cage, Deadon the Commando, Lynch the Hunter, Kane the Mercenary, The Bandit, and Cain. Marion continued speaking to the mercenaries concerning their purpose to being inside the facility. As she talked, Danton was focused.

"There is a prize at stake." Marion said. "Only those such as yourselves are capable of retrieving it. For it will bring to you a bigger future and more opportunities to come. Now, the rules are simple, during this obstacle course, defeat all of the other mercenaries and come out on top. Although, no killing. There are other jobs to offer."

"For what gives?!" Lynch the Hunter uttered.

"Don't concern yourself, brother." Kane the Mercenary replied. "We have our ways to get around it. You know."

"Ah."

"I hope you'll all have some fun with this." Marion concluded. "I know you will."

Everyone talked among themselves while Marion left their presence, returning to her office, however, Danton saw her and followed. Lynch and Kane gazed around at the other mercenaries, scoffing. They turned to see Tessa walking past them.

"Where are you going?" Lynch asked.

"None of your concern."

"Listen." Kane said. "We'll all in this game together. How about you join us and make it to the finish."

"I'll make it on my own."

"Don't do anything you'll regret, woman." Lynch said, stepping forward.

"Is that a threat?"

"Depends on your decision."

Tessa turned and walked away. Lynch didn't take it kindly and went to follow, only to be stopped by Kane.

"Not right now. We'll get to her later."

Marion reached her office door and Danton came from behind as the door opened.

"What is all of this?!"

"All of what?"

"This mission with the Don? It was all a ploy to get me here? To participate in this game you've constructed?"

"In a manner of speaking."

"You played me like a fool!"

"I did not. This is an opportunity greater than the mission you were given. What could be better than finding a crime lord other than a game. A game of mercenaries. All out for the same prize."

"What is the prize you've promised them?"

"I can't give you that information. Classified."

"Classified? From me? After all I've done?"

"Defeat the other mercs and win the game. You'll find out that way."

"You said no killing. I only know how to kill when there's opposition in my way."

"Then, you'll have to find a solution to avoid slaughtering them.

Besides, not all of them will be a problem for you. Just a few."

"I don't work well with others."

"You and Gunbaine turned out well." Marion noted. "Seems you two didn't go and kill each other in Enigma City."

"We have a mutual respect."

"I'm sure you do after your pact in Retropolis fell through."

"It didn't fall through." Danton said. "We just came across an enemy who knew us well. Very well."

"And I'm sure you want another opportunity to make it right. For yourself and your pride."

"I'll get my chance one day."

"Do yourself a favor and keep your eyes on this game. Win it and maybe, you'll get that chance. Lose the game and you may not. Your choice."

Danton nodded with thoughts running through his mind. He turned to the door and looked back to Marion at the desk.

"Where's the first phase of this game taking place?"

"In Manchester. There is a ball taking place. It'll be filled with wealthy patrons of course. I'll be sending you and the mercs out there. You'll find out why when you do."

"Will it require killing one of these patrons?"

"Perhaps. Maybe. Who's to tell."

Danton smirked and walked out of the office. Marion sat still with a grin on her face, overlooking a file containing information on all the mercenaries.

Danton walked back out into the front, seeing the mercenaries still in place, talking to each other. Tessa was nowhere to be seen. Lynch and Kane stood against the all, speaking with several V.A.U.L.T. soldiers. While, walking to the outside, Deadon stepped in front of him, measuring his uniform.

"We're a lot alike." Deadon said.

"In appearance, yes." Danton replied. "However, in skill, we've yet to determine he case."

"Perhaps, in this game, if we cross paths, we'll find out."

"You don't want to test that theory."

"It's my job to test all things. Prove them to see if they're indeed fact."

"The fact will become your end if you continue to speak in this manner toward me."

"Throwing out threats already and the game hasn't even begun."

"If you want to stay in the game, you'll keep quiet."

Deadon nodded, stepping away. Danton walked outside and left the headquarters. Returning to his homestead as always. He rested for the remainder of the day. The other mercenaries had places prepared for them. Similar to Danton's stead. The following morning, the mercenaries were contacted individually and were privately taken to the airport, where they were flown off to England.

Now in Manchester, the mercenaries gathered at a facility owned by V.A.U.L.T. themselves. Within the briefing room, Marion arrived and instructed the mercenaries on the details of the game and what it features. She began to tell them of the ball later that night. Speaking that the mercenaries should prepare themselves for the night. Find a way to blend in with the crowd of patrons and visitors. The objective of this part of the game will be told when nightfall comes around. The mercenaries went to their own places of stay for the rest of the day. Preparing themselves for the ball in any way they can.

Danton sat in his room, mediating. A knock echoed from the door, jolting him from his meditation. He stood up and opened it, seeing Marion as she walked in.

"Why have you come?" Danton asked. "Why visit me?"

"Because I wanted to see how you're doing. Before you head out to the ball."

"A ball you orchestrated. For your little game."

"This is only a game fit for mercenaries. You are one of them. One of the best."

"And you expect me to find the patron and win this portion of the game?"

"I know you will."

"Have you spoken to the other mercs? Besides Smalls?"

"I've spoken with Balthazar. She seems thrilled to be involved in such a game."

"The girl's a treasure seeker. Not a mercenary."

"She has skill." Marion referenced. "Very precise in her craft."

"I've heard from those she's stolen from."

"And none of them are here to capture her. Besides, isn't that a task only fit for a mercenary?"

"I've never had to opportunity of confronting her. She's too young for her own good."

"Maybe you can talk to her. Put some sense into her."

"Better you than me."

"You better than me to talk to her."

Danton sighed.

"Why'd you really come?"

"I've come to tell you it's better if you go into the ball incognito. You don't want the people to see a fully dressed mercenary scurrying around the ball."

"You want me to wear a two-piece suit and join in?"

"Only if you want to find the patron quietly."

Danton nodded with a smirk. He approached the door and Marion knew what he meant as she walked past him.

"I guess I'll be seeing you at the ball tonight?" Danton asked.

"You'll find out when you show up."

Marion left as Danton closed the door. He turned around and exhaled quietly before returning to his mediation. Upon mediating again, he glanced over toward the chair against the wall where his Maveth mask sat, staring at him. He gazed into the eyes of the helmet. Feeling the urge growing.

Elsewhere in Manchester, the mercenaries were ready. Yet, only a few of them were visited by Marion in similar fashion as Maveth. Once nightfall had approached, Danton exited his residence, wearing a suit with no tie. He approached the front, finding a vehicle waiting for him. He scoffed.

"Figures much."

Danton entered the car as he drove off. Inside the car sat Marion facing him. He laughed within himself, shaking his head.

"I wasn't aware we'll be arriving together." Danton said.

"It's all for the diversion."

"And the other mercs? How will they be arriving?"

"Each one has their own style. They'll do what they know."

They arrive at the ball, seeing it crowded with people of Manchester. Danton and Marion enter together and quickly, Danton scanned the area, seeing Tessa standing on the second-floor balcony. On the other side were Kane and Lynch, dressed in suits of their own. Passing by Danton and Marion were five individuals, he looked at them and recognized who they were without question.

"Didn't know the Exchange Force knew how to dress well." Danton said.

"Everyone has their ways." Marion replied. "I'm sure you're looking for the patron."

"I am. Where is he?"

"He?" Marion questioned with a grin.

She pointed in front of them toward a woman. From her appearance, she had to be someone of authority within Manchester. An experienced woman in the political field. She was the patron. Danton saw her and how she conducted herself to the others.

"Who is she?"

"Someone important to this city."

"What is the objective of all this?"

"You'll need to get her out of here."

"Get her out? For what purpose?"

"This place is about to get a little loud."

"What are you talking about, Marion? Tell me."

"Get her out now. I'll meet with you back at your residence."

Marion left the ball, leaving Danton standing in the room confused. He turned toward the patron and approached her. She looked at him with questions.

"You don't know me, ma'am. But, I've been informed to escort you out of here."

"Escort me out? For what cause?"

"I'm not certain. However, trust me and I can assure your safety."

Before she could answer, Deadon burst through eh doors, guns blazing. The people panicked upon the sound of the firing, running amok inside the room. Danton held the patron down and ran with her to the outside.

"What is going on?!" She asked.

"Stay out here. I'll find out what's happening inside."

Danton returned to the room, seeing only Deadon standing, facing him. Two machine guns in his hands.

"The Death-Bringer in a suit?" Deadon joked. "What has the world come to."

"This is how you come to a ball? Shoot up everyone. Aren't you aware of the patron?"

"I am. But, here's the thing. I'm a mercenary. Like you. I kill who I'm paid to kill. Same as you. However, it seems our deals have crossed paths. I saw you take the woman outside. I've been sent to kill her."

"I've been told to protect her."

"Have you? Seems our paths are crossed after all."

Danton jolted his arms and out of the sleeves appeared two pistols. Sleek and precise in size. Deadon scoffed at the sight of them.

"Clever man. You believe those peashooters will outperform my rounds?

"Only way to find out, Commando." Danton replied. "Your move."

"My move it is."

Deadon fired the first shots as Danton dodged them with his speed. Firing back, Deadon bolted to the opposite wall of the room, taking more shots as Danton continued. Deadon fired back and the two mercenaries sat still, waiting for the other to attack.

"Tired already?" Deadon mocked. "It isn't your style, Death-Bringer!"

"The night is still young, boy."

On the opposite side of the room, Bandit ran in and started shooting toward the people near the doors. Gunbaine bolted in and started firing toward Bandit, who ducked underneath the nearby counter of wine and champagne. Gunbaine paused his shots.

"Why are you killing them?"

"This is a moment of fun for men like us. Take some shots and enjoy the night."

"I can't let you kill them. They are not our target."

"I pick my own targets, Smalls."

On the second floor, Tessa is being harassed by Lynch and Kane. She ran down the corridor to avoid them. They followed as she entered a room and shut the door. Kane ran into the door, yet it was too dense for his weight. Lynch shook his head with shame, pointing toward Kane's glock on his side.

"Think wisely, man." Lynch suggested.

Kane looked at his firearm and gestured with a nod humor toward Lynch. Lynch kicked the door open and they ran in. The room itself was only a lounge room. Two sofas against the opposite walls facing each other. A small table set with a lamp and magazines and books of British Literature. Lynch kicked the table.

"The hell did she go?!"

"She couldn't have gone far, man." Kane said, running to the opened window. "Hey, you think she jumped?"

Lynch approached the window and looked out, only to see the pavement of the ground. Tessa was nowhere in sight. Lynch shook his head again, turning away from the window as Kane closed it with a slam.

"She's still here on the property." Lynch uttered. "All of us are."

"That brings the question. We're still hearing the shootout downstairs. That was Gunbaine, Deadon, Bandit, and Death-Bringer. Where are the others?"

"Who?"

"The Exchange Force, Cage, and the big guy?"

"They're here. Somewhere. Maybe they'll find Tessa for us. Then, we can relish her in our own ways."

They continued to search the estate and turn corners down the hallways of the second floor. After their third turn, they saw five figures facing them from the other end of the hallway. Kane jolted, raising his gun.

"The hell are they?"

"The Exchange Force." Lynch said. "Let's clean up the competition."

"Absolutely!"

Lynch and Kane fired toward the Force, who have removed their casual attire for their armored gear. The Hunter and The Mercenary fired down at the force as two of its members rushed toward them with swords. Downstairs continually Maveth and Deadon fire rounds as Gunbaine and Bandit do the same. Gunbaine ran out into the firefight between the Death-Bringer and the commando, ducking down and taking a shot toward Deadon before diving behind the counter, directly in Maveth's presence. Maveth wasn't keen on seeing Gunbaine at the moment and neither was Gunbaine.

"Can't you see I'm busy!"

"As am I."

"You wouldn't have come over here without some kind of plan."

"Where's the patron?"

"I got her out. She's clear."

"So, what do we do about these two?"

Bandit walked out, getting Deadon's attention. Bandit held his hands up with guns in tow. He approached Deadon calmly.

"I'm on you side here." Bandit said. "Let's take these two out and return to the base. Clear the competition."

Deadon thought for a second and agreed with a nod. The two turned toward the counter and shot it up. Maveth and Gunbaine held their own to avoid the incoming rounds. Outside of the estate, Tessa moved stealthy to get out of the land. Before she could, she was grabbed by Cage. His smile was terrifying and his eyes were wide. Tessa struggled, but Cage was too strong for someone very lean.

"I need another mark on my list!"

"I'll mark you up!" Tessa said, kicking Cage back.

He let her go and grabbed her again. She continued kicking him and quickly stopped as Cage turned around, seeing Cain standing. Cain grabbed Cage by his neck and tossed him against the estate wall. Tessa backed away slowly as Cain saw Cartavious was knocked out from the impact. Cain turned toward Tessa, helping her to her feet. Tessa was in fear of Cain for his large size and intimidating presence. His eyes showed no pupils and his mask summoned fear.

"Go." Cain said. "Make sure you return to your residence safely."

"Thank you." Tessa replied.

"No need."

Tessa made her way back to her residence. Cain entered the estate, hearing the gunfire from both the first and second floors. Cain moved upstairs, finding Lynch and the other Kane fighting the Exchange Force. Cain stomped the ground, quaking it. The Force stumbled as did Lynch and Kane. They turned, seeing Cain standing still.

"Shit." Kane said.

"The hell is he supposed to be?" Lynch asked. "Beast wanna-be?"

"Return to your residences." Cain said. "This part of the game is over."

"Who are you to give us orders?" Lynch asked.

Cain ran with superhuman speed and shoulder tackled Lynch to the wall and turned to the others. Hoping they'll fight back, yet they chose not to and left the second floor to save their own lives. Cain looked down at Lynch, who's grunting in pain and walked back downstairs toward the ball room.

Once Cain arrived downstairs, he saw the gunfire between Maveth and Gunbaine against Deadon and Bandit. Cain knew he couldn't just run in the middle of the gunfire. He shrugged his shoulders and reached into his belt pocket, pulling out small pellets. He tossed them into the room and they explode upon hitting the floor, stumbling the four armed men. They looked over, seeing Cain as he tossed another pellet into the room. This time a smoke bomb. As the smoke took over the room, Cain measured the four men and nodded.

"This portion of the game is over. Now, onto the next."

After Cain finished speaking, police sirens echoed from the outside, causing the mercenaries to escape quickly. Once they were outside and away from the estate, Maveth looked around and only Gunbaine was in his sights. Deadon, Bandit, and Cain were gone

III

UNIFICATION OF SKILLS

The next morning, Danton trained in his residence before leaving Manchester. The mercenaries were taken onto the plane and brought to a private island. Owned by a wealthy partaker who's funding the game. Marion gathered the mercenaries together. However, Cartavious Cage was not present among them. As he was defeated by Cain back at the ball.

"This is how this portion works." Marion said. "Each of you will be placed on a particular part of the island, where you all must arrive at the mansion. Once you're inside, you must find the briefcase. Silver, little chromed touch. Grab it and bring it to the copper. On your own, no team ups concerning the case."

"Pardon," Lynch uttered. "If I may?"

"Go ahead."

"You're saying basically on this island, anything goes."

"Anything besides killing. There's no need to kill each other when other opportunities await."

Lynch grinned, glaring toward Tessa on the other end of the room. "Good for me."

"What's inside of this case, Marion?" Danton asked. "Sure, it's something important."

"It is. Intel on our competitors."

"Hmm. Which one?"

"You might find out once inside the mansion."

Danton nodded with a grin. Standing back against the wall of the briefing room. The Exchange Force stood quietly. So did Gunbaine,

Deadon, Bandit, Tessa, and Cain.

"That is all. You'll all be flown to the island at once."

"And will you also be there?" Danton asked. "To keep your eyes on us?"

"Unfortunately, I have some other business to attend. However, I will be present when the round is over."

"Sure you will."

Marion sent them off and the mercenaries were flown to the island. A place sitting in the middle of the Indian Ocean. Danton observed the island from the air. It seemed familiar to him. He's seen this island before. Been to it once. Danton turned to his front, seeing Deadon sitting.

"We aren't done, Death-Bringer."

"What's your play, Commando?"

"Once we step foot on the island and the round begins, I'm taking you out of this picture."

"That so?"

"Oh, you know it is. I'll be remembered as the victor and the one who eliminated the famed Maveth."

"Don't get cocky yet. The round hasn't begun."

Deadon scoffed. Leaning back in the seat.

"Cockiness sets in the bold."

"Never heard that before. Sounds cheesy."

"You'll see."

The plane landed on the island, particularly on a place designed for air-landings. The mercenaries stepped off the plane. The officials on the plane began to yell toward the mercs to reach the mansion. Danton placed on his helmet and Deadon had him in his sights. Deadon put on his mask, keeping his eyes on Danton.

"My eyes are on you."

"Shut up and reach the mansion." Maveth replied.

In the air above them, several helicopters flew over, heading toward the other end of the island. Danton looked at them closely, seeing an image on their sides.

"T.I.T.A.N.?" Danton said.

The mercenaries ran into the wilderness to reach the mansion. Within the wilderness, Lynch and Kane made it their purpose to chase down Tessa as she jumped up into the trees to reach the mansion. Gunbaine and Bandit went full speed, firing round at each other to only hit the trees. Maveth made his move for the mansion and Deadon walked quietly with his eyes on him. Cain walked calmly through the forest as the rounds flew in front of him and behind. He was not threatened nor caught off guard by the shots. Cain knew the rounds weren't aimed at him, and he didn't care. His only concern was the briefcase. The Exchange Force were scattered on opposite ends of the island, each one making their move to the center. A tactic they've used countless times on missions.

On the other end of the forest, T.I.T.A.N. agents bolted out of the helicopters. A dozen agents in total. All lead by Agent Marshall Henshaw. Gun in hand, dressed in all black besides the white buttoned short-sleeved shirt as he walked toward the mansion. He directed the agents toward the mansion, setting them inside the three-story home. Centered at all points of entry. From the doors to the windows. Agent Henshaw entered the mansion's front doors, kicking them open. Inside the mansion, it was clean. Detailed for a place hidden on a private island in the middle of the ocean.

"Make sure you have your spots! Keep your eyes opened at all times!" Agent Henshaw commanded. "V.A.U.L.T.'s hired operatives will be arriving soon."

Maveth walked through the forest to find the mansion, seeing it's the back end. Above him, Tessa jumped from the trees to the mansion's second floor like a panther, entering one of the second-floor windows. Maveth chuckled at the sight, running toward the back doors. Behind him were Gunbaine and Bandit, still shooting at each other as they went around the corners of the mansion. Deadon walked up to the mansion and entered with Cain following in the distance.

Inside the mansion, Maveth moved around the first floor, seeing the T.I.T.A.N. agents ahead. Hearing their steps from the upper floors.

Maveth's ears were keened to his surroundings. He stepped back behind one of the walls of a room. The room itself appeared to be a lounge of sorts, cushioned seats were sitting in front of a counter while sofas were against the walls.

"Shit." Maveth mumbled. "She could've told us."

Two of the agents moved closer to the room and before they could take another step inside, Tessa jumped down from the staircase, kicking the rifles from their hands and tripping them on the ground. The other agents saw her and began firing as she ran back up to the second floor. The agents followed her, giving Maveth the opportunity to make his move. He ran past the staircase, looking at the mansion's interior.

"Who lives here?" He asked himself.

Maveth went down a hallway, leading toward the living room. He went to enter but saw Agent Henshaw with three agents looking around. Maveth backed himself against the wall with his eyes focused not on the agents, but Henshaw.

"Sir, one of the mercenaries was sighted outside."

"Which one?"

"A big guy. Wearing a mask covering his mouth and nose."

"Cain. Make sure you move quietly around him. He's not to be taken lightly."

"Yes sir."

The agents returned to the outside. Maveth held his gun in place, ready to fire. Outside of the mansion, Gunbaine and Bandit continue their shootout, bringing themselves to the attention of the agents. Gunbaine saw them in the distance and they fired toward him. He ran, ducking down behind the brick wall surrounding the pillars of the mansion. Bandit moved to the other end, shooting one agent in the chest.

"These damn fools!" Bandit yelled. "Do you know who you're dealing with?!"

The agents retaliated and fire back toward Bandit, who dodged the coming rounds and returned inside the mansion. Gunbaine looked over at the edge of the wall, seeing the agents rushing into the home chasing Bandit. Gunbaine shook his head.

"We'll see how he'll do."

Inside of the mansion itself, Bandit continually ran as the agent chased and shot at him. Taking every turn possible through the hallways and rooms, he made the move and eventually ran into Deadon, who was prepared for a shootout.

"Why are you standing in here?" Bandit asked.

"To catch these fools off their guard."

The agents bolted into the room, which was a gaming room with arcade machines set on the walls with a pool table to the left of Deadon and Bandit. Deadon raised his firearms. The agents held theirs still. A standoff is in place with Bandit holding his six-shooter aimed at the agents.

"You are to come with us now!" An agent commanded.

"You're giving us orders?" Deadon asked. "We don't work for your kind."

"Either you come with us or we have to shoot!"

Deadon turned to Bandit, who was grinning with excitement. Deadon moved his focus back to the agents, his fingers on the triggers. He held them tightly and cocked his head. The agents stood firm yet were shivering in a slow fashion. Deadon noticed it and found his mark.

"Very well." Deadon said.

Deadon and Bandit fired at the agents, who only released several shots back, yet, they missed the mark. The agents fell to the floor as Bandit walked over them, shooting them in the chest and head to make sure they're down. Bandit proceeded to look the bodies for anything useful they might have carried around such as money, credit cards, and suchlike. While Bandit was looting, Deadon caught the sound of footsteps outside the door. He paused and raised his hand toward Bandit, who stopped what he was doing.

"What is it?"

"Someone's coming." Deadon said, slowly raising his firearms toward the doorway.

Bandit was ready, standing beside Deadon. Their arms ready to fire as the footsteps inched closer. The sound of them grew with each step. Once the footsteps were loud enough to be near, Deadon and Bandit saw someone standing at the door. The figure was large as it entered the room, looking down at the dead agents.

"Ah." Deadon said. "It's him. The big guy."

Cain had entered the room. He knelt to the agents, closing the eyes. Bandit was confused and attempted to kick one of the agents' bodies. Cain looked up toward him before raising himself up. Bandit held his hands over his head while Deadon was calm and his weapons were down.

"Respect the dead." Cain said. "Whether friend or foe."

"And what if I don't agree with that sentiment?" Bandit asked.

"You won't make it out of here."

"You can't kill us, big man." Deadon said. "Woman's orders. This game is not designed to kill us."

"I'm not going to kill you."

Cain turned back, shutting the door to the room. Bandit raised his guns toward Cain in fear.

"The hell's he doing?" Bandit asked.

"Put your guns down." Deadon said. "Before you do something foolish."

Cain turned back to the mercenaries. His eyes were red. No pupils and the breathing from his mask sent chills down Bandit's body. Chills of fear and chills of the unknown. Bandit held his shooters still, but his hands were sweating, and his fingers were slowly slipping from the triggers.

"Bandit, put your guns down." Deadon said once more. "Put them down!"

"You think you can shoot me?" Cain asked. "Are you up to it?"

"Don't push me." Bandit replied. "I'll do it."

"Bandit, put the damn guns down!" Deadon yelled. "Before he annihilates you."

"No." Cain said. "I'm not going to annihilate him. If he takes the shot, I'm going to curse him."

"You don't think I'll do it?"

"Depends on you. Is your character worth the opportunity at taking the shot? Or are you only in fear because of who stands in front of you?"

"Bandit. For the last time, put down the guns!"

Bandit kept the shooters steady as he breathed heavily. Deadon dropped his firearms and rushed toward Bandit. Cain stood still, waiting for the answer to come forth. Bandit screamed in making a choice and fired the shooters. The rounds pierced Cain's chest armor, bouncing off and falling atop the bodies of the agents. Cain looked down at the bullets. Deadon swiped the shooters from Bandit's hands, however it was too late. Cain stepped forward, rushing into Bandit, slamming him through the wall into another room, which was a guest bedroom. Bandit was on the floor as Cain walked toward him, grabbing him by his head as he tossed him into the walls of the room. Deadon picked up his firearms and fired them, shooting Cain in the back. Cain stood still as the bullets bounced off one by one. Deadon ceased firing as Cain turned around and rushed toward him, doing the same actions he had done to Bandit. The two mercenaries were knocked down, yet they moved slowly and in much pain. Cain sighed and left the room through the opening of the wall.

    Elsewhere, as the mansion game went on, Marion sat inside a room with several armed men. The room was dark with dirty walls, appearing to be made of concrete. Only a hanging light from the ceiling and one door. To enter and to exit. The men were not with Marion nor were they affiliated with V.A.U.L.T. They were with the guest who had entered the room. He carried with him a sword and was well-dressed. Marion knew him instantly.

    "Mr. Conley." Marion greeted.

    "Ms. Eldric. I am delighted you've managed to meet on these terms."

    "Any other way doesn't seem truthful."

    Conley removed his coat and sat down at the table, facing Marion. His men stood by his side of the room.

    "I'm going to call you Conley while we're here." Marion said. "No need to bring up your other name."

    "What of that name?"

    "It's more for the criminal intent. Something to throw around at other rivals."

    Conley nodded.

    "But, that's not why we're here."

"No, it is not."

Marion reached over toward her bag, taking out a file. The file came from her office and she slid it over toward Conley, who opened it and saw the pages and the photos which were in place. His eyes went up from the file toward Marion.

"You have these mercs playing in your little game?"

"What's the problem?"

"Maveth's in this. Why?"

"You know him well?"

"Can't say I don't. We've crossed paths very recently. However, I thought The Swordman had gotten to him. Sent him off to Pegasus or killed him."

"No. He was never captured. Truthfully, he made his escape. Gunbaine did as well."

"So, I can see." Conley said, seeing Gunbaine's page in the folder. "So, what's the solution to all of this?"

"Which ever one wins this game will get an opportunity at a bigger prize. The reason you're here right now is because you are familiar with such prizes."

"Basically, in short, you're giving one of these mercs the chance at a high-priority job. Something they would not pass up. Money-wise?"

The doors opened and Conley's men raised their arms up quickly. Marion glared at the doorway with a smirk. Conley turned around to see who was entering as he could hear the footsteps. Marion stood up to greet the incoming visitor.

"Glad you could make it." Marion said.

Entering the room was Kex Kendrick, dressed in his casual white suit and shoes. With him was his assistant Beatrice Mercer. They approached the table and Kex sat on the edge of the table with Marion to his right and Conley to his left. Beatrice stood against the wall, facing Conley's men. Kex began applauding.

"When I was given the call, how could I turn this down."

Marion looked toward Conley and turned back to Kex. The meeting between the two intrigued her. Never has anyone in their status ever encountered one another. Ever since the appearances of the rising heroes and the *Battle of Retropolis*, things have changed drastically across the world.

"I have to ask, you two haven't met one another before have you?"

"No." Conley said. "We have not. I don't do much work with businessmen of his stature."

"I'm not those men. But, this is the first." Kex replied. "The first of many I hope."

Kex extended his hand toward Conley. Conley stared. Unsure of Kex's nature.

"Are we on familiar terms?" Conley asked. "Concerning the purpose of this meeting?"

"I know of your concerns about your sword-wielding ninja. As I am sure you're familiar about the titagod flying over my city."

"Taltus? He's the one you have a problem with?" Conley questioned. "Now it makes sense. You're one of the ones they brought down during the Battle of Retropolis."

"That I am."

"I take it they're not aware of your status of being a free man once more?" Marion asked.

"They aren't aware of my current whereabouts and I would like to keep it that way."

Conley nodded and shook Kex's hand. Uniting the agreement of the meeting to a complete beginning. Marion was astounded at the work in which could be done with Kex and Conley working together and alongside V.A.U.L.T. An opportunity not fit to bepassed up. A possible unification between them would shake the foundations of the criminal underworld.

"Since you're here, you should take a look at these."

Conley slid the file over to Kex and as soon as he saw the pages and the photos, he was intrigued.

"These are the ones you're working with?" Kex asked Marion.

"They are. See any that intrigue you?"

"Oh, I do. Very much so."

"Now, shall we get to the business at hand?"

"Not without me." A voice said from the door, gaining everyone's attention.

Walking into the room after speaking was A.B., with Lieutenant Gage Hark leading her in. Marion stood up. Conley and Kex were at a loss for words. Hark measured Conley's men and saw Beatrice. He nodded with his AR strapped and held tightly to his chest. The gun was loaded and prepared for any means necessary. Beatrice watched his every move and he did hers. Skilled individuals the two of them are. Gives A.B. and Kex something to show and a means of respect.

"You were in the Force?"

"One time or another."

"Which field may I ask?"

"Marines." Beatrice smirked.

"I can see clearly."

Hark nodded.

"It shows."

A.B. sat at the table, facing Kex, who was confused about jer sudden appearance. He's heard of her workings behind the scenes. Intrigued a bit. Perhaps. She nodded.

"Interesting to see the four of us here as the world continues moving onward."

"Better they do not know why we're here." Conley said. "I take it you're the one who leads that group of baddies."

"Baddies?" Kex asked.

"Enforcement Order." Marion said.

"That unit. Ah, I see."

"I see you've shown the file around, Marion."

"That I did. Conley and Kendrick are certainly interested."

"That's good. I suppose the two of you know anyone in your areas who could be a good fit for my organization."

"I'm sure there are plenty." Kex gestured. "I can make some calls."

"Indeed, you could. How about you, Conley or should I call you J?"

"Conley will do."

"Very well."

"Retropolis is full of opportunists. Crime lords, scavengers, horrors beyond the normal mind of men. I'll make some rounds and send you the

Intel. Hell, Pegasus is full of choices for you. Might as well head over there sometime and check out what is available."

"Excellent. But, let's get back to the matter at hand."

"Certainly." Conley replied. "Kex?"

"Absolutely." Kex grinned, handing the file back to Marion.

"Then, let us begin." Marion grinned.

Back at the mansion, Tessa ran past several T.I.T.A.N. agents chasing her. Downstairs on the first floor, Cain walked, casually knocking down agents as the rounds bounce off his chest, arms, and back. On the second floor, Maveth moved through the agents, as he had warned them not to get in his way. After slewing them, he found himself staring off with Agent Henshaw, whose gun was set on Maveth's head.

"Death-Bringer. Figured we would meet again."

"Henshaw, you do not understand what's happening here. This is all a game set up by V.A.U.L.T."

"That right? Then, where are the V.A.U.L.T. soldiers? The crew? The soldiers? The agents? Why are there only ransacking mercenaries running loose on this island?"

"Because it is a test for us."

"A test? Of what kind?"

"The winner gets a high-paying opportunity. You know how this all works."

"Once I did. But no longer. I'm taking you in Danton. You and the rest of these guys."

"I can't allow that." Maveth replied, raising his gun.

As the two stood off, Gunbaine bolted in the room, quickly seeing Henshaw, who's gaze turned toward him as did his gun.

"Seriously." Gunbaine said.

"Smalls!" Henshaw replied. "You too? What's going on here?!"

"I've already explained it, Marshall." Maveth said. "Put down your weapon and let us be."

"As I've already stated, I cannot allow that."

Gunbaine fired a shot toward Henshaw. Maveth shoved Gunbaine as the fire didn't impact Henshaw, who moved to the other side of the room, diving down. Gunbaine fell to the floor, looking up toward Maveth.

"The hell was that for?!"

"He doesn't need to die." Maveth clarified. "Believe me, he's not worth the kill."

Maveth helped Gunbaine to his feet and the two mercenaries left the room right as Henshaw stood up. He saw them leave and shook his head. Henshaw went ahead and contacted the agents who were still in the mansion to keep their eyes open for Maveth and Gunbaine. Maveth and Gunbaine ran down the hall, reaching the front room of the mansion. They stopped. No signs of agents or the other mercenaries.

"We're the only ones left?" Gunbaine questioned.

"I doubt that."

They quickly hear pacing steps coming from behind them. Once they turned to look, they saw Tessa running. She ran right into them, standing next to Maveth, leaving Gunbaine in a moment of confusion. Tessa pointed down the hall where she had come.

"They're following me."

"Who's following you?" Gunbaine asked.

"I have an idea." Maveth noted, seeing Lynch and Kane in their sights.

"Shit, looks like they're still alive." Lynch said.

"No issue for us." Kane replied. "We can deal with them easily and leave the girl for ourselves."

Maveth placed his gun back into his holster and pulled out his sword. Gunbaine stood firm with his weapons loaded and ready. Tessa exhaled as she took out her staff. Lynch and Kane laughed, mocking the three. Lynch reached toward his back, revealing he had a staff of his own. One used for hunting.

"Let's get this over with." Lynch said.

IV

HIS MARK SCORCHES

Lynch and Kane rushed toward Maveth, Gunbaine, and Tessa as the fight began. Maveth used his sword against Lynch's hunting staff. Kane fired shots at Gunbaine while Tessa lunged at him with her staff, Kane dodged the incoming blow and continued shooting toward Gunbaine. The two fired back at one another continuously with Tessa dodging in between the gunfight. Maveth and Lynch continued their bout with the sword and staff. Lynch shoved Maveth to the wall and pressed him against it with the end of the staff on his chest. Maveth grunted as he pushed Lynch back.

"You can't win this game." Lynch said. "This is my time."

"Only if you can make your way out of this mansion still on your feet."

Lynch went for a left kick toward Maveth's right knee, et, Maveth's reflexes were too quick for Lynch to connect the attack and Maveth swiped his sword against Lynch's leg, slashing him as the blood seeped out. Lynch limped stepping back with Maveth moving forward. Lynch swiped the staff to avoid Maveth's incoming close range. However, the Death-Bringer stopped and looked over toward Tessa.

"Balthazar!" Maveth yelled.

Kane punched Gunbaine and Tessa moved over, tripping the Mercenary with her staff. As she had done that action, she heard Maveth calling her name. Glancing over, seeing Lynch holding his leg in pain with Maveth signaling her to come over with his finger. Tessa went over and stood next to Maveth, looking in disgust toward Lynch.

"Best you have the last hit." Maveth said.

"You can't kill me!" Lynch yelled. "Those are the rules of this game. I am to be still alive when this is all over!"

"Yes, I cannot kill you." Tessa replied. "But, I can hurt you. Hurt you enough to remember it was me who eliminated you from the game."

Lynch scoffed, rubbing the blood from his leg onto his hand and swiping it in the faces of both Maveth and Tess. Maveth rushed at him with the sword, set to impale him in the chest, but Tessa stopped him. His anger could get the better of him and she could sense it. She nodded and Maveth knew as he looked over, seeing Gunbaine and Kane now in a fistfight.

"Take care of him." Maveth told Tessa. "And help us with this last one."

"Will do." Tessa smiled.

Maveth ran over to assist Gunbaine while Tessa looked down at Lynch with her staff gripped. Lynch laughed.

"If only you let us have our way. This shit could've been much different."

"It's where it needs to be. If I ever see you again outside of this game, I will kill you."

"Will you now?"

"Don't tempt me otherwise."

"Piss off!"

Tessa smacked the staff across Lynch's head, knocking him unconscious. Afterwards, she turned to see Maveth and Gunbaine against Kane and ran over to help them.

On the second floor, Henshaw regrouped with the remaining agents as they prepared an ambush on the first floor. Henshaw sought to take out Maveth, Gunbaine, and Tessa by any means. However, as he and the agents walked down the hall, the exchange Force was waiting on them. Their armor glared with the incoming sunlight of the dusk.

"Fire!" Henshaw yelled.

The agents let out their rounds toward the Force, but their armor was too dense for their bullets to penetrate. Something Henshaw is familiar with. He stomped his foot, commanding the agents to return to the helicopter outside. Once the agents made a move to evacuate, the Force came at them with attacks from all corners. Henshaw ran and as he continued running, he ran right into Cain. Henshaw raised his head, looking up at the brute figure.

"I have no quarrel with you." Cain said. "Leave the Exchange Force to me."

"Bit, you're a mercenary. I have to bring you in."

"Leave." Cain commanded. "Or else this mansion shall be your grave."

Henshaw nodded in agreement, he ran down the hall, eventually entering the front room seeing Maveth, Gunbaine, and Tessa fighting against Kane the Mercenary. Maveth looked and saw Henshaw. He pointed down the hallway as other agents came running past him to the outside.

"He's coming!" Henshaw told Maveth. "Prepare yourselves!"

"Who's coming?" Maveth questioned.

Henshaw and the remaining agents entered the helicopter and left the mansion grounds. On the second floor, the Force finished killing the agents who could not escape. The leading member heard the fighting downstairs.

"We must go and end this game."

Once the Force took a step toward the steps, Cain was already there. Breathing calmer than most. The Force stood their ground, posed for the fight. Cain was already prepared. No need to put his arms up or to make a stance. His posture of standing still was enough to project fear into his opponents.

"Forgot about you." A member said. "This will be challenging."

"You must remember. My mark scorches all who come into my path. This day, you five have done so."

"Bring it, big man!"

The Force jumped on Cain, attacking him from every corner they could find. Cain shoved them back, grabbing the lean member of the

Force and smashing him into the floor, causing the entire floor to tremble. Downstairs, dust fell fro steeling, gaining Maveth's attention. Tessa also saw the dust and could hear the loud bangs from above.

"What was that?" She wondered.

"Trouble." Maveth said. "And it's coming our way."

Cain fought the remaining four, taking them out with slams into the floor, the walls, and the ceiling. He left the leader last. The leader was as big in size as Cain. A perfect match of sorts, one Cain preferred in fights. The leader punched Cain several times in the face before Cain grabbed him by his throat, ripping his armor from his body and throwing him off the balcony as he fell to the first floor. Gunbaine kicked Kane the Mercenary near the balcony as the body fell next to him. The fight had paused as they each looked up toward the second floor and could hear the loud footsteps coming down from the stairs.

"Oh shit." Gunbaine uttered.

"I know." Maveth said. "I know."

Kane himself turned around as the footsteps reached the first floor and now to their knowledge, Maveth looked outside to find it was now nightfall and Cain was standing in the room. Gunbaine raised his glocks and Tessa had her staff ready. Maveth stood still, watching the room and everyone who was in it. It clicked into his mind. This is all who is left of the game. Deadon is eliminated. So is Bandit and even the Exchange Force. it was now down to the five to see who would become the victor of Marion's game. Cain had stood over Kane the Mercenary, who walked up to him, staring at him.

"So, we share a common name." Kane said. "How about you and I team up to take these guys out. Leave the game to ourselves?"

"No." Cain said.

"If you say so…" Kane raised up his gun and went to fire it, but Cain grabbed his arm, breaking it as he lifted him up. Kane screamed in pain, dropping the gun from his hand.

"You are too weak." Cain said.

Cain tossed Kane the Mercenary out of the window to the outside. He turned, seeing Maveth, Gunbaine, and Tessa. He walked toward them very, very slowly.

"It is now the four of us." Cain said. "I will take care of you swiftly and collect whatever the prize may be."

"We will not back down!" Gunbaine yelled. "You hear me!"

"Surrender isn't something we're used to." Tessa added. "I'm sure you know that."

Cain nodded.

"I respect your decisions."

Cain quickly moved like a bull toward them, shoving Maveth into the wall as he grabbed Gunbaine by his head and threw him outside of a window. Tessa ran at him with the staff, hitting his legs, arms, and neck. Cain shrugged the attacks off and backhanded Tessa to the ground. Maveth stood up, seeing Tessa down and Gunbaine outside. He set his focus on Cain.

"I knocked you back for a reason." Cain said.

"And that reason is?"

"You're the one I wanted to meet. The famed Death-Bringer."

"Well, today's your fucking damn day."

Cain chucked under the mask.

"I've always wanted to know what it was like to defeat a man of your caliber. You've come across many warriors who could match you."

"I have. Most of them are dead."

"Well, we'll see how this day turns out."

Cain posed himself, ready for the fight. Maveth took the moment to think. He saw that Cain had no weapons in hand. Maveth's a fair guy. He raised one of his guns toward Cain. Cain waved it off.

"I have no need for firearms or swords or staves. My hands are enough. My feet are enough. I am enough."

Maveth set down his weapons. All of them and stood up facing Cain with his fists balled up, his feet in position. Cain nodded.

"Now you're thinking like a true fighter."

"Only one way to see who's the true fighter." Maveth said. "What are you waiting for?"

▼

THE DEATH-BRINGER VS. THE CURSE

Cain moved like a raging bull toward Maveth, ramming him into the wall of the room. Maveth kicked, punched, and uppercutted Cain as he held him. The wall cracked from the impact. Maveth double-kicked Cain back and he ran toward the big man, jumping over his head and hitting Cain with a roundhouse kick. Cain stumbled and turned around slowly toward Maveth. Cain shrugged himself.

"You're good." Cain uttered. "You have skill."

"I have a lot more in me."

"I see that."

Cain lunged over, pummeling Maveth in the chest and stomach with his fist. Maveth fell to his hands and knees from the attacks as Cain stomped him in the back. Maveth held himself up as the foot crashed atop his back, right in the middle. Maveth did not let out a noise of pain. He took it in, shoving Cain back before delivering a series of jabs to Cain's face and a head butt. Cain backed up with several steps and Maveth ran toward him, spearing him against the wall. On the floor, Tessa's eyes opened, what she saw Maveth and Cain going at it. Too hurt to raise up and help him, Tessa's eyes closed.

Cain grabbed Maveth by his neck, slamming him into the floor and dragging him across the room. Cain raised the Death-Bringer up to his feet and tossed him outside through one of the remaining windows. Maveth rolled across the ground. He picked himself up before seeing the downed Gunbaine beside him. Gunbaine still lives, he's only knocked out. Maveth could tell by hearing Gunbaine's calm pulse. Cain walked out from the front doors, moving toward Maveth.

"They say you are the Death-Bringer." Cain spoke. "The Slayer of Heroes. I must know to be certain, are you truly who they claim you to be? Or are you just another man with a title yet to be claimed?"

Maveth stood up, stumbling on his feet. He faced down Cain as his helmet is shattered and cracked across the eyes. Maveth removed his helmet, revealing his face toward Cain. Cain saw how young Maveth was, from there Cain knew how much experience and knowledge he possessed. Enough to match a fifty-year old veteran in the force. Cain stomped the ground, shaking it to cause Maveth to stumble once more in his place. Maveth did not stumble. He held himself together.

"Answer my question." Cain said. "Are you who they claim you to be?"

"I claim to be only a man on a mission." Maveth said. "A man looking for his next duty. A man who will stop at nothing to accomplish a task. Any task. Who am I? I am Danton Thomas to those who call me friend or brother. To the world, I am Maveth, The Death-Bringer. The Slayer of Heroes."

Cain applauded. Showing some respect for Maveth. However, it did not matter as Cain speared Maveth into the ground. The dirt flying upwards and landing on Maveth's face. Cain stood over him. His eyes glaring red and his breathing deep. He placed his right foot atop Maveth's chest. Maveth fought back, punching Cain's knee and leg. The attacks did not faze him. For his leg was too large to be harmed from Maveth's punches.

"It appears I cannot kill you, Death-Bringer. Much like the others out here. I can only leave you all in a deep sleep. Only to be awoken to a defeated dream. That is the fate of your kind. All will know of your fates and they will understand the curse has been sealed."

Maveth exhaled. Looking Cain in the eyes.

"Fuck your curse."

Maveth rolled himself from Cain's foot as he collapsed to the ground. Cain swiped toward Maveth, yet he ducked under the attack and punched Cain in the throat. Cain paused, holding is neck and stepped back. Maveth looked on and continued his punches, kicks, and attacks on Cain.

Wearing the big man down. Cain stumbled and fell to one knee. Maveth ran and double-kicked Cain in the face, cracking his mask and Cain fell down. Maveth stood over him and started pummeling Cain in the face with sharp punches. He continued the attacks until he heard the sound of a helicopter approaching. Maveth ceased the attacks and looked up to the night sky, only to see a V.A.U.L.T. helicopter landing. Maveth walked away from Cain toward the helicopter, seeing Marion stepping off and approaching him. Marion looked around at the mansion. Seeing the broken windows and the bodies of the agents and mercenaries in her sight. She chuckled.

"I take it this was eventful."

"The game's over. I've won."

Marion looked behind Maveth, seeing Cain on the ground, slowly moving. Cain went to raise himself up yet fell back to the ground. Marion shook her head as Maveth nodded, wiping the blood from his face.

"You didn't tell me you owned this island."

"And why would I have done that?"

"No reason."

"Looks like it was a tough one." Marion said. "However, you got through it. Alive and well."

"Appearing can be altering if you're not aware of the causes."

"You have kept up yours in a manner of sorts. None of the mercenaries appear to have been killed. The game is over. You've won, Danton."

"So, what's next?"

"You go home. I will contact you regarding the prize. I'm sure it will take to your liking."

After some time, the mercenaries were all gathered by V.A.U.L.T. and returned to their primary areas. Cain had disappeared from the mansion grounds, unable to be found. Danton returned to his home and rested. Several days had passed and Danton received a phone call from Marion, telling him to meet her at the headquarters. Same office as usual.

Danton traveled to the headquarters and entered Marion's office. Yet, this time she was not alone. Sir Onyx and Kex Kendrick were also present in the office. Danton was caught off guard and Marion calmed him in his slow uncertainty of appearances.

"They are here for you."

"For me? I've already worked with Onyx. But, Kex Kendrick. I am not familiar with his methods."

"But you've heard of me?"

"I have. Many who have paid for my services have mentioned you by name. claiming your goals for this world are far out there. Some have called you a psychotic."

"That's only a word replaceable for a genius mind."

"Why are the two of you here?"

"They are here because of the prize." Marion said.

"The prize? What is it? Money? Gold? An island to call my own?"

"It is something much more valuable." Sir Onyx replied. "Something you crave deeply in your soul."

"You better not be wasting my time."

"We're not." Kex said. "Onyx, tell him of the prize. Your side of it, at least."

"His side?"

Onyx grabbed a file which was sitting on Marion's desk and handed it to Danton. He opened it and saw what was inside. Danton's eyes widen, gazing up at the file and Onyx.

"Is this true?"

"It is." Marion said. "Onyx isn't the only one who has one to show you."

Kex handed Danton a file of his own. Danton opened it and saw the details inside. He looked up to Kex.

"You wish me to face him?"

"You defeated the mercenaries. I'm sure you can handle the titagod."

Danton closed the file and set it down on the corner of the desk next to him. Kex nodded, glaring at Danton and the file folder.

"Another time." Danton said. "However, this one I am interested in."

"Figured you would be." Onyx replied. "I always knew you were looking for a rematch."

Danton closed the file, grabbing it and Kex's file. He turned toward Marion and she nodded with a grin.

"I'll take the tasks. These are truly prizes to behold for a mercenary such as myself."

"Are you sure you're ready for this?" Marion asked. "After what you've been through, can you handle another set of bouts? Is it any good for your health?"

"I'm with the lady on this one." Kex added. "Can you complete the contracts you've been given?"

"Kex, do not doubt the man." Onyx said. "He's proven to me he can accomplish anything that comes in his way. I trust in him and his skill set."

"How soon shall I get started?" Danton asked.

"How soon can you get there?" Marion asked.

"I'm on my way now." Danton replied. "Thank you for this opportunity."

Danton stopped in his steps and turned back to Marion.

"I must know. How's Tessa?"

"The huntress? She is doing well. Already on another treasure hunt last I was told."

"Good to know."

"What's it to you?" Kex asked. "She an old lover or something?"

"Something else. Reminds me of something else."

Danton left the office with the files. In his truck, he placed the file which Kex gave him down in the seat and opened the file from Onyx. He grinned as he read the details and saw the photo of the target. A silhouette of a figure moving through the city. Carrying with it a sword. He savored the opportunity and the coming moments ahead.

"We meet again, *Myth-Walker*."

MYSTERY OF THE MUTANT-THING

After a night out of investigating a series of demonic attacks across Washington D.C., Gabriel Abraham, known throughout the world as Abraham The Devil Hunter returns to his workplace called the Revelation Center. Entering his office area as his fellow partners have also went out into investigations themselves. Abraham reads through a series of files laid out on his desk, ranging from poltergeist activity in a suburban area to folkloric figures popping up in many areas throughout the country.

"This is just too much to deal with at one time." Abraham said.

He looks over to another files that is titled, *"The Mystery of The Mutant-Thing."* Grabbing his attention, he opened the file and started reading the information within. He recognized some of the locations that were written down of the Mutant-Thing's possible whereabouts.

"This isn't too far from here."

Turning through the pages of the file, Abraham heard the front door to the building open. He raised his head, looking to see someone inside. Not seeing anyone, he leaves his office and walks out to the lobby area. Unable to find anyone standing around, he returned to his office. Abraham entered his office and seen a man standing behind his desk, reading the files of the Mutant-Thing.

"Who are you?" Abraham said.

The man looked up at Abraham and nodded his head.

"I'm Travis Vail. Some call me the Spirit-Seeker."

Why are you here, Mr. Vail?"

"I am here on the case of the Mutant-Thing mystery and I happened to hear your place was nearby. So, I figured you would have some information regarding the mystery and it appeared to be the truth. This file you have here gives much information."

"If you needed information, you could've went to some other place or even called in to let me know you were coming."

"That's not my style, Abraham. I appear out of nowhere as the wind blows and goes."

Vail placed the file back onto Abraham's desk and walked over toward him.

"For the best, I can ask that the both of us should work together on this mystery in order to discover its truth."

Abraham thought to himself while Vail waited patiently for an answer.

"I can assist you in this mystery, Mr. Vail."

"I appreciate it."

"So, we just go off to this dark wilderness?" Abraham said.

"No. We go to London."

"Why London?"

"I have a friend over there who could give us a helping hand."

Entering London, England at the brink of day, Vail and Abraham walk through London for hours on end with Abraham mostly following Vail around the big city.

"Why are we here exactly?" Abraham said.

"We're here to meet someone who can help us further this mystery. They're in the same field as the both of us."

They approach a Law Firm building and enter it. Inside Vail walked toward the front desk, speaking with the receptionist while Abraham looked around the interior of the room and could sense the small presence of spiritualism around the building.

"Me and a friend are here to see Ms. Cindy Lawson. Is she here right now?"

"Sorry, but she left about an hour ago."

"She did." Vail said. "Thank you anyhow."

Vail walked over the Abraham, seeing him circling his head around the room. Vail tapped him on the shoulder to get his attention.

"I know what you're doing and its best to keep it to yourself for a little while. Until we find out partner here."

"You can feel the spiritualism in this place, and it isn't benevolent energy."

"I am aware of that. Which is why we have to leave this place now."

Leaving the Law Firm, the two walked down the streets of London, passing by the Big Ben. Vail stopped and stared at the tower for a moment. Abraham looked at him and looked at the tower.

"What is it, Vail?"

"Here."

"What about here? What's over here that's important to this case?"

"This is where she will be tonight."

"Who is she?"

"Our helping hand. We'll come back here at nightfall and our partner should be here."

They waited until the night had fallen over London and the moon shined its light brightly above the city. Vail and Abraham returned to the Big Ben with Vail looking upward to the tower, in the far distance, he could see someone standing up atop the tower, looking over the city.

"There she is."

"May I ask who this woman is?"

"Cinderella." Vail chuckled.

"Cinderella? As in the fairy tale Cinderella? Not a possibility."

Vail turned to Abraham with a smirk on his face.

"You hunt demons for a living. I send spirits to the Other Side and you mean to tell me that Cinderella doesn't exist. Yet the world doesn't have any belief in the things we hunt down and eliminate."

"I see your point there. But, how could this be a reality. How did she even get up there in the first place?"

"She has her ways, Abraham. She can tell you more about it than I can."

Up on the ledge of the Big Ben, Cinderella looked around the city of London, monitoring it for any threats lingering that night. She looked down and could see Vail and Abraham standing.

"What is he doing here?" Cinderella said.

She jumped down from the tower, using her coat to glide herself through the air before landing in front of Vail and Abraham.

"I never knew you could do that?" Vail said.

"The coat is made of some materials that allow me to do such a thing."

"I know you're going to ask me why I am here and I will tell you why."

"Tell me then."

"Me and Abraham here need your help on a small case that we're doing together."

"Abraham as in Abraham The Devil Hunter?"

"You've heard of me?"

"The words that surround your hunt for demons goes a long way. Inspires some to become just like you. Others deem you crazy and psychotic for doing such a thing."

"I've been told."

"What is this case that the two of you are working on exactly?"

"The Mystery of The Mutant-Thing." Vail said. "Ever heard of it?"

"I was mentioned once in the office as some kind of teenage joke, but the disappearances of many prove it to be more than just a joke."

"This dark wilderness location exists?" Abraham said.

"It exists. I've been there before on some matters concerning the supernatural."

"Where is this wilderness, Cindy?" Vail asked.

"In Canada. Within the Ontario providence."

"Around some city called Retropolis?"

"That's right."

"Thank you for the information." Abraham said.

"I'm going along with you guys."

"I knew this would happen." Vail said. "That is why I agreed with it before coming to you."

"Why would you want to come along with us?" Abraham said.

"Because I only know where the wilderness is. Other than that, I know someone who lives around the city who can gives the three of us a better way of handling the area."

"Who is this person?" Vail said.

"Have the both of you ever heard of the Creed of Swords?"

"I've done some studies upon it. Only to know its considered a legend."

"Once during an investigation." Vail said. "Why?"

"Because the help we'll need is a mentor of mine."

They traveled across the Atlantic Ocean heading to Retropolis. Entering the city at the time of night, walking through the city, they see a police car chasing down a pair of criminals through the streets.

"Never been to this place." Vail said. "Is it like this all the time?"

"Pretty much." Cinderella said. "He should be here at any moment now."

"Who will be here?" Abraham asked with curiosity.

They gazed around the streets. From the corner appeared roaming, a black and silver vehicle pass them toward the criminals' car.

"What was that?" Abraham wondered.

"My mentor." Cinderella smiled.

From the car, jumped out The Swordman, dressed in his hooded cloak and Kevlar suit, latched himself onto the top of the criminals' car. Breaking the hood window and pulling the driver out of the car before jumping off the as it rammed itself into a tree near the sidewalk. Cinderella, Vail, and Abraham proceeded to walk toward the scene. Though not with much haste. Yet, they were in a hurry. Stepping closer, they witness The Swordman interrogating the criminal driver as the other one is laid out on the sidewalk. Unconscious from the crash.

"Where is Fear?" The Swordman said.

"I don't know." The criminal said.

"You work for her. You know where she is."

"She never tells us anything. Especially when it concerns locations."

"When you wake up, make sure she knows I'm coming for her."

"What? What do you-"

The Swordman head-butted the criminal, knocking him out. He

turned around seeing Cinderella, Vail, and Abraham walking toward him.

"Cindy." The Swordman nodded. "Why are you here?"

"These two men need you help on a case they're solving."

"Travis Vail and Gabriel Abraham."

"How do you know about us?" Vail said.

"I've studied your works. I'm aware of what the two of you do for a living and how much you put into it."

"This is something I never expected to happen." Abraham said.

"Why do you need my help, Vail?"

"We're looking for a place known as the dark wilderness. It's supposed to contain the Mutant-Thing according to its legendary mystery."

"The Mutant-Thing is real."

"You know?" Cinderella asked.

"I've encountered the creature a few times during some of my novice investigations. It's a creature Man should not tamper with."

"We would prefer to see the creature firsthand before we come to our own conclusions." Abraham noted.

"I understand your meaning." The Swordman paused. "Very well, I will lead you to the dark wilderness. If you cannot handle the creature yourselves, I will accompany you."

"What are we waiting for?" Vail said. "Lead the way, Mythological Man."

The Swordman ignored Vail's sayings. "Get in the car."

"What car?" Abraham asked looking around the streets.

From behind The Swordman drove up the *Assassin* or the *Swordmobile* as it's called by the residents of Retropolis. They get into the car, surprise it fits up to four individuals. The Swordman drives off down the streets.

Entering the dark wilderness, The Swordman stood guard, removing his sword out of the sheath. Ready for combat. Cinderella was also prepared to fight if it became necessary. Vail walked through the wilderness, reminiscent of his past time of entering a similar wilderness, encountering an army of druids ranging from adults to children.

"Make sure you're on edge." The Swordman said. "Prepare yourself for anything."

From the trees, something moves past them, rumbling the ground beneath their feet and shaking the trees surrounding them.

"Earthquake?" Abraham said.

"No. It's the creature. It's making itself known."

"That's rather quick." Vail said.

The ground shakes and from beneath it arose the Mutant-Thing. Roaring toward them with anger. The creature was covered in roots, dirt, and grass. The Swordman and Cinderella were prepared to face the creature. Vail and Abraham stood by watching. Vail pulled out his ritual book, staring at The Mutant-Thing.

"Seems the mystery has been solved."

"If the creature makes any move to attack, you send it back into the ground, Vail."

"I will do so, Swordman. Trust me."

The Mutant-Thing roared as it swiped its arms toward Swordman and Cinderella. They moved out of its path quickly to avoid an attack. Swordman jumped above the creature, slashing it with the sword. Cinderella kicked the creature and delivered a small series of blows to its back and chest. Vail raised his hand up in the air.

"I got this." Vail said.

Vail started reading from the ritual book, slowing sending the Mutant-Thing back into the ground. The creature fought back, but Abraham attacked the creature with holy water and chanting words along with Vail. Working together, they send the Mutant-Thing back into the ground and leave the dark wilderness.

The following days, Abraham and Vail continued to meet at the Revelation Center, concerning cases that the two were working on. From the doors entered Papa Afterlife.

"What are you doing here?" Abraham asked.

"I am here on urgent information that concerns the two of you."

"What kind of urgent information?" Vail wondered. "We're listening."

"I have a plan to bring together people such as yourselves to combat a coming malevolent threat that will bring the earth to its very knees."

Vail and Abraham approach Afterlife. They nodded.

"Explain away." Vail gestured.

THE CURSE OF THE MUTANT-THING

I

DETECTION OF THE ELEMENTS

With Demonticronto defeated, the newly formed team of Travis Vail, Gabriel Abraham, Cinderella, Creed, Death Chaser, John Terror, Ghost of England, Visitant Outlander, and Dark Manhunter head their separate ways. Amongst them in the battle was the Mutant-Thing, whom left the area, returning to its own estate deep into the wilderness. While mediating, the Mutant-Thing sensed something sinister and it made its move east, toward the border of Manitoba.

Sometime later, a series of strange murders were committed within and outside the city of Winnipeg. Entering Winnipeg are two detectives. Keen in their skills. Detectives Cole Yeager and Lewis Knight enter the police station to learn more about the murders. Greeting the two is Chief Bill Thompson, who walked them to his office.

"Good to have you guys here." Thompson said.

"We got the call and figured it was something worth doing." Lewis replied. "Now, what is truly going on?"

"Where to start? Ah, we've been receiving several reports of bodies being found out in the woods. Apparently, they add up to a series of murders. Are they committed by the same suspect? We don't know and that's why you two were called up."

"Wait a second." Cole jumped in. "You called us here to find the suspect? Without any evidence to the case?"

"Only evidence we have are the bodies in the woods."

"How many bodies are we talking?" Cole wondered.

"A dozen. Maybe more."

"Ah shit." Lewis said. "Sorry, I wasn't sure it was that many. Thought it might've been five or six at the most."

"Who's at the sight now?" Cole asked.

"A few of our patrolmen. Keeping the place secure from prying eyes. You know how people are these days. Always filming something for social media."

"Generational things." Lewis scoffed. "They come and go."

"One more thing I must ask." Cole said.

"Speak it."

"How come you didn't call one of those 'risen heroes' to solve this case?"

"We don't have no heroes in Winnipeg."

"I see."

"Anyway, while you two deal with the case on the outside, we have a reporter who's already on the case speaking with possible witnesses."

"A reporter for what?" Cole questioned. "Lewis and I can talk with the witnesses."

"I agree to that." Lewis said. "Why bring in someone else when we're already here?"

"To broaden out the case. She will go around and question those who may have some insights to the murders. Be it family members of the deceased or those who might have seen something strange these past several days. You'll probably bump into her on your way around the city or when you return back here."

Yeager nodded, standing up from his seat and walking toward the door. Knight turned to him and looked over to the Chief. The Chief only pointed at the door to which Knight shrugged his shoulders with a nod, standing up and walking out of the office with Yeager.

"You could've said you wanted to head out now." Lewis said.

"I went to the door." Cole replied. "What other signal is there to add on?"

Traveling out near the wilderness of Winnipeg, Cole and Lewis stepped out of their vehicle, seeing several officers surrounding a pile. From their perspective, the pile appeared to be only mounted trash. Until they walked closer and saw arms and legs covered in mud and blood. Lewis covered his nose without hesitation while Cole continued walking closer. No expression showed or appeared. Cole was collected as he stepped toward the officer.

"You guys must be the ones they talked about."

"We are." Cole said. "We'll take it from here."

The officer nodded and stepped away as Cole kneeled toward the bodies. Their stench strong as Lewis knelt down as well, covering his face with a cloth. His eyes went in several directions. Both from the bodies and toward Cole. His eyes locked in on Cole for a second as he shook his head.

"This smell ain't bothering you or something, eh?"

"No. The smell does not command my body to respond to its own concerns."

"The hell that's supposed to mean?"

"Means I have ultimate control over my body than the bodies we see in front of us."

Lewis scoffed.

"Oh, good for you."

Cole searched through the bodies, seeing arms and legs of men and women. Cole leaned in closer and caught a glimpse of fur. Confused, Cole stood up and walked toward one of the nearby trees, looking down on the ground as he picked up a stick. He returned to the pile, using the stick to move the bodies.

"What are you doing?" Lewis wondered. "Cole, what's the stick for?"

"There's something else here. Something other than people."

Using the stick, Cole moved the bodies, uncovering a smaller pile of dead animals. Lewis stepped back, covering his face even more as Cole leaned in further. Looking at the animals, Cole nodded.

"Elk." Cole said. "Looks like some beavers as well."

"The hell's happening out here?" Lewis said.

"We're dealing with something that shares no discrimination between human and animal. This thing kills whatever it desires."

"What kind of person does this." Lewis replied.

"I don't think it was human." Cole added. "Something else."

II

LAW OF NATURE

A young woman stepped outside of her car in front of a home which appeared to be separate from the nearby suburban area. The woman carried a journal as she approached the front door and knocked. She waited and the door opened, revealing a woman similar to her age. She glanced at the woman and the journal.

"Who are you?"

"I'm Cassandra Day. I'm here to speak with you concerning the murders."

"And why would you speak to me about murders?"

"I was informed you might know what's happening here. What may have caused them."

The woman went silent. Her eyes moved left and right before she sighed, allowing Cassandra to enter her home. Once Cassandra had entered, the woman took a quick glance around the front of the home before shutting the door. The woman led Cassandra to her dining room table, where Cassandra sat down. The woman walked over to her coffee pot, pouring a cup.

"You want a cup?" She asked.

"No thank you." Cassandra replied. "I'm well."

The woman picked up her cup and sat down next to Cassandra.

"I never got your name." Cassandra said.

"My name's Morhana."

"Morhana." Cassandra said. "That's an intriguing name."

"It's foreign in many parts."

"Forgive me, but, that name sounds like it would belong to a witch."

"I am a witch."

"Oh." Cassandra paused.

"No need to be afraid. I'm not a sinister one."

"Well, I'm here to see if you may know what's been happening here."

"Regarding the murders?"

"Yes."

"I will tell you for starters, the cause of these murders are not only natural. They are also the cause of a supernatural force."

"A supernatural force?"

"You can't believe all of those murders were caused by a simple serial killer."

"There's records of it occurring in many places."

'Is that right?"

"Yes." Cassandra said. "I've been across this country and a few others to realize that murders such as this have happened before."

"Did you ever find the cause of the murders? The suspect?"

"Only for a few."

"What of the others?"

"The suspect remains a mystery."

"To the natural eyes."

Cassandra sighed, writing in her journal. Morhana raised herself up in the chair to get a glance. Cassandra spotted Morhana's movements, glancing at her from the journal.

"Just curious as to what you're writing."

"I'm writing what I need to solve this mystery."

"And I guess I'm a helper to your cause?"

"A minor one at the moment."

"Still good enough."

"Quick question." Cassandra said. "Your witchy tactics? How did you become one?"

"I was born this way."

"You were born a witch?"

"I was born into a coven. My mother was a witch as was my grandmother. They taught me the ways of sorcery and one I was of age, I was welcomed into the coven with open arms."

"Where is this coven now?"

"Underground. Although, we move around in the open secretly."

"How come?"

"Because, there are forces out there who seek to rid the earth of my kind."

"Let me guess. Witch hunters?"

"More than hunters. Sorcerers. Spiritual forces."

"And how do you face them?"

"By using what I've learned in my youth. They primarily use magic as their resource of power and I use it against them."

Cassandra closed the journal. Morhana's gaze was set on the journal.

"So, if I were to go by what you've said, I should be searching for the supernatural element to this case?"

"That would be your best bet."

"And what if you're wrong?"

"I'm never wrong." Morhana scoffed.

Cassandra nodded as she stood up from the table, grabbing her journal.

"Thank you for your time."

"No. Thank you."

Elsewhere, Cole and Lewis travel to a laboratory in the areas of Winnipeg. After gaining information from the officers and forensics, they make their way to speak with a scientist who may have some details concerning the suspect to the murders. Lewis parked the car in front of the laboratory and Cole stared. Lewis noticed Cole's silence and his stillness. Looking back between Cole and the lab.

"What's the issue?" Lewis asked.

"Something's not right about this place."

"Where are you getting this from? The door or the surroundings?"

"Both."

"Look, let's just go in there, speak with this guy to see what he knows, and we'll be out of this place before the sun sets."

"I know." Cole said.

"You know."

"I know."

The detectives enter the laboratory and quickly, they get the glimpse at the scientist who's operating at such a quick speed. Moving back and forth between desks. Lewis looked at the scientist's attire and scoffed.

"He sure dresses the part."

"The part?" Cole questioned.

"You know. The white coat, glasses. The whole gear set."

"Ah." Cole sighed.

Cole stepped forward, knocking on the desk nearby. The scientist jolted, turning around to see the detectives. He glanced toward them, looking at their attire. He raised his finger, pointing at them in a frantic fashion.

"Are you two students?"

"No." Lewis answered. "We're not students. We're detectives."

"Oh. But why would detectives be here in my lab on this day?"

"To ask you some questions concerning the murders." Cole replied.

"The murders? What murders?"

"You aren't aware of the murders in this city?" Lewis wondered.

"I'm afraid not."

"The hell you've been this whole time." Lewis asked. "Stuck in this lab or something?"

"What my partner is trying to say is how do you not know?"

"I keep to myself. Mostly."

"What's your name by the way?" Lewis asked.

"I'm Dr. Larry Grint."

"Grint?" Lewis said. "What kind of name is that?"

"A unique one."

"Sounds like one." Cole added.

Grint turned back toward his desk, Cole stepped forward looking atop the table, seeing nothing but papers and folders. Lewis looked around the lab, nothing interest him nor gave any indication that Grint may know something. Lewis shrugged his shoulders.

"I think we hit a dead end."

"You're certain?" Cole asked.

"I am. The guy's not giving us anything. Hell, he's not even paying attention to us."

"Oh. I almost forgot!" Grint yelled.

"And that is?!" Lewis asked loudly.

"I saw trails leading into the woods several days ago. I wasn't sure what is what or where it came from."

"Trails of what?" Cole asked. "What were the trails made of?"

"It looked red. Like a bright red."

"You're talking about blood?" Lewis said.

"I assume so. Because the trail led to the pile of bodies."

Cole turned toward Lewis, a still expression. Lewis only let out a sigh and shook his head, turning toward the exit.

"Anything else?" Lewis asked, rubbing his eyes.

"Nothing so far."

"There is it." Lewis turned away.

"Thank you for your time." Cole said.

"Sure thing, gentlemen."

Lewis and Cole exit the lab and stand on the sidewalk next to their car. Lewis placed his hands on his side, shaking his head while gazing down. Cole was still. No expression. He turned toward Lewis.

"What now?"

"Let's give the site another glance."

"A glance for what?" Cole wondered.

"Humor me this once."

The detectives returned to the body site to find more details. Upon arriving, they discover they're the only ones there. The officers who were previously in place around the site were gone as were the forensic scientists. Lewis began to worry and Cole only walked closer to the bodies. Lewis, feeling uneasy placed his hand over his holster.

"Something off about this place." Cole said.

"You're just now realizing it." Lewis answered.

"No. I mean there's someone else here."

Lewis looked around. Only seeing the trees and the road. He tossed his arms in the air.

"I don't see anyone out here besides you and me."

"Not a human being." Cole said. "Something else."

Cole stared into the wilderness, Lewis could see Cole was focused on something. As he turned toward the tress, he saw what Cole was staring at. A tall figure, shrouded in the shadows of the trees. Yet, the figure stood over nine feet in height as its presence brought sheer terror over Lewis. Cole's eyes were set on the figure as Lewis went for his gun, raising it up toward the figure.

"The hell is that?!" Lewis yelled.

"Don't shoot!" Cole screamed. "We're not sure why it's here yet."

The figure did not move nor make any noise. It only stood still, staring at the two detectives. Lewis was shaking as his hands began to sweat. Cole kept Lewis calm as he stepped forward toward the woods.

"The hell are you doing?!"

"Trying to get a better look."

"You see how tall that son of a bitch is?!"

"I do and I'm not concerned."

"Cole! Get your ass back over here!"

"Just calm down, Lewis." Cole responded. "I got this."

"You don't got shit!"

Cole had stepped close enough to reach the trees and he stood still. He raised his head to get a better look at the figure and what he saw he couldn't understand. Looking into the figure's eyes, Cole nodded and began to step back slowly. Lewis watched on as Cole returned toward him and only nodded at the forest. Lewis looked at Cole and turned back toward the trees, seeing the figure had vanished.

"The hell'd it go?"

"Deep into the forest." Cole said.

"How do you know?"

"It's hard to explain."

"The ride back to the station is long enough for you to explain."

Cole sighed, opening the car door.

"Hope you'll comprehend."

"Comprehend what?"

They left the site, returning to the base. Once they entered, everyone inside could hear Lewis ranting on about the incident. Lewis continually screamed toward Cole and Cole stayed silent as they entered the Chief's office. The Chief saw the commotion, standing up from his desk.

"What's this all about?"

"We went back to get a better look." Lewis said. "For more information. Little did we know we were being watched."

"Watched? By who?"

"Not a who. A what."

"Some… thing." Lewis answered. "It was strange."

"Cole, what's he talking about?"

"We went back to the body site after our visit with Dr. Grint."

"You spoke to Dr. Grint?"

"Yes sir."

"And what did he say about the murders?"

"Hardly a damn thing." Lewis responded. "the guy's a crackpot. He wasn't even giving us attention. Just busy with whatever the hell he was doing inside that lab."

"And the stalker in the woods?"

"It wasn't human." Cole said.

"What's that supposed to mean?" The Chief questioned. "What do you mean by 'not human'?"

"The thing was tall." Lewis said. "Had to have been over nine-feet at least."

"Is this true, Cole?"

"It is. I got a closer look."

"Yeah. This jackass decided to step forward near the thing. Go ahead, Cole. Tell him what you saw."

Cole sighed.

"I saw the figure in its full form. Its body was made of bark. Leaves growing from its limbs. It carried the stench of dew and its eyes were bright like the sun. It didn't speak, but it communicated in my mind. Like it spoke to me true some kind of brain wave."

"You talking psychic stuff?" the Chief asked.

"I am."

"Well, I guess I'll break it to you guys. I've heard of this being before."

"You have?" Lewis asked. "Seriously?"

"Yes. I only thought it was just some kind of joke to scare away tourists or to attract tourists. Either way, it gained some attention several months ago."

"What is the thing?" Cole asked.

"Some of the locals call it the Environment Man."

"Environment Man?" Lewis said. "Like a man who monitors the environment?"

"Not a man. A spirit. A ghost. Whatever it is, it's not human nor was it born human. The legends state the Environment Man was created and designed to watch over the environment at all cost. No matter the location or the scenario. Some incidents recall the being always present near deceased animals or humans. The fact that you two saw it at the body site only confirms there's something strange going on in this city and we need to get to the bottom of it."

"I agree to that." Lewis replied. "But, what are we going to do next? The doctor was a dead-end. Where's that reporter you spoke of?"

"She already made her rounds. She spoke with a witch apparently."

"No shit?" Cole said. "Does she know about the Environment Man?"

"Who's to say. But the witch told her there's something supernatural involved with the murders. So, if that's enough to go on."

"This shit is getting weird." Lewis said. "Definitely for me."

"Well, you can start at another site."

"Another pile?" Cole asked.

"Not exactly. The site is presumed to be a residence for the culprit. Perhaps, the murderer left something behind. I'll let the two of you head out there to find out."

The Chief handed them a map and on it was the detailed location of the second site. Lewis nodded, wiping the sweat from his forehead as Cole folded the map, putting it in his pocket.

"We'll come back with the details." Cole said.

"I'm sure you will. Also, be on the lookout just in case you run into him again."

"We will." Lewis said. "Armed up this time."

III

EVERYTHING HAS A SEASON

Cole and Lewis made the drive up to the secondary site. They see the location and the ruins. Lewis shrugged his shoulders, turning to Cole. He pointed toward the building.

"Is this what I believe it to be?"

"Another lab." Cole answered.

"You're sure this is the spot?"

"I'm sure. Chief marked it on the map clearly."

Lewis stepped forward near the laboratory door. Seeing a padlock, he sighed.

"Someone wanted to keep this place shut."

"And who do you have in mind?" Cole asked.

"A crazy scientist. As always."

Cole pulled the lock as Lewis took a gaze around the area.

"Would be better if we had the key."

Lewis' attention quickly turned toward the tree line behind the lab. Cole looked on, hearing some rustling. Lewis reached for his gun with speed, aiming it toward the woods.

"Something's watching us again."

"It's not the Environment Man." Cole said.

"How do you know? You see him?"

"No. Because the rustling is multiplied."

"Meaning?"

"There's more than one person in those trees staring at us."

From the trees walked out over a dozen figures. Shrouded in black robes and hoods. They stepped forward slowly toward the detectives. Lewis yelled, holding his gun steady. Cole only glared, slowly going for his weapon.

"The hell's going on in this city?!" Lewis screamed.

"Who are these people?"

"How should I know!"

"Their apparel." Cole noticed. "They look to be part of some group."

"More like a cult if you ask me!"

The hooded one moved toward the detectives, their arms stretched out. The fingers shaking as they reached closer. Lewis kicked one in the chest and backed up. Cole only moved away from them. It reached the point where the two were backed up against their vehicle as the hooded ones circled them. Corning them in full. Lewis shook his head with the gun in hand. He was ready to fire. Cole only shut his eyes and raised his head.

"What are you doing?" Lewis asked. "Praying?"

"You could say that."

Once the hooded ones had their hands on the detectives. Lewis screamed and fired a shot, killing one of the hooded ones. The death didn't not shake them nor stop them. They kept coming. Lewis went for another shout, however, the ground began to quake. Cole's eyes open as he looked toward the trees. The hooded ones ceased, turning around to the woods. What they saw was a large crack emerging from the ground, separating the grassy plain from the concrete ground of the driveway. The crack stopped directly at the feet of the hooded ones. They glared down at the crack as Lewis and Cole slowly stepped back. The ground shattered open as the detectives saw the mutant-Thing attack the hooded ones. Snatching them by their heads and tossing them into the woods. The hooded ones all went in for the attack. Circling the Mutant-Thing, climbing him due to his immense height. Lewis looked on, seeing the Mutant-Thing was as tall or taller than the Environment Man.

"That's not the Environment Man." Lewis realized.

"It's something else." Cole said.

The Mutant-Thing exploded himself, impaling the hooded ones through their heads and chests. Their bodies dropped to the ground as the

Mutant-Thing glared toward the detectives. Lewis slowly lowed his gun and Cole only stared.

"What is that?" Lewis wondered.

"Something beyond our understanding."

The Mutant-Thing nodded and turned back, bellowing into the crack and it closed itself as the Mutant-Thing disappeared. Lewis looked down, noticing the crack was gone.

"The fuck's going on here?"

Elsewhere, Cassandra made her next stop at Dr. Grint's lab. Surprisingly, Grint allowed her inside his lab. While there, Cassandra questioned him on the recent findings involving the bodies. Grint laughed, confusing Cassandra.

"You know, some detectives were here earlier. They asked me about the same thing."

"Did you tell them anything?"

"Not much."

"Why not? You're not aware of it?"

"I am aware. However, it is not any of my business."

"But, you live here. What happens here must certainly be on your mind when you're out in the public."

"One would believe such. Yet, it is better to keep your mind on your own affairs. Leave the others to their own concerns. Otherwise, you might cause trouble that shouldn't never have been."

"Well, I'll ask you this one question. What are you working on?"

"Ah. Something which will be used in the near future."

"For what purpose?"

"To make Winnipeg better. The environment better. Hopefully, once it's revealed, the countries of the world will accept it and my work will be spread across the world."

"You want to make the world a better place?"

"Doesn't everyone to some extent."

Cassandra nodded, putting her journal into her bag.

"So, you're not aware of anything. No strange sightings of any kind?"

"Nope."

"Thank you for allowing me to speak to you."

"Same to you, madam."

Cassandra had left the lab with Grint continuing with his work just as he did with Cole and Lewis. Back at the department, another detective had arrived after a call with Chief Thompson. She walked in and went straight for the Chief's office. She knocked on the door to get his attention and as he saw her he welcomed her inside the office.

"Go you've made it, Detective Salvatore."

"You called. Said something major was happening and I couldn't miss it."

"Yana, what's happening here, will need as much attention as possible."

"Where do I start?"

IV

<u>NEW FACES</u>

Cole and Lewis returned to the office. Walking through the lobby toward the chief's office, they stop and see the new detective in the interrogation room with a suspect. Lewis confused, pointed while gazing at the other officers passing by in the lobby.

"Who's she?"

"That's not the reporter." Cole answered.

"You're sure?"

"I'm positive."

Lewis shook his head and waved his hand.

"I'll ask the chief."

"By all means. Oh, you're going to tell him of what we saw out there?"

"Which part? The druids or the monster from the ground?"

"Better to tell both."

Lewis sighed as he entered the office. While Lewis spoke with the chief, Cole watched Detective Yana interrogate the suspect. The suspect in general appeared as a mid-sized man. Cole watched his movement as Yana spoke more questions. The thing which fascinated Cole was the calculator sitting on the table. Why a calculator instead of a Smartphone Cole wondered. However, he approached the door and opened it. Yana turned around, seeing Cole.

"I'm sorry to interrupt." Cole said. "Me and my partner didn't know there was another detective here on similar work."

"I'm Yana." She extended her hand. "Yana Salvatore. I come from a town nearby."

Cole shook her hand with a nod.

"Nearby. Are you here to help with the murder investigation?"

"I am. Which is why I'm questioning this man."

Cole turned toward the man, seeing the calculator up close and the man's apparel. Which was only red buttoned shirt and black slacks. His hair was medium length, passing his ears and his facial hair was kempt to a degree. Cole pointed at the calculator.

"Don't have a phone?"

"I do. But, the calculator has given me much freedom."

"Noted."

"This man is Waid Givens. Calls himself the Calculator Man."

Cole stared. His eyes going back and forth between Yana and Waid.

"Calculator Man?"

That's what he said." Yana said. "He seems to know something greatly about the investigation."

"Knowing what?"

"He states he calculated the true suspect."

"Calculated?" Cole asked. "With the calculator?"

Yana sighed.

"Yes."

"And where do we go to find this suspect?" Cole asked Waid.

"You don't know?"

"How can I? You're the one with the answers today."

"My calculator estimated the suspect is always centered around the cemetery."

"Cemetery?" Yana said.

"What cemetery?" Cole asked.

"The one where the eeriness is always welcomed."

"Huh?" Yana said. "What's that supposed to mean?"

"It means the environment feels very, very strange. Like beyond this world. Beyond nature."

"How can we take this for face value?"

"You can't. Only you can estimate the numbers to calculate the location."

Cole took a moment of thought. He nodded.

"I'll track down which cemetery presents this eeriness you're talking about."

"Are you going out there?" Yana asked.

"Me and my partner will head on out there. It's what we do mostly."

Cole exited the room and as he shut the door, Lewis approached him from the chief's office. Lewis wiped his forehead and took a moment to breathe.

"What happened in there?"

"What happened in there?" Lewis said, pointing at the interrogation room. "You spoke with the new detective?"

"I did."

"And the suspect in there?"

"Waid Givens. He calls himself the Calculator Man."

Lewis stared.

"The fuck's that?"

"I don't know."

"He calls himself the Calculator Man? Seriously."

"Yes, he does."

"This case is getting stranger by the hours. How long do we have to keep this going?"

"Right now, we focus on getting it done. Now, he said he knows the location of the true suspect."

"Does he now? Where is this spot?"

"A cemetery."

"You're kidding me."

"I'm not."

"Ok. What cemetery?"

"He didn't say."

"And you believe him?"

"He only gave a small detail."

"Like what? Find the cemetery where the bodies raise up from the dead?"

"Not exactly. Said the cemetery where the suspect is presenting a form of eeriness."

"You're joking right now. Please tell me you're joking?"

"Afraid not."

Lewis nodded, glaring at the interrogation room. He saw Yana and she moved to the side, revealing Waid for Lewis to get a look at him. Lewis stared, seeing Waid holding up the calculator.

"What's with the calculator?"

"It goes with his name."

Lewis silenced himself and turned away.

"Let's just find this cemetery." Lewis said.

"Agreed."

While Cole and Lewis headed out to every cemetery they could find in searching for the eerie one, another detective had arrived at the office. Chris Harper. The chief contacted him in helping Detective Yana with their part of the case.

Cassandra traveled out into the wilderness after receiving another word from Morhana about a spiritual occurrence deep in the forest. Cassandra stopped her car and walked into the wilderness just as the sun was setting. With the surroundings growing dim, Cassandra took out her flashlight and searched the area. Unsure of what to find, she pulled out what appeared to be a compass. However, this compass was glowing. The colors reminded her of the northern lights only instead of the green, there was violet.

"Now, where do I go?" She asked herself.

She continued walking in the wilderness as the snow fell over her. The ground was covered in snow as she began to pick up her feet to continue walking. Nightfall had come and Cassandra was still in the forest. She looked around, seeing nothing but trees and snow. With that moment, she heard a loud breathing sound coming from the trees.

"Who's here?"

The breathing continued, followed by rustling snow and low thumping sounds. The thumping could be felt under Cassandra's feet and they began to grow in volume and feel. The compass ringed loudly as the violet colors transformed into a dark red. Right at the moment, the breathing had ceased. Except for the one huff of breath which was behind

Cassandra. She slowly turned to see the source of the breathing and found herself staring at a colossal figure. She could only point out the horns, the legs, and the eyes.

"What are you?!" she screamed.

Cassandra started stepping back as the figure huffed once more and dragged its feet into the snow. Its breath could be seen through the chilly air. With the moonlight, Cassandra was able to get a better look at the figure. Seeing it's a hybrid of a man and a bull.

"A minotaur." She said softly.

The beast began to charge toward Cassandra and before the horns could touch her, the beast was pulled back by a larger entity hidden in the shadows of the trees. Cassandra moved herself to see and she saw the minotaur struggling to get away from the Mutant-Thing. The Mutant-Thing was covered in snow and was nearly camouflaged in the wilderness. The minotaur went to fight back, punching the Mutant-Thing with his man-like hands and rammed the Mutant-Thing with its horns. The horns went for another strike and the Mutant-Thing grabbed them, breaking one of the horns. The minotaur screeched as it trampled away. Cassandra stood still, gazing at the Mutant-Thing in awe.

"Who are you?" she asked.

"Leave this place." The Mutant-Thing commanded.

"Leave?"

"Go now."

"But, what should I tell everyone else? You saved me."

"Leave." The Mutant-Thing said once more.

Cassandra took in the words ad nodded before returning to her vehicle. Once she entered her car, she looked back at the trees, not seeing the Mutant-Thing. She sighed as she drove away from the woods.

V

HYBRID OF MAN AND BEAST

While Cole and Lewis were away from the office, Detective Harper had met with Yana and they began to question another suspect, who dimmed himself only a witness. The man claimed to have the ability to control the weather and brought with him a suit. A sleek uniform decorated in the colors of silver and red. He stated it was made of nanofibers, which the detectives quickly tossed away. He also included goggles and a wristwatch. Although, the wristwatch was not an actual watch. It was the source of his theory to controlling the weather.

"How is this possible?" Harper asked.

"Simple! You put on the suit and the watch. Afterwards, you have the power to change the weather to whatever you so desire."

"We're not buying this guy's games." Yana said. "He can't be a witness."

"Listen, Mr. Marston."

"Um. Mr. James Marston. But, call me... The Climate Control."

Yana looked around and shook her head in shame and let out a depressing sigh. She fanned away Marston as she approached the door.

"I'm done for the night." Yana said, exiting the room.

"Can I go now?" Marston asked.

"No." Harper replied boldly.

Dr. Grint continued working in his lab as the snowfall began to increase. The chill in the air didn't faze the scientist or interfere with his work. It in truth, enhanced it. Grint continued working more during the snowfall than the early hours where there was only calmness in the air. Grint stood over a large vertical table. Pulling tubes and cords from the surrounding walls, attaching them to a larger object on the table. Grint walked over to the desk and flipped a switch. There, a peculiar fluid moved though the tubes and entered the large object. The object itself appeared as what some would call a cocoon.

"In just a matter of sure moments. My work will be finished. A creation between man and beast."

VI

A VISITANT STRANGER

Cassandra returned to her apartment. She laid down her belongings on the table and as she walked toward the bedroom, she flipped the light switch and the lights flickered. Strange to her as the lights worked well earlier in the day. Unsure as to the occurrence, she flipped the switch again, turning the lights off. Flipping it again, the lights turned on and she paused herself, backing up against the closet door.

"Who are you?" She asked.

"Do not fear me, Cassandra Day." The visitor spoke. "I am here on your behalf."

"But, how did you get in here?"

"I have my ways. Ways beyond the borders of the natural realm."

"Are you a ghost?"

"I am not. I am known across the realms as the Visitant Outlander."

"I've never heard of you."

"Many have not. Few have encountered me. Now, you are one of the few."

"Why are you here?" Cassandra asked. "Why visit me?"

"Because of your reaction to the Mutant-Thing."

Cassandra relaxed herself, walking out of the bedroom to the living room of the apartment. Within seconds, the Visitant Outlander was standing in the living room, startling her. He understood and gave a slight nod, showing his understanding.

"You know of the creature?"

"I do. I was around before it even existed."

"How old are you exactly?"

"Far older than the world you see today."

Cassandra nodded.

"The creature did not attack me." Cassandra noted. "I'm not sure why. It looked like it was trying to save me."

"The Mutant-Thing did not harm you because you have not been tainted."

Cassandra paused, glaring at the Outlander.

"What do you mean?"

"You are a virgin. The Mutant-Thing cannot harm a woman who has not yet been married. It's a balance of nature."

"So, why come to me?"

"To tell you you're in danger if you continue down this path."

"It's my work. My job is to find out who's responsible for the murders."

"And what have you come to?"

"I believe there's something supernatural happening here. It explains you standing in my apartment right now, doesn't it?"

"Does it?"

"How can I know?"

"You spoke with Morhana earlier."

"Yes. She seemed to know something others did not."

"She knows more than she's letting you on."

"What do you mean?"

"Morhana is a witch. As you are already aware. Yet, you do not know her place within the confinement of this world. Morhana is currently hiding from others beyond even her control."

"I'm not getting what you're saying? Who's beyond her control?"

"Powerful entities outside of the borders of humanity."

"I have to ask. Are they responsible for the murders?"

"No."

"So, since you know so much." Cassandra said. "Then, you know who the murderer is."

Outlander grinned.

"I know who's responsible."

Cassandra approached Outlander, seeing his height was far over her own. She sighed, taking a step back. She sighed.

"Can you tell me who it is?"

"You've already met him."

"Him?" Cassandra jolted. "Who?"

"Take the moment to meditate. Then, it will come to you."

Cassandra walked over to the table, grabbing her journal. she turned back and the Outlander was gone. Without a noise or sudden movements.

"And he's gone."

Cole and Lewis traveled across the regions of Winnipeg to the cemeteries. The trail led them toward the last cemetery. They parked the car and walked through the gated entrance and out into the field of graves. Lewis held out the flashlight to keep a look around. Cole walked slowly behind him with no flashlight. He only wanted the moonlight to show him around. The field was covered in snow which annoyed Lewis.

"Didn't expect this much snow out here."

"Snow was said in the forecast."

"Oh good. What's the name of this one?" Lewis asked.

"Elmwood."

"Elmwood, huh. The place looks closed."

"Well, to the public it is."

"And us?"

"We're here on business."

"Good point. The place is giving me the creeps."

"You just now noticed?"

"Yeah. You don't appear to be a little shaken up out here."

"Because I sensed it as we drove up here."

Lewis scoffed, shaking his head.

"Figures."

Walking through the cemetery, they looked at all the headstones, seeing the names of the deceased. Lewis continued searching around as Cole showed his respect to the graves around him. While walking, Lewis stopped in front of one headstone, seeing no inscriptions. The grave was also set next to a tree.

"Hey, Cole. Come look at this."

Cole walked over, seeing the unnamed headstone. His eyes focused and he sighed. Lewis was uncertain. Waving the flashlight around the headstone and the grave. Lewis spotted several spots of fresh dirt in the mix with the snow. The appearance seemed to indicate to Lewis the grave had been buried in recent hours.

"I wonder who's grave this is?" Lewis said.

"Don't." Cole said. "Don't bother with it."

"Why the hell not? This don't seem strange to you?"

"Oh, it does. Very."

While Cole stepped back from the grave, Lewis bent down, moving the snow from the grave, finding the dirt. Lewis grinned as he started wiping the dirt. Cole went to grab him and a decaying hand arose from the dirt, snatching Lewis by his tie.

"The fuck is this?!" Lewis screamed.

"Move back!" Cole yelled. "Move back!"

Cole grabbed Lewis and pulled him from the hold. They moved back with their guns in hand as the hand rose from the ground, exposing the body. The figure which came out of the grave looked decayed from head to toe. Lewis was terrified and Cole was intrigued. The figure was dead, but it's behavior was as if it was not dead.

"There's zombies now." Lewis asked.

"How would I know." Cole replied.

"I wasn't asking."

Lewis fired a shot and it had no effect. The deceased one screeched and behind the detectives emerged a disembodied spirit, which was visible to their eyes. The spirit grabbed the deceased one and returned it into the grave, sealing the dirt over its body without a fight.

"What is that?" Lewis wondered.

The spirit turned back toward the detectives and nodded. Lewis and Cole were unsettled. Both frozen in place and hesitant to move for their firearms.

"What are you?!" Lewis yelled. "The hell are you here for?!"

"I saved your lives."

"Saved our lives?" Cole said. "How and why?"

"You were trespassing on the grave of the Restoration Man. I am the one who keeps those such as himself in line to the natural order."

Lewis waved his finger back and forth between the spirit and the grave. The sudden appearance of a spirit made Lewis feel unsure to his surroundings this night. The snow and the chilly air did not help. The spirit kept its composure in a unusual way toward the detectives. Cole only stared in a creepy awe of the spirit. Questions began to linger in his mind. What should he ask and what does the spirit know.

"Restoration Man?..." Lewis said while catching his breath. "You're dead too or something?"

"That man is called the Restoration Man?" Cole asked.

"He is. He cannot be killed. If he's every brutally harmed, he will rise once more. It is his nature and his curse."

"And you're not like him?" Lewis questioned. "Like, if I were to shoot you, the round wouldn't harm you?"

"How can it? My body isn't made of this natural world such as yourselves."

"But, you were once human?" Cole said. "Weren't you?"

"I was once alive like the two of you. Now, I am a spirit who wanders and protects."

"Your accent." Cole said. "You're not from around here are you?"

"I was once known as Robert Shaw. Now, I am only known as the Ghost of England."

"You're from England?" Lewis asked. "Like London, England?"

"I am."

"So, why are you here in Canada? In Winnipeg?"

"I was summoned here by the Restoration Man's rise. You interrupted his sleep."

"The dead don't sleep." Lewis replied. "He was, is dead."

"I see you're not keen on the workings of the land beyond. No matter, leave this cemetery and continue on with your case."

"You know we're on a case?" Cole said intriguingly.

"Yes. Who you're searching for is not here. In fact, you've already spoken to them."

"What are you saying, ghost?" Lewis asked.

"Go and the answer will come."

The Ghost of England disappeared into the night sky. Lewis placed his gun back into his holster while looking at Cole, who was only focused on the sky. Trying to see if he could catch a glimpse of The Ghost.

"You see all this shit?" Lewis asked.

"Yes."

"And you're not bothered by any of this? Anything we've encountered these past hours?"

"Not really."

Lewis shook his head and shivered from the cold air.

"I'm going home." Lewis said. "I need some sleep after all of this nonsense."

VII

THE TRUTH OF ACTIONS

The following morning after the events which transpired, Lewis and Cole returned to the office and as they walked in, Cassandra was standing at the chief's door talking to him. Lewis pointed.

"That must be the reporter he told us about."

"Who else could it be."

Walking past them was Yana and Harper. They moved with haste toward the interrogation room. Cole wondered what the purpose for their speed was. He approached the interrogation room door as it closed and inside he saw the two detectives questioning another possible suspect. Only this time, the supposed suspect was very active and seemed a little shaken. Lewis walked over next to Cole, glancing through the door window.

"Another one?" Lewis asked.

"No. This one's different. He's not responsible."

"After what we were told, of course not."

Lewis rubbed his chin, trying to get a clear hearing through the window. He stopped himself and sighed.

"You wanna see what they're talking about?" Lewis asked.

"After you."

Lewis opened the door as Yana and Harper turned around to see him and Cole walking in with Cole shutting the door stealthy, even though the other detectives can see him. Harper stood up, pointing toward them and giving a glance at the door. He scoffed with a smirk.

"Trying to be ninjetic?"

"*Ninjetic?*" Lewis said. "Is that a word?"

"It is now. I'm not sure why you two are in here. But, this is myself and Yana's operation at the moment."

"Well, we came in to see if you needed a few extra hands." Lewis replied.

"Extra hands aren't needed if you're just questioning a potential suspect."

"I'm not a suspect!" The man said at the table. "I'm a witness. A clear witness."

"A witness to what?" Cole asked. "What did you see?"

"I saw everything."

"What's your name, son?" Lewis asked.

"Pablo Lopez."

"Pablo." Harper said. "Tell us how you know everything?"

"I worked for the government for a time. Saw some things they were operating on and I couldn't partake in it no longer."

"What kind of stuff?" Lewis asked. "Give us something."

"I worked in the scientific field. I saw tests. All kinds of tests."

"You're gonna have to give us more than just tests, Pablo." Harper said.

"I agree." Cole added.

"Ok. I was working alongside another scientist. His last name started with a G. But his first name was Larry. That I remember. we worked on hybridizations."

"Hybridization?" Cole said. "What kind of hybrids were you working on?"

"The mixing of man and beast with certain elements of nature."

"Like plants?" Lewis asked.

"Yes."

"Wait." Cole said. "You said the scientist you worked with was named Larry?"

"Yes. I can't remember his last name. We usually went by first-name basis in the lab. It was his protocol."

"You know a scientist named Larry?" Yana asked Cole.

"In a matter."

Cole turned toward Lewis and Lewis nodded. The two exited the interrogation room, standing by the door. Lewis gazed around at the other officers walking past them through the lobby area.

"You know who he's talking about." Cole said.

"Yes. I know. What are we going to do about him?"

"We could pay him another visit."

"You think he would allow us back in after our first visit? The bastard didn't even pay us any attention. Why would he listen to us now?"

"Because we have evidence of his involvement."

"The kid never said he was involved."

"But the Ghost did." Cole noted.

"The Ghost didn't give us much to go on."

"He gave us enough. Dr. Grint is the killer."

"So, what's our next move?"

"Let's dig up whatever we can on Dr. Grint. Find out what he's been a part of."

"And how are we going to do that while working on this case?"

Cole looked over to the chief's door, seeing Cassandra. Lewis noticed and nodded.

"Let's see."

They approached Cassandra as she was finishing up her conversation with the chief. She turned around just as they stood next to her. Lewis extended his hand.

"Detective Lewis Knight. We haven't had the chance of meeting."

"Oh. You're the two detectives working on the same case."

"We are. I'm Detective Cole Yeager."

"Nice to meet the both of you. So, what have you uncovered so far?"

"We believe Dr. Grint is the killer."

"How did you come up with that conclusion?"

"The two other detectives are speaking with a witness in the other room." Lewis said. "He told us the scientist he worked with is named Larry. Dr. Grint's first name is Larry."

Cassandra nodded.

"Then, what's your next move? Interrogate Dr. Grint into admitting to murder?"

"No. we need to check Dr. Grint's background to make sure the witness is telling us the truth."

"And you want me to dig into the history books?"

"You read out mind." Lewis grinned.

"Very well, I'll go see what I can find. Once, I do, we'll meet up back here then?"

"Sure." Cole replied.

Cassandra headed out and went into extensive research. Gong as far as to travel to libraries to research the scientific history surrounding Grint as his name was featured across various articles all speaking on hybridization and the proposed future of humanity becoming more than just human. Cassandra found little, but nothing with much weight. After she traveled to laboratories settled across Winnipeg and discovered old files and documents which were labeled *confidential* by the government. Inside the files were photos and documents speaking of a hybridization project. The names she read on the files were many, only one stood out in bold."

"Timothy Fegan?" Cassandra said.

The file documented Timothy Fegan being the test subject for the hybridization project overseen by Grint and his team. In the file was an image of the team and Pablo was present, only referred to as an intern. The remaining files detailed Fegan's disappearance from the public eye and the project went into darkness. There was nothing else available to the public concerning the project or Fegan. The team was broken up and Grunt was fired from the project and went into hiding, presumably finishing up the project on his own. Cassandra placed the file in her bag as she left the laboratory.

VIII

THE HIDDEN BEAST

Cassandra returned to the office where Cole and Lewis waited. She approached them hastily, pulling out he file she found. Lewis grabbed it and opened it, seeing the details. Cole glanced over, seeing the black and white photographs.

"Where did you find this?" Cole asked/

"I did some looking around. Came across one of the old labs in the city and discovered this in the archives."

"This states Dr. Grint was involved in some crazy shit." Lewis said. "Does anyone else know about this?"

"If they do, they're keeping themselves very quiet and very hard to find."

"Grint isn't hard to find." Cole added. "We should go and ask them about this."

"Yeah."

"Wait." Cassandra said. "I'm going along too."

Lewis scoffed with a short laugh.

"Look, I know you want to come with us and record all of it, but, this might get deadly and we don't need someone caught in the crossfire."

"You saw what was in that file. There's not telling what Grint is working on right now. He could be finishing what he started. You'll need all the hands you can get."

"She has a point." Cole said.

"Don't help her." Lewis grunted. "Very well. Just do not get in our way."

"You'll barely know I'm even there."

They went toward the door as Yana and Harper were walking back inside. They stopped, seeing them. Yana was uncertain of their motives and called out to them. Cole turned back, nodding to Lewis and Cassandra to head to the car.

"Where are you three going?"

"We have a lead on the case. We're going to pay someone a visit."

"And that's why the reporter is tagging along?" Harper questioned. "You sure she can take care of herself?"

"We'll see once we're there."

The three left the office and made their return to Grint's laboratory. Immediately, they noticed a strangeness in the air as soon as they pulled up. Exiting the vehicle, Cassandra looked around in the air, Lewis noticed her movements and glanced upward.

"What is it?" Lewis wondered.

"There's something in the air. Something's watching us."

"Like what?"

"I'm not sure."

"What does it feel like?" Cole asked.

"It feels… it feels evil."

The energy in the air communicated with Cassandra, turning her attention toward the door of the lab. She pointed as Cole and Lewis looked in the direction. With a nod, she knew for certain the energy was coming from within the lab. Lewis nodded and reached for his gun, rushing toward the door and kicking it open. Cole and Lewis had their guns up, aimed at Grint while Cassandra remained behind them. Grint was working on the table as he was prior.

"Put the tool down." Lewis said. "Turn around."

Grint stopped, holding the tool in his hand. He turned around slowly to see the detectives. What Grint held in his hand was a large kitchen knife. Lewis' eyes enlarged as he stepped forward with one foot. Cole glanced at Lewis' movement.

"Put the knife down." Lewis said.

"What's going on here?" Grint asked.

"The knife." Cole said. "Put it down."

"But, why? What's happening here?"

"Put the fucking knife down!" Lewis screamed. "I won't ask again!"

Grint nodded. Putting the knife down on the table. Lewis sighed. Cole remained steady and Cassandra was silent.

"We know what you were working on." Cole said. "The secret experiments."

"Experiments?"

"Yeah." Lewis said. "Some shit called hybridization."

Grint grinned.

"What's funny?" Cole asked.

"I guess it would've came out sooner or later."

"What came out?" Lewis questioned. "The hell you talking about?"

"My work. It has never ceased."

"And I assume that's what you've been doing here ever since?" Cole said. "Trying to complete your work?"

"Of course."

"So, you're the cause of the murders?" Lewis questioned.

"They were only failed subjects to the cause."

"You admit you killed them?" Cole asked. "And the animals too?"

"All subjects which failed to endure the trials of perfection."

"You're sick." Lewis said. "A sick man."

"Sick is just a term used by the illiterate to describe brilliance."

Grint backed up against the table, putting his hand atop a control panel. Lewis jerked his gun forward.

"Step away from the table!"

"Sure. Sure."

As Grint moved, his finger pressed the black button on the panel and the lights flickered. Distracting the detectives, Grint made a run for it deeper into the lab. Lewis noticed and ran after him. Cole went to follow, telling Cassandra to remain at the door just in case. Cole ran and reached Lewis, who had stopped in his steps, seeing Grint standing at the vertical table with the cocoon.

"What is that?" Cole said.

"My ultimate creation. I believe it's time to be awakened."

"Do not make a move." Lewis said. "One more move and I will shoot you."

"Go ahead and do your work. I will do mine."

Grint took a step toward the table and Lewis fired a shot, Grint ducked as he pressed a green button on the table, in which separated the tubes from the cocoon and from there, the cocoon began to shiver, moving with intensity as Grint stepped back against the wall. Lewis and Cole were uncertain of what to do, so they aimed their guns toward the cocoon. After a minute, the cocoon busted open and from it arose a towering figure. Its figure appeared humanoid, but its hands, feet, face, and eyes appeared very much like an animal. A mixture of a human, a bear, and a wolf. The creature screeched and it was loud to the point it reached Cassandra.

"What was that?" She questioned.

Grint applauded the creature, standing beside it. The creature glared over toward Grint, who nodded with a smile.

"You are reborn!" Grint said. "No more are you Timothy Fegan!"

"Fegan?" Cole said.

"Yeah." Lewis replied. "The man from the file."

"You are now known as The Hybrid!"

Lewis and Cole began firing at the Hybrid as Grint moved out of the way. The bullets did no harm to the Hybrid's body as the hair was dense enough to preserve the body from gunfire. The Hybrid humped down from the table, swiping the detectives out of its path and bolted into the wall, crashing through as it ran to the outside. Cassandra looked around, hearing the explosion and when she walked over to the side of the lab, she saw the Hybrid, running on all fours into the wilderness.

"He's done it."

While the Hybrid ran through the wilderness, seemly making its way toward Winnipeg, the Mutant-Thing arose from the dirt in a far region, sensing the Hybrid's essence and hearing the screeching. From there, the Mutant-Thing melted into the dirt and moved with speed, following the path of the Hybrid.

IX

THE WAYS OF SCIENCE AND MYSTERY

The Hybrid made its entrance in the downtown region of Winnipeg, frightening the civilians as it began hurling vehicles into the air, slamming its arms into the pavement, shaking the ground. The police had arrived and exited their vehicles. Their firearms aimed and ready. The Hybrid saw them and showed a grim smile before charging toward them. The rounds went off, firing at all ranges toward the Hybrid. The bullets did nothing as they bounced off the fur. The Hybrid moved with a much greater speed, tackling the officers against their own vehicles, crashing them into one another. The Hybrid screeched and went further into the city.

Back at the lab, Lewis and Cole followed Grint as he made his escape into the basement of the laboratory. Cassandra entered the operating room, seeing the vertical table and the massive hole in the wall.

"Where did they go?"

She looked around and turned her attention forward. She moved and glanced over to her left, seeing a portion of the brick wall was moved to the side, revealing a set of stairs going down. She didn't hesitate. Figuring Lewis and Cole went down, she was going as well. Pacing herself down the stairs, she could hear faint echoes of Lewis shouting Grint's name followed by gunfire. Stepping foot on the ground, leading into a narrow hallway with water flowing on the ground, she noticed Cole standing in the distance. Moving faster, she caught up to him and he was not pleased.

"Why are you down here?"

"I saw something outside. It was massive."

"Yeah. That was Grint's experiment completed."

"The project he was working on? That was the subject?"

"Yes. That subject you saw rushing into the woods was once Timothy Fegan."

"Ok. Where's Lewis?"

"Catching up on Grint's trail. I'm here just in case the doctor makes a u-turn."

"I can help out, you know. Find a way to lure Grint out and-"

"You're better off back at the car."

"And what if Grint gets out of your sights? What then?"

"Lewis and I have it covered. Just wait back at the car. Please."

Cassandra let out a short sigh and turned back. Once she did, Lewis ran toward Cole, grabbing her focus.

"Did you find him?" Cole asked.

"This place's a maze. However, he somewhere down here."

"Then, let's find him."

Lewis looked over Cole's shoulder, seeing Cassandra. He shook his head.

"Why are you down here?"

"Trying to find you two."

"Did you see the big thing bolt out of the wall?"

"I did. It went into the forest. My guess it's going somewhere crowded."

"The city." Lewis said. "Every damn time."

"Look, we need to find Grint now. Sun's going down soon and we don't need to be out here at night."

"The hell we don't" Lewis agreed. "Let's get this over with."

While they searched for Grint in the sewer-life tunnels, they were ambushed by several dwarfish entities. They attacked with slashes to the legs before vanishing in the air. Only leaving a small echo of laughter following their attacks. Lewis looked around as the light in the tunnels were growing dim. Cole held his gun steady, and Cassandra remained at the entrance to the tunnels. In her right hand however was a glock.

"You see those things by any chance?" Lewis asked.

"Just a quick glance."

"And what did they look like? Besides elves?"

"Hobbits."

"Great. So, Grint's down here making fantasy characters come to life."

"They've always existed, Lewis. It's just they remain in hiding."

"And how do you know this?"

"History speaks of it."

Lewis nodded.

"That's good. Didn't know you were a historian as well. Must work well in your other endeavors."

"Comes and goes in favors."

"That's great. Now will any of that history shit help us find Grint or not?"

Cole stared and before he could answer, Grint jumped in front of them, holding a knife in one hand and a gun in the other. Cole and Lewis held their firearms aimed at Grint. Neither of them hesitated in their steps. Their boldness intrigued Grint to continue stepping further.

"One more fucking step and I will put your ass down!" Lewis yelled.

"This has to end one way." Grint said. "Only one of us must survive."

"Make your move." Cole said.

Grint nodded, tapping the knife on his forehead. He lunged with such speed at Lewis with the knife. Lewis fired a shot, knocking the knife from Grint's hand and Lewis snatched Grint by his lab coat and tossed him against eh brick wall, pummeling him in the face and stomach with his fists.

"Don't kill him." Cole said as he watched. "We need to bring him in."

Lewis delivered one more punch to the face before exhaling and raising himself up off Grint's body. Grint laid on the floor, giggling with blood pouring down his face. Lewis and Cole shook hands.

"We done our duty." Lewis said. "Let's bring this bastard in."

"NEVER!" Grint screamed, raising up from the floor.

Grint reached into his lab pocket and took out a taser, quickly holding it against Lewis' ribs. Shocking him as he stumbled and fell to the floor. Cole looked on, firing his gun at Grint, who moved out of its path before throwing the taser into Cole's face. Cole stumbled in his steps and Grint kicked him to the floor.

"Such fools! A scientist is always prepared!"

Grint looked down, seeing Cole's gun. He grabbed it.

"A pity I can't use my own. Seeing how it fell somewhere in this area." Grint said. "The water must've washed out elsewhere. No matter, using your own against you is a message proved just enough."

Grint aimed the gun toward Cole's forehead and a gunshot fired. Grint stared into space as he glared up toward the entrance, seeing Cassandra standing with her glock aimed. From the muzzle moved smoke and Grint had realized he was the one shot as he never had a chance to pull the trigger. Grint chucked and fell to the ground with a bullet wound in his chest. Cole snatched his gun from Grint's hand and stood up, holding his head. He went and checked on Lewis, helping him up as they exited the tunnels, returning to the car.

"What about Grint?" Cassandra asked.

"We'll tell the others and they'll pick him up. He's not going anywhere."

Lewis sat in the back seat, still shivering from the electricity as Cole drove into Winnipeg.

Once they arrived, they saw the city in distraught, civilians running in mass as gunfire sounded in the air. Lewis remained in the car as Cole and Cassandra walked out, moving through the people. They continued further before finding several officers shooting and being killed by the Hybrid.

"Oh no." Cassandra said.

"We have to do something."

"We can't face that thing."

"We have to find a way."

While they thought, the ground quaked. Shaking to the point of grabbing the Hybrid's attention. The creature stood firm as the ground in front of him arose and underneath the rising concrete and dirt was the Mutant-Thing. Its red eyes glared toward Hybrid as the Hybrid screeched, dragging its right foot into the ground.

X

THE CURSE OF THE MUTANT-THING

The Mutant-Thing ran and tackled the Hybrid into the ground, pulling the creature by its head and slamming it into the nearby trees. Cole and Cassandra moved to a further distance to avoid the flying debris. The Mutant-Thing walked over toward the downed Hybrid, covered in bark and leaves, which arose, slashing its claws into the Mutant-Thing's chest. Stumbling the Mutant-Thing in his steps, the Hybrid grabbed the Mutant-Thing by its throat and slammed it into the pavement and stomped its chest. The Hybrid lowered its head and screeched in the Mutant-Thing's face before the Mutant-Thing grabbed the Hybrid by its jaw and pulled it onto the concrete, swiping the Hybrid's foot from its chest and reversing the attack. Now, the Mutant-Thing stood over the Hybrid with its foot on the creature's chest.

"You... do... not... belong..." The Mutant-Thing said.

The Mutant-Thing used both hands, grabbing onto the Hybrid's head and began struggling against the creature. Cole and Cassandra watched on as they saw the Mutant-Thing using all its strength as he tore off the Hybrid's head with its blood pouring and spreading. The creature is dead and the Mutant-Thing tosses the head across from Cole and Cassandra. they looked down and gazed up, seeing the Mutant-Thing's eyes on them. Cassandra nodded.

"It is done." The Mutant-Thing said, as it walked into the nearby river and evaporated away.

Afterwards, Lewis was taken to the nearby hospital and the officers had arrived at Grint's lab. They confronted him as he made it to the upper floor trying t escape. The officers had their guns on him. Grint was surrounded.

"Dr. Larry Grint, drop the gun!"

"Only one of us is making it out of here alive."

"Drop the gun!"

Grint nodded with a smirk before turning the gun on himself. News had spread the next day of Grint's suicide and everyone knew he was the one responsible for the murders. Chief Thompson thanked Cole, Lewis, and Cassandra for their help. The case of Winnipeg's mysterious murder was solved. However, the Chief handed the detectives a letter. They opened the letter, which requested for their assistance in a case surrounding a growing fear in paranoia. Cole glanced at the location of the case. He nodded.

"We going to Retropolis?"

"Might as well." Lewis said.

Cassandra had returned to her home in Vancouver and as she entered, she found a visitor sitting down in her chair next to the couch. The visitor stood up and greeted Cassandra.

"How did you get into my home?" She asked. "And why are you here?"

"My name is Doctor Donald Fortune and I am here to speak to you concerning the witch, Morhana."

"Why speak to me about her? I only questioned here concerning the case in Winnipeg."

"I know of the case and the assistance of the Mutant-Thing. I understand it and I give my gratitude for the creature's help with humanity. But, I am not here to speak to you concerning the Winnipeg case. I am here to ask you some questions."

"Why? What kind of questions?"

"Important ones that could save your life. Because something is coming and its growing fast. To put it to you simply, you're in its crosshairs."

THE LONE OUTLAW: TARGETED

1875. An old town in the Northern West of Canada. Four men dressed in dirty suits and hats exit out of a nearby saloon. They laugh and yell at each other. Enjoying the company. Each of the hats were a different color to differentiate the four men from those outsides of their circle. From the looks of them, they maintained control over the entire town. From the sheriff's department to the poorest one in the town. Their hats were gray, brown, white, and black.

"We've done everything we could've possibly achieved." The Black Hat said.

"In this town we have." The White Hat responded. "Yet, we haven't found him yet."

"I'm sure he'll come across our path sooner than later." The Brown Hat said. "He has to. You know the mindset of a man like him. Full of anger and yet, no direction."

"You really believe what you've spewed from your mouth?"

"What else can you describe such a man like him?"

"Men like him make no mistakes. Their mind is always set on the mission. Until the mission is fulfilled, they're never satisfied. Never."

"He'll show himself." The Gray Hat said with vigor. "Trust my words, boys."

From their left, they could hear footsteps. Boots touching the ground with a clicking sound following the steps. Coming across them in the distance is a brown horse with its rider. The horse ran toward the four hats and stopped within only a few feet from their faces. The four hats were concerned and unaware as to who's riding the horse. Truthfully, the only thing that peaked their interests was the horse and the potential to have the rider join their circle.

The rider removed himself from the horse, dressed in all brown clothing with a black duster and hat. His face was hidden by the brim of the hat and his hands were set on his sides. He started to walk toward the four hats and they still weren't sure of what to make of the whole scene. The man in the brown hat stepped up toward the rider.

"Who the hell are you supposed to be?"

"Why you hide your face from us?" The Gray Hat referenced with a grin. "Show your damn face so we can know who you are,

boy."

The rider stopped and started at the four men. His face still hidden and his hands motionless on his sides. The man with the black hat stepped forward to the rider. Their faces near one another. The rider was not moved by the man's presence.

"Listen and listen good. Show us your face. You have nothing to lose. Besides your horse, of course."

"Enough of this." The White Hat yelled. "Quit playing hide and seek with us and show us your face. Who are you? Tell us your name."

"The Lone Outlaw." The Rider replied.

The four men shook in their boots. Taking minor steps back from the rider. They've heard of him across the Northern West. What he's done and the things he can do if necessary.

"It's... It's him." The Black Hat trembled in his speech. Pointing at the rider.

The rider swiftly moved his right hand, shoving his duster back and revealing his holster. From there, he fired shots at the man in the black hat, killing him with shots to the chest. He continued from there, turning toward the men in the brown and gray hats.

"Anything you wish to say?"

"You son of a-" The man in the brown hat yelled.

The rider fired once more, hitting the man in the brown hat through the chest. His eyes glared onto the man in the gray hat. Both standing completely still, their pistols directed to one another. The man in the gray hat quickened in his steps. Shuffling the pistol in his hand. The rider watched him tremble.

"You're going to turn yourself over-"

The rider shot the man in the gray hat with the pistol and he fell to the ground, lying next to the men in the brown and black hats. Their hats sat on the ground motionless to the coming wind. The man in the white hat stared down at his fallen partners of their circle. His eyes moved slowly to face the rider, who's pistol was already aimed for him.

"You're the last man standing."

"What's it to you? You killed my boys!"

"Are you concerned?"

"Listen here, you're the guy we were discussing days prior. Yet, they were right. You brought yourself over to us and killed them. Killed the believers and left the unbeliever alive. All I ask of you right now is to turn yourself in for the crimes you've committed, and these murders are added to that list of crimes."

"I haven't done anything wrong."

"Have you now? Look around, boy! Look at what you've done to these three gentlemen."

"I've done this land a service. A great service."

"You've only committed three murders. That's all you've done right now. My boys were right, you're one crazy bastard."

"Good." The rider said.

"I have no choice." The White Hat said, reaching over to his holster. "You've given me no other choice, boy, but to put you down."

The rider fired at the man in the white hat. The gunshot blasted through his head, leaving a hole through the white hat as it fell to the ground. The dirt began to hover in the air as the wind started to pick up. The rider gazed around, feeling the chilling air coming. He looked down at the man in the white hat's body and spat on him.

"Justice and vengeance are all that is left for me in this world. I can only choose one of them. And I have chosen vengeance."

The rider climbed atop his horse and rode away as thunder started to roar in the clouds above the small town. The bodies of the four men remained on the ground as the rain started to fall.

TRAIL OF VENGEANCE

LATE TRAVELS

The rain fell over the dead bodies of the Four as the Rider rode off. Sometime later, the city began to hear of more stories surrounding the famed mysterious rider. Hearing of his heroic actions across all of Canada and portions into the northern United States.

Silver City is one of the top cities of the nation. It glistened like a ghost town, but it was filled with people. Riders rode through the muddy streets on their horses as prostitutes stand on the corners. One horse in particular, white, is coming up to the City Hall building. The horse stopped and its rider leaped off. The rider was known in the city as Jack London. A young, handsome gentleman to many of the women and a potential apprentice and ally toward the men. He made his focus toward the City Hall. Jack entered, going up the stairs, passing by visitors throughout the building. Reaching the second floor, Jack had stepped into the main office.

"Governor." Jack said, standing at the desk.

In front of Jack was a desk, surrounded by soldiers and behind the desk sat a man of African descent. His position in the Hall was deemed unpopular to a few of the city's residents. His countenance was clear as was his purpose for his place. Brute, fierce, and born to lead. This man was Lieutenant Cullen Mason. Realizing the Lieutenant was sitting in the governor's desk, Jack stepped back with confusion. Cullen raised his hand, relaxing Jack.

"The governor isn't here at the moment. As you can see."

"Where is he?"

"Do not worry. I will be taking his place until he returns."

"Returns? Where did he go?"

"Some important business. Seemed like a family matter."

"I understand. Well, sorry sir. Btu, I've come here with some urgent news."

"I would expect it nonetheless. Why else would you be here. So, what have you come to tell me?"

"There was a quadruple-murder near the area of Yukon."

"Yukon?" Cullen said, leaning back. "The causalities? Their names?"

"Names were unknown. But, we do know the killer."

"And this killer is?"

"The people call him The Lone Outlaw."

"The Lone Outlaw." Cullen nodded. "An interesting title to proclaim for a mysterious figure."

"I guess you've heard of him before." Jack said.

"Indeed I have. My soldiers have heard the stories of this Outlaw going throughout the country. Saving lives and not even taking a ounce of gold for his troubles. Seems like a folktale to me. But, you've come with news of his presence nearby. He's probably come into the city without us even knowing."

"What's should we do?"

Cullen waved his hands and the soldiers took their leave out of the office. With only Jack and Cullen in the office, Cullen offered Jack a seat and Jack kicking his legs went and took the seat. Once Jack was comfortable in the chair, Cullen stood up out of his and approached Jack directly.

"Keep it simple. Keep a lookout for this lone outlaw. We must capture him."

"Capture him?" Jack wondered. "I thought we were only going to find him and see why he's helping people."

"No. the man's a criminal. An enemy of us all. His little acts of heroism could easily be turned into acts of an invader. We don't even know if he was even born in this country. Let alone if his actions as pure. Track him down as best as possible. I will do what I can on my end. Once we find him, everything will show itself."

"I'm sure you have something in mind to find him?"

"As a matter of fact I do. I've already sent out one of our most trusted men to the location where this Outlaw is claimed to reside. Once he finds him, all our answers will be certain."

"I understand you clearly, sir."

"And what of the other one? Thaine Tucker."

"What of him?"

"Has there been anything of him recently? Any sightings or encounters?"

"None that we've come to discover."

Cullen nodded and returned to his seat.

"Very well. You may go."

"Yes sir."

Jack turned and left from the office. Cullen leaned forward to the desk with his hand on his chin. Thinking.

An individual rode upon a black horse, entering the small area of Maverick Town. A gruff-looking man with eyes of a vicious killer. His dirty brown duster looked to mix with the ground. The people in the area call him Thaine Tucker. Tucker entered through the shining lights of the Maverick Town street. Thaine rode into the city, yet no one recognized him. Not even with his face clearly seen. He took this as an opportunity to make his name known amongst them. His appearance with a full-grown beard seemed to impress the women. Thaine watched them as they exited through a building. Looking at its structure and hearing the faint sound of music coming through the doors, Thaine knew it was a brothel and bar. Making his stop, he stepped off from the horse and walked into the building.

Thaine glanced through the interior of the brothel, catching nothing but bare-chested women surrounding the bar and tables. He grinned as he walked through, so did the women. One woman, proceeded to approach him, donning a silky white dress, a dress which quickly caught the eyes of Tucker as he removed his hat.

"Looks like you've come here to find a good time."

"A good time can be anytime, milady. However, right now is not so. I'm here looking for a Mr. Jonathon Wayne. Is he here?"

"Lucky for you, he's here." She moved in closer with a smile. "Follow me."

Thaine went and followed the prostitute down the hallway past the bar, seeing several doors on both sides. Watching her steps, Tucker knew the prostitute was leading him to the main office. How Tucker knew where the office was within the brothel was something he kept to himself. Not everyone can know the methods of Thaine Tucker. Standing in front of the door, hearing the music in the background. She knocked. Within a second, she heard the response to enter as did Tucker.

They entered the office and the prostitute walks over to the desk. Sitting at the desk was a handsome, arrogant man, wearing his favorite brown suit and cowboy hat. He raised his head, looking up toward the prostitute and behind her he saw Tucker. Thaine grinned.

"Mr. Jonathan Wayne, I presume."

"That I am." Wayne said, turning to the prostitute. "Woman, who have you led into my office?"

"Sir, he requested to see you by name."

Wayne nodded as he looked unimpressed. He sighed and waved his hand.

"Thank you otherwise. Please sir, come and sit."

"That I will do."

Thaine went and sat down in front of the desk, facing Wayne. The prostitute stood by the door, watching the two men staring at one another. The tension in the air began to make her uncomfortable. Wayne's eyes leaned over to the prostitute and he saw her standing with a slight shiver. he smiled and told her to leave. She went and shut the door.

"So, tell me sir, who are you and why have you come to see me?"

"Because, you're the owner of this establishment. I'm here to collect my share of the profit."

"Your share? Share of what?"

"The hell do you think? I made an agreement with the previous owner of this place and we settled on a fifty-fifty deal. Such was a simple agreement. I see now, you're the new owner and I believe you should keep this deal. No need to cause trouble."

"Trouble? By you?"

"Who else?"

Wayne scoffed.

"For starters, the previous owner never told me of a co-partner in the business. So tell me, just who the fuck are you supposed to be?"

"Who the fuck am I? I'm Thaine Tucker."

Wayne leaned closer, staring at Tucker. He rubbed his eyes and continued to stare. Tucker shook his head and waved around his hat.

"Looking for something?" Tucker laughed.

"Oh shit. Tucker? Oh! I remember now. I didn't recognize you with the beard."

"It's a recent growth. So, you do know of me?"

"I do. The previous owner, Mr. Barnes had informed me of another partner who shared a stake in this place. He only referred to them as Tucker. Never told me your first name."

"Because we spoke on business terms. Last names only."

"I see. I see. So, you've come here to collect your share of the place?"

"Why else would I have come?"

"Well, I could. But, as all businesses work, once a new owner is in place, the previous deals do not continue further."

"You're telling me I came all this way for nothing?"

"Yes. But, we could however make a deal. Between us this time."

Tucker leaned back and scoffed.

"The fuck we have to make a new deal for? I already had one and it branched over once Barnes sold the place to you. It's all part of the deal. Regardless of ownership."

"That's not how I do business."

"So I can tell."

"Look, I have an offer for you. Let's make ourselves a deal right now. Between you and I. Once the deal is in place, you will have your share and more."

"And that's supposed to be all?" Tucker waved his arms.

"And I could throw in one of the women out there. I'm sure one of them will suit you well."

"To lay down with one of the women out there? Ha! No. I never play with the product. Not my standard."

"Then, you're missing out, my friend."

"Missing out?" Tucker said. "What are you implying?"

"I've tasted my share of these women. It was the only way I could know if they were good for business."

Tucker nodded slowly, leaning stealthily toward the desk.

"Just out of curiosity, how many of these women have you laid with?"

"Five."

"Five? Ah. Five. Quite a number for a beginner."

"I know right!"

Thaine laughed with Wayne before he bolted up from the chair and fired shots into Wayne's chest four consecutive times. Wayne leaned back in the chair, touching the wounds as he moved slowly. Struggling to breathe. Thaine walked around the office, holding the revolver in his hand. He paused and turned toward Wayne.

"Oh, that's right."

Thaine fired another round at Wayne through his head. With Wayne's body hanging from the chair, Thaine placed the revolver back in its holster and let out a slow sigh.

"Five it was."

Thaine exited the office as the same prostitute who greeted him walked by and into the office. Seeing the body of Wayne in the chair, she let out a loud fearing scream. Thaine grinned as the bar and brothel visitors began to move in terror. Walking back to the outside, Tucker sat atop his horse and rode off, leaving Maverick Town in a sense of fear. A method he's too fond of.

Sometime later in Silver City, Jack sat in the saloon, taking in a drink. From the doors, the sound of clicking boots echoed, grabbing his attention. Jack looked over toward the bar and saw the dirty brown duster and hat. For a split moment, Jack believed him to be the Outlaw, only for that thought to wallow away as the Outlaw doesn't dress in such colors according to the witnesses. The stranger had his drink and sat at a table across from Jack. He drank and caught the eyes of Jack staring.

"You see something?"

"Nothing much."

The stranger scoffed. Standing up from the table, he made his move toward Jack's table and took a seat. Jack sat up with hesitance.

"I didn't ask you to sit here."

"I know and I don't give a shit. But, you're giving me strange looks and I don't take that lightly. Who are you?"

"Who are you?"

"I'm Thaine Tucker. Only the few may know me around this city. Seems today, you've become one of them."

"Tucker." Jack said. "The figurative on the run."

"Fugitive?! No boy, I'm not a fugitive. Just a businessman with certain standards which society refuses to believe."

"I've heard of all your works. The terrible things you've done."

"They're not terrible. They're practical."

"You're just like that Outlaw roaming around out there. Doing whatever it takes to live for yourself."

"Outlaw! You talk of him? Oh, you think I'm just like him, huh? Some kind of hero to the people? Well, I'm no hero. I'm the guy who gets shit done regardless of praise or hatred."

"From what I've heard, you're just a selfish man looking out for your own fame."

"You're damn right. And who the hell are you?"

"I'm Jack London and I report to Lieutenant Cullen Mason."

Thaine scoffed with a smile, clapping his hands lightly to avoid eyes from the others.

"You work for him? This is something. So, let me guess? He's sent you, his little errand boy on a mission to find me and the Outlaw, huh?"

"That's right."

"And what are your orders once you find them?"

"To bring them in. By any means."

"Oh. Any means. That's nice."

Tucker cocked his head as his hand slowly reached down toward the holster.

"You really believe you can bring me in? You can't be that dumb."

"I follow orders. It's what is required of me."

"Boy, let me give you some advice. Following orders blindly will put you into an early grave. A suggestion I might add. Don't go blind into the fight. Like you're doing right now."

Thaine's hand raised above the table. No sign of the revolver as he chuckled. Standing up from his seat as he took one last gulp. Taking his leave, Jack rose up and grabbed Tucker by his shoulder.

"I won't let you leave this bar."

"Boy, best you get your hand off my shoulder. Before you end up without it."

Jack with a slight hesitant to remove his hand, when and done so. Thaine grinned with a muffled chuckle to follow as he exited the saloon. Jack stood in the middle of the bar, seeing the eyes of the others on him. Shaking his head, he too left the saloon.

Elsewhere in the outskirts of Silver City and not far out from Maverick Town, Lieutenant Cullen's hired man, Constantine Welles rode out alone into the dark of the night, toward a deserted landscape. Scouting the area, Constantine only found an old shack with a horse standing by. Jumping from his own horse, he approached the shack through the shrouding mists and the vocals of owls, just as he made one step closer to the shack, the door bolted open like a gust of wind. Constantine quickly raised up his revolver. His eyes locked onto the entrance. Seeing nothing but a dim candlelight.

"Whoever's in there, step outside."

While he waited, the sound of creaking wood crawled up Constantine's spine as from the doorway appeared a shadow. Inching closer t the outside as the moonlight shined upon him, the figure revealed himself to be the Outlaw himself. Seeing his presence, Constantine grinned.

"Looks like you've been found."

"On what circumstances have I been discovered?"

"You know why? I've been sent here on orders to bring you in. dead or alive."

"Orders under who's authority do you follow? Mason's?"

"You know him too well and his methods."

"Best you turn around and leave." The Outlaw commanded. "No need for another death this night."

"I'm not leaving until I've completed my order."

"Son, you do not want to take this any further."

"I'm here. Therefore, I must complete what I've come for."

The Outlaw paused, gazing back toward Welles. His eyes were locked on. Welles held his position with the revolver drawn. Seeing as how Constantine did not make a move to turn away, the Outlaw sighed and kindly took his return into the shack. Taking one step inside, a round fired from Welles' revolver into the air.

"I meant what I said." Constantine spoke. "I'm taking you in. Dead or alive."

The Outlaw turned around to face Welles and the two stood at arms. Both their eyes were locked onto the other. Welles smirked, seeing the opportunity of taking out the famed Outlaw. It appeared that's what he wanted regardless of Lieutenant Cullen's orders. The Outlaw on the other hand, only saw an intruder to his solitude. An invader who was forewarned and disregarded the decency which was allotted to him. Outlaw's hand was steady on the handle of his revolver. His demeanor ### calm. Welles began to sweat, taking the moment to wipe his forehead, both fired their shot. The air cooled while the gunfire's echoed had filtered away.

"Check your chest." The Outlaw said.

Welles looked down and felt his chest, feeling the warmth of his own blood as he glanced at his hand covered in it. His legs buckling as he stumbled to the ground. The Outlaw approached him as he raised his revolver to gain a shot. The Outlaw placed his hand over Welles' revolver and lowered it.

"I will get my shot." Welles muffled.

"No. No you will not."

Welles laid on the ground, coughing up blood as the Outlaw stood over him. Not in triumph, but in shame. In the shame of Welles' own self-will. The air was cool enough to keep Welles stable for a few seconds.

Although it wouldn't have mattered much in the end. The Outlaw stood by Welles' side as his breath began to decline in minutes. Welles attempted to speak, only for the Outlaw to silence him. Suggesting he keep his breath and not to waste it on idle words.

"Should've taken my advice. I did not want to end it like this. You're not on my list."

Welles laid back as he exhaled his last breath and his blood poured from his chest. The Outlaw sighed and walked back to the shack, taking a look at Welles' horse. He nodded.

HITMAN OF THE OLD WEST

In the morning light over Silver City, a horse ran into the streets, bringing the attention of Cullen and London. The horse made its stop in front of the city hall where Cullen instantly saw a body laying over the horse. Signaling his men to retrieve the body, he and Jack watched as they removed the body from the horse. The horse shook and galloped away.

"Seems Welles did not complete the task." Cullen uttered.

"What should we do?" Jack questioned. "Should I go ahead and send out word to the men?"

"No need. I already have someone who can do the job."

"If I may ask, who do you have in mind?"

"You'll see him soon enough." Cullen answered, returning to City Hall.

Elsewhere back in Maverick Town, Thaine had overtaken the brothel and bar establishment. Countless men entered and relished in the sight of women and whiskey. Thaine walked throughout the brothel, greeting the men and seeing their lustful gazes toward the women. Thaine knew he made the right decision in his own mind. Making his return to his office, the prostitute he met previously entered and handed Thaine a paper. Grabbing it, Thaine looked calmly. Sighing as he sat the paper down.

"Where did you get this?"

"It's what came in."

"Did you see who delivered it?"

"Some man who came by the entrance. He came and left the paper on the bar. Didn't give a name nor anything else."

Thaine nodded and glanced back at the paper.

"Thank you for giving me this."

"It's my job."

"I understand. However, one must ask. You don't seem to be afraid."

"Afraid?" She said.

"Yes. You saw Wayne's body in here. Bleeding out after I shot him. You stayed."

"Well, to be honest, I have nowhere else to go."

"No family?"

"No sir."

"Well, you have no reason to fear me. I did what had to be done. Wayne was an untruthful business partner and business had to be done. He was the only target. No one else."

"You don't have to explain it to me. I get it."

Thaine nodded with a grin.

"Sure. Sure."

Grabbing the paper again, taking another glance. Thaine sighed and laid back in the chair.

"Appears I'll be paying them a visit. Subtly."

Within the office of City Hall, Cullen sat at the desk with his men standing by at the door. Jack sat down across from the desk as Cullen began to speak with a visitor. The visitor looked almost like a wrangler. Although, not a wrangler they're familiar with. The clicking sound emitting from his boots to his slanted hat. His countenance was somewhat of a cocky nature. Yet with confidence. His gaze would gloom over those not in his favor. Cullen began to tell him of the Lone Outlaw and the crimes he's committed. The wrangler smacked his gums and leaned in toward the desk.

"Any idea where this man is?"

"Last seen on the outskirts of town. Probably still out there. Can't have traveled far."

The wrangler gave Cullen a nod and stood up from his seat. Jack rose up from his own seat in response. From there, Cullen stood up and extended his hand.

"Do we have a deal, Mr. Duke Rogers?"

"Yeah. We have a deal."

The wrangler and Cullen shook hands with each other giving a slight nod of respect.

"How soon do you want this man turned in?" The wrangler asked.

"How soon can you move?"

"I got you. They don't call me Longshot for nothing."

With the wrangler taking his leave, Jack approached Cullen with questions concerning the man's whereabouts and his purpose for being summoned into the City Hall. Cullen quietly sat back down at the desk and sighed.

"Because Jack, that man is the key to bringing in this Outlaw. By any means."

"You're saying you gave him permission to kill the Outlaw?"

"If it comes to that, yes."

"And what if he doesn't?"

"Then he'll bring him in. look, everything is going well. The man's a mercenary-for-hire. His only motivation is to be paid in full. He's already received half. Once he finds this Outlaw and either kills him or brings him in, he'll receive the other portion. No need to worry. Things will work out for the better."

LADY IN RED

Moving through a mining facility in droves were a group of men. Two of them were rushing back and forth between the mine and their carriage with chests covered in locks. Tossing them in the carriage and back to the mines. While making their quick moves, one f the men held a chest and went to turn toward the carriage only to find himself in the gaze of the Outlaw. Dropping the chest to the ground, signaling the attention of the other men. They looked with stares as the Outlaw's gaze was set on the man in front of him.

"Are these chests yours?"

"Not exactly. They're for a few friends of ours. Nothing more."

"Then, why rush? Seems if they belonged to your friends as you say, you wouldn't have no need to rush."

"He's not the one in charge here." said one of the other men, stepping forward. "You see, sir, these chests, they do belong to a friend of ours. This is not a thieves' game. Only a pickup."

"A pickup? Then, why move in such speed?"

"Because our friend requested we do. So, we wouldn't run into other thieves or strangers such as yourself."

The Outlaw nodded, taking a look at his surroundings. Seeing only some trees in the distance to the mine's entrance and the sound of a train moving in the distance behind him.

"The friend you continue to speak of. What is his name?"

"I'm afraid we cannot divulge such information. Especially with those outside of the range of information."

"You have no choice. His name."

"We cannot say."

The Outlaw quickly bolted out his revolver to the forehead of the thief, startling the others as they stepped back. The thief breathed heavily feeling the coldness from the revolver against his forehead. The Outlaw's eyes remained focused. Unmoved.

"You have another opportunity to answer me. I am a just man. I kill only those necessary."

"Ok! I'll give you the name."

"I'm waiting."

"Weldon. Ray Weldon."

The Outlaw held the revolver steady and pulled it away from the thief's forehead.

"Where will I find this Ray Weldon?"

"He moves between Silver City and Maverick Town. He doesn't stay in one place."

"So, I'll have to make my rounds. That's fair enough."

The thieves remained still. Their nervous nature could be felt across the air. The Outlaw gave them a nod and placed his revolver into his holster. Cocking his head toward their carriage, he gave them leave. Without a second to pass, the thieves leaped onto the carriage and rode off. The Outlaw watched as they fled and looked down at several gold coins which were left behind after the chest's fall. picking up one of the coins and examining it, the Outlaw knew this Ray Weldon operated with some powerful people.

In Silver City, Jack went and gathered several of Cullen's armed men. Their objective was set in motion after a brief discussion with Cullen the day prior. Jack and the men prepared a search through Silver City for Thaine Tucker. With the wrangler on the hunt for the Outlaw, Cullen believed Jack would be best suited to track down Tucker and bring him in. Jack's plan was a simple one: To search every populated location in Silver City for Tucker and if they ended up finding him, they would arrest him without haste and bring him in before Cullen.

"Sir, what happens if he doesn't surrender?" One of the armed men questioned.

"Ugh." Jack breathed. "We can't just kill the man. He must be served justice."

In another distant location, the thieves who fled from the Outlaw's sight had returned to their base. Bursting inside like animals, they were quick to pause in front of their leader, Ray Weldon. A man of a brutish stature, yet his drinking would make many look in another direction. Weldon stood up, trembling the ground as he approached the thieves. Searching their hands and seeing three chests and some gold coins.

"Where's the other one?"

"The other what?"

"The damn chest! There were four."

"I dropped it."

"You dropped it?! The hell would you drop a chest full of my money?!"

"Sir, we were found."

"Found by whom? Officials? Gunslingers? What? Who?"

"Some stranger. He dressed like an outlaw."

Weldon scoffed, shaking his head as he gulped another drink.

"You mean to tell me some stranger came to you guys and you left in fear?"

"Sir, his gaze was not of this world. He had to have been some sort of ghost."

"Ghost? You saw the damn thing! He wasn't some ghost." Weldon sighed. "What is the last thing you know of him and my chest?"

"The chest is still near the mine and the stranger said he's coming to see you."

Weldon rose up and snatched the thief, tossing him outside of the base. Taking a second to catch his breath, Weldon turned around toward the others.

"It appears we have someone n our trail. Thanks to all of you. Now, I must put out the word. I have someone who will deal with this stranger while the rest of you return to the mine and collect whatever's left. Now go!"

Later in the night, the wrangler had arrived at the shack where the Outlaw and Constantine Welles had their confrontation. Moving with much quietness, the wrangler searched the shack, kicking down the door. He entered with his six-shooter aimed steady. Within the shack was only a worn-out bed, a dining table with two chairs and a closet. The air was covered with the stench of gunpowder. That was enough to confirm the workings of the Outlaw in the shack. Yet, there was no living sign of the Outlaw to return to the shack. His place there was done and he had moved on. The wrangler sighed and stepped out of the shack.

The next morning, Weldon sat inside the base with his men surrounding him. Some had prostitutes sitting on their laps. From the opening door entered a woman gowned in red. Hair as dark as the night, yet cut to the ends of her ears. Her eyes sparkled before the men and Weldon stood up to greet her.

"Our lady in red. Good of you to come."
"Nice sending out the word for my assistance. What is it you need?"
"We have a problem."
"I'm listening."

LOOT OF THE TRADE

During the mid-morning, Thaine rode into Silver City, covering himself in a cloak and gaiter. Leaving his horse across from City Hall, Thaine quickly moved across the road toward the Hall. Taking a slight moment to listen, he could hear the ongoing conversation between Cullen and Jack. Thaine smacked his gums hearing the muffled talk.

"He's still inside."

Thaine took the time to overhear the conversation. Within a mere moment of minutes, the voices stopped, following the sound of an opening door. Thaine raised his head, peeking through the window as he saw Cullen and Jack exit the office. With them no longer inside, Thaine pulled a blade from his boot and picked against the window, creaking it open. Thaine slowly entered the office and searched through the drawers of the desk. Pulling out papers detailing the ongoing events surrounding Silver City and Maverick Town.

"What is this?" Thaine questioned, reading the other paper.

Upon the paper were small, documented details of a coming war between the Northerners and the Natives of the outskirts. Thaine was unaware of the Natives, having yet to encounter them. Now knowing they're somewhere near the areas of both towns, Thaine began to question his work and methods. Seeing another opportunity on the horizon to cause more trouble for Cullen and his gang of soldiers.

"Best I take this one. Leave the rest."

Thaine quickly folded the paper into his coat and jumped from the window to the outside as a soldiers approached the door, taking a look inside. Seeing nothing, the soldier turned back and walked away. Outside,

Thaine chuckled as he cocked his head and walked down the road toward the residents of Silver City.

Ray Weldon sat in leisure within his base as his men walked back and forth carrying chests filled with gold. With each man passing, Weldon grinned at the glinting speck of the coins. As he admired the continuing appearance of gold, the door to his base opened. Not expecting any visitors, Weldon sat up in his seat, seeing the silhouette of a duster and hat standing. The figure entered as the door shut behind him. From there, Weldon stood up as his men were paused in their steps. Weldon took a moment to measure the man and nodded.

"And who are you supposed to be?"

"Ask your men. They know of me."

Looking at his men, seeing sweat forming upon their foreheads as the chest in their hands started to tremble. Thinking back, Weldon knew it. He faced the man as he commanded his men to return to their duty.

"You're the bastard who threatened my men at the mine?"

"I didn't threaten them. I warned them."

"Where I'm from, talk like that is a threat. You were going to kill them and take my gold."

"I have no need of your gold. I only seek justice."

"Justice for whom?"

"For all who desire it."

Weldon laughed, facing his men with a large smile as his men chuckled softly. Hidden under their muffled mouths. Weldon pointed at the man, shaking his head after hearing his words.

"And who are you supposed to be? The savior to the Northern West?"

"I am the Outlaw who brings forth justice. Even from the crooked actions you yourself serve."

"Who do you work for? The government?"

"I work for the people. Nothing less."

"Look here, fellow. I've already been told of your actions and I have someone looking for you. A shame they're not here to take you out."

"I'm sure we'll meet soon. Everyone often does."

The Outlaw turned away toward the door. Before his hand could reach the handle, the sound of a crashing chest bolted through the base.

The Outlaw slowly turned back as his right hand was pressed against his revolver's handle. Weldon remained still, shrugging his shoulders while yelling at his man to pick up the chest and gold. The Outlaw's hand pulled away from the revolver's handle and to the door. Once he opened the door, taking one step out, he paused.

"Forget something?" Weldon chuckled.

"No. only to warn you."

"Warn me of what?"

"If I catch your actions out here again, I will come for you."

The Outlaw stepped out of Weldon's base as the door closed behind him to nothing but silence. Even Weldon's men were afraid of what the Outlaw might do if he returns. However, Weldon was not afraid as he yelled again to his men to return to work. Shaking his head in annoyance of the visit, Weldon sat back down in his chair.

"Nothing to worry about." Weldon uttered. "Our assassin will take care of him. I know she will."

THE VIGILANTRESS STRIKES

Lieutenant Cullen returned to his office later in the day and quickly noticed something within was off. Glancing over at the window behind his desk, he walked over and saw the glass slightly pushed outward. His eyes widen as he never opened the window during the day nor the days prior. Yelling for Jack, the young man ran into the office to see Cullen pointing at the window.

"Someone was here." Cullen yelled. "Someone was inside my office!"

"Sir, there was no one here after we left."

"The window is pushed outward. As if someone came in from the outside."

"Are you sure, sir?"

"I am. I need to check my desk. If something is missing, it proves my point."

Opening the drawers in haste, Cullen scrambled through the papers, tossing them atop the desk and around. Jack stood still as the papers flew through the air by Cullen's speed. Reaching toward the bottom drawer, Cullen searched and quickly stopped. Taking another look inside and only responding by slamming his fist on the desk, startling Jack for a second.

"It's gone!"

"What is gone?" Jack questioned. "Sir, what is missing?"

"The damn papers! Shit! I've been robbed. Jack, send out word to the troops. Tell them to search for a thief in the city. They're still lingering around here. Be it man or woman. They must be found and brought in before me."

"Yes sir."

Cullen stormed out the office with Jack following him to the outside. As they both stepped outside, taking a gaze at the city's civilians, Jack approached three soldiers whom were standing by, telling them the details of their new mission. The soldiers took Jack's words and followed him to their horses. Watching the soldiers take their leave with Jack, Cullen took another gaze at the civilians. Watching their hand gestures and the body language. Cullen was keen to discover whom the thief could be even though he already had several conclusions in his mind.

Elsewhere in another area, the Outlaw rode through the opened desert of the north, making his way toward a location where Weldon's operations were continued. Making haste to reach the spot before the day's end, the Outlaw's horse is startled by something moving in the distance. The Outlaw paused as the horse refused to continue further.

"What is it, boy?"

The horse shook itself as it refused to continue moving forward. The Outlaw stepped from his horse with his revolver in hand, taking slow walks to see the object standing in the desert. The object stood upright just as he did. Walking closer, the Outlaw could tell it was another human being, cloaked in a black duster and brim hat.

"State your name before I have to shoot." The Outlaw stated.

"I have no name. only a purpose." said the figure.

"Your voice? You sound like a woman. You are a woman, aren't you?"

"I am." She replied, lowering the gaiter from her face. "What business is it of yours?"

"You tell me? Why would a woman standing alone out in the desert in the path of riders? Looking for someone in particular?"

"I have my reasons."

"As do I. Best you move out of my way. No need to escalate this any further."

"I will not move. I do not know you or your business in this region. As far as I can see it, you're trespassing."

The Outlaw sighed with bitter in his breath. Looking down, he raised up the revolver and saw the woman held one of her own. He nodded with a slight smirk on his face. Her face showed a smile of her own, letting him know she was aware of his actions.

"Are you sure this is what you want to do?" The Outlaw asked.

"If I have to, yes."

"It appears we have ourselves a crossroads."

"One you brought to yourself."

"Enough of this, woman. Move aside."

"And why should I move out of your path? Who are you that I should obey your words?"

"I am the Lone Outlaw and I am on a mission to stop a criminal from continuing his work."

"The Lone Outlaw?" She said slowly. "No. you're him?"

"You're heard of me?"

"I heard of what you did in Silver City. Taking out the Four Hats on your own. Many would have never done such a task. Even if they were capable of achieving it."

"Then they are nothing but fools. Someone had to take the task and I did. Four criminals are dead and now I hunt down those who remain."

The woman nodded, removing her hat, fully exposing her fair face and blue eyes. She removed the scarf from around her neck, completely showing her smile as she placed her revolver back into its holster. She walked over toward the Outlaw and extended her hand. Looking at it, the Outlaw stayed silent as he shook her hand.

"I'm on a mission as well."

"You? On what mission requires a woman such as yourself to stand in the middle of a travel path?"

"There's someone who took something from me many years ago. I learn how to defend myself with every weapon that was within my sight. After about three years, I am here, doing my part to protect the innocent."

"And who are you hunting down?"

"Lieutenant Cullen Mason."

The Outlaw remained paused, placing his revolver back in the holster. Taking a look at their surrounding sand only seeing dirt with small fragments of grass as the wind bellowed around them. In his own mind, the Outlaw began to answer his own questions as to why the young woman would be looking to take down Lieutenant Cullen. What did he do to her that made her into the woman he's standing by. Before asking the question, she answered it without even his notice of interest. From her mouth, she stated Cullen had began a manhunt against her after their brief encounter in Silver City. Cullen set a bounty on her head and she fled into the wilderness to defend herself. Eliminating all the hunters who came for her by Cullen's command. Now, she waits for Cullen himself to arrive as she can release the final blow.

"And have many other hunters made themselves known since?"

"Not as many as before. I assume he believes I've ran too far into the United States. Otherwise, I'll be shooting down bounty hunters to this day."

"I see. I'll tell you this. The reason I'm in this area is to find a mining site that's being operated by a man called Ray Weldon. A thief stealing gold and claiming it as his own."

"There's a small town down the path. I've seen only a few men every other day taking carriages back and forth with crates of gold. Never questioned where they came and went with such a trove."

"Then this is the spot. I must confront his men and warn them of the price they might pay for Weldon's foolishness."

The woman nodded as she looked down the path toward the mine's direction. Shaking her head to her own mind, she moved aside as the Outlaw's horse walked over toward him. Petting it with a chuckle in her voice. The Outlaw went onto his horse and thanked the woman for her honesty.

"Nice horse you got there." She smiled.

"He's a keeper. One of the things I'm grateful for."

"So, what will you do once you stop the men at the mines?"

"I will speak with Weldon and give him an update concerning his work. Afterwards, I will deal with Cullen's men."

"His men? He's hunting you down too?"

"For killing the Hats. It appears we make enemies wherever we go."

"We could work together against him and his soldiers. Put it all to a stop much quicker than either of us could anticipate."

"We could." The Outlaw answered. "Yet, now is not the time."

The Outlaw moved past the young woman as she stood watching him move on the trail. The horse paused and stepped as the Outlaw turned around to face her.

"One other thing." The Outlaw said. "You never told me your name."

"My name has been lost to the desert. The people only call me the Vigilantress."

"Vigilantress? What have you done to gain such a title?"

"I have my works ahead of me."

"Appears you do." The Outlaw answered. "Do me a favor."

"Sure."

"Keep watch on this trail for any of Weldon's men. Or even Cullen's soldiers."

"I'm always on watch." She answered.

The Outlaw gave her a nod as he rode off down the path. The Vigilantress turned and walked over to the side, sitting down as she twirled the revolver around her finger.

CIVIL DUTIES AND DEATH TO RIGHTS

Riding down the path, the Outlaw had reached the small town which the Vigilantress spoke of. Passing by a small wooden sign which read, "Welcome to Maverick Town" Entering the old town, seeing people walking on with fear encompassed upon their faces, the Outlaw knew there was something oppressing the Maverick residents. While riding into the town, he looked ahead and saw three gunslingers antagonizing a lone man who was riding his cart through the street.

"I cannot allow that to continue." The Outlaw said under his breath.

Riding over towards the three men, they heard the galloping of the horse coming up behind them as they turned, seeing the Outlaw with his two six-shooters aimed and he fired upon them, killing them in front of the old man. The Outlaw's horse stopped as he leaped off and approached the old man, checking on him to see any injuries. Searching him, he found no injuries and the man was thankful for the Outlaw's sudden arrival.

"Go about your business." The Outlaw said.

With the old man thanking him before taking his leave, the Vigilantress herself rode into town, quickly coming up upon the Outlaw. Her face was in distress as she leaped from her horse and ran toward him. Tugging on his sleeve as she looked back at the entrance to the town. The Outlaw started to wonder; what was she afraid of?

"They're here!" She said. "Lieutenant Cullen's men. They're here."

"I see them." The Outlaw responded, gazing ahead at the horses entering the town with the soldiers and in front of them was Jack.

The Outlaw stepped upon his horse and faced them, leaving the

Vigilantress with confusion and terror as she continued to ask him what he would do since they've arrived much earlier than she expected. The Outlaw looked down toward her and back toward Jack and the soldiers. With a nod, he informed her he would speak with them and whatever happens after will simply happen. Otherwise, the Outlaw already had business to take care of in the town regarding Weldon and his mining crew of thieves.

"What if they start shooting?" She asked.

"Then shoot back."

Riding off to meet with Jack and the soldiers, the Vigilantress stayed back near the saloon of the town and watched as the residents all gazed their eyes toward the Outlaw's rushing move to meet with them. Coming up near them as Jack ceased and the soldiers paused behind him. Jack turned back and gave the soldiers directions to follow as the Outlaw reached them in the road.

"Look who've we found." Jack grinned. "The famed Outlaw of the Northern West."

"I am not here for troubling causes. I came for a mission."

"A mission? And does that mission include killing more men?"

"Yes. Thieves who've been robbing the poor of their wealth and necessities."

"Then, let us help you in this matter. Give the people back what's been stolen."

"I will not. If you were truly a good cause, you would've done so in Silver City. Yet, my actions there prove your words are flawed and laden with poison. However, the poison comes from your boss. You're a different lad."

"Truth be told, I am not like my boss. But, I must follow commands just as any soldier. It is our place."

"Your place. Not mine."

Jack shook his head and nodding before facing the Outlaw once more.

"Look, we didn't come here to start a shootout. We've come to find a woman. The people call her the Vigilantress. Might as well ask you if you've seen her through your travels?"

"I saw a woman on my way here. Down the same path you came from."

"And you're not aware as to where she might've gone?"

"She told me she would be sitting on the side of the road. Waiting for Cullen's men to arrive so she could take them out. Guess, you and your men should consider yourselves lucky she didn't."

Jack gulped and turned back to the soldiers. Whispering something to them as the Outlaw could only watch. Jack nodded and looked back to face the Outlaw and smiled.

"Very well. We'll be on our way to inform Lieutenant Cullen of the news. Take care of yourself, Outlaw."

"I will."

From there, Jack and the solders turned back and rode out of Maverick Town with the Outlaw riding in the opposite direction. Riding back toward the saloon, the Vigilantress stepped out with her eyes facing the entrance the town. When she looked, she saw Jack and the soldiers leaving. A sigh of relief exhaled from her body as the Outlaw looked down at her with a nod of respect.

"They asked for you."

"And you didn't give me up."

"I didn't. No reason why I should've."

"So, what's next?" She questioned. "We both know they'll be back eventually."

"Then, best you prepare yourself for such a time. Meanwhile, I have matters to attend to near the mines. Take care of yourself, my lady."

"I will."

THE LONE KID

The Outlaw rode past Maverick Town and had reached the location of the mines. Taking the moment to stop, he leaped from his horse as he heard the muffling voices of men coming out of the mine. Finding a place to hide himself near the rocks, he watched as two men exited the mine, both carried with them chests. The chests were in similar fashion to those the Outlaw saw when he encountered Weldon's men in the woods.

"His men." The Outlaw whispered.

Before the Outlaw could make a strike, a young man bolted from the other side of the mines, holding a revolver in his hand, aimed at the two men. The men paused in their step seeing the young man.

"What are you going to do with that?" One of the men questioned.

"You're thieves." The young man answered. "You're stealing from the people of Maverick Town. I cannot allow you to leave."

The two men looked at one another and back toward the young man. Within a second's passing the men busted out with laughter. Laughing and patting themselves on the back, confusing the young man. With the revolver in his hand slowly trembling, the two men pulled out revolvers of their own, terrifying the young man as he held his up even higher. The Outlaw couldn't watch any longer and came out from behind the rocks, taking fire at the two men, quickly killing them in mere seconds to the young man's own fear.

"Next time when you try to confront a pair of thieves, do so with much quietness."

The young man gave the Outlaw a nod of understanding. The Outlaw nodded back and asked of the young man's name. the young man sheathed his revolver and stood firm.

"My name is a mystery to the people. I prefer to be called the Lone Kid."

"The Lone Kid?" The Outlaw said with a chuckle. "That so?"

"Is there something wrong with it? Is it childish or not a name thieves would fear?"

"No. it's your name. do so with it as you wish. Just concentrate on honing your skills first. Then the name will take care of itself."

"I'm sorry, sir. But, how do you know all of this?"

"Because. My name, my real name is Clint Winston. However, the people of this land and beyond only know me as the Lone Outlaw."

The young man's jaw dropped like he won some kind of prize out of the blue. The Outlaw knew why he was giving such an expression. He's heard of his actions prior to their meeting and with that information given to him by just a sheer expression, the Outlaw grinned while hanging his head.

"You're him?! The Outlaw who killed the Four Hats!"

"Yes I am."

"But, do you know the good you've done for the people of the city? With the Hats dead, you've provided a better life for the people. They can dwell in their homes without fear. Because of your good deeds, you've given them a glimpse into a life of peace."

"Good to know." The Outlaw replied, turning back toward his horse.

"Where are you off to now, if I may ask such a thing?" The Kid spoke.

"I came here to stop the thieves. Seems with your interference, that task is done."

"And where are you off to now?"

"Silver City. There's other business that needs tending."

"Well, if I may ask, will you require assistance in your tasks of bringing forth justice?"

The Outlaw looked at the Kid with a hint of humor, yet, he was impressed by the young man's tenacity to join in the fight and to help others. The Outlaw went ahead and told him that he should continue practicing his skills, such as his stealth if he wants to avoid being seen by thieves, bounty hunters, and suchlike. The Outlaw nodded and stepped upon his horse and rode off from the mines.

Back over in Silver City, Thaine remained as Lieutenant Cullen was outside of the city on his military duties with a meeting with the Governor. Thaine went and acquired a brothel of the city with the income arriving from the brothel in Maverick Town. Inside the brothel, Thaine sat in his office as the sounds of a filled bar with prostitutes laughing and men cheering, Thaine began overlooking the papers he took from Cullen's office. Seeing all the details and with mire time to examine them, Thaine had enough. Balling up the papers and tossing them into the fireplace. Thaine sat back in the chair with his head hanging over. His eyes focused on the ceiling as his mind wandered off. Three minutes had passed before Thaine picked up his head, cracking his knuckles and neck. He took another minute to pause and stare into space before his eyes glazed over toward the fireplace, seeing the embers rising from the burning papers.

"Yeah." Thaine said to himself. "I'm going to do it."

THE HIGH COST OF LIVING

Thaine quickly arrived in Silver City and began attacking the officials. From the soldiers of Cullen's command to those who were on other business affairs. Thaine did not care for the civilians as several of them were caught in the crossfire. Moving through Silver City, Thaine made it his mission to cause disruption to all of the towns in the land. With his escape from fire in Silver City, Lieutenant Cullen learned of Thaine's actions and immediately sent out his forces to track him down and kill him on site. Thaine rode off into Maverick Town and had done the same, coming into conflict with a few bounty hunters who were looking for Thaine regarding his past actions of avoiding justice.

"More boys seeking trouble." Thaine cackled.

"You're not getting past us this time around."

"Oh, I think I will."

Thaine took out his revolver and fired a shot, hitting a sack of dynamite near one of the saloon posts which he had placed there before the hunters' confrontation. With the explosion, Thaine took his escape from Maverick Town. Riding off into the unknown, Thaine laughed in the cold air, taking in the thought of Cullen and his soldiers on his trail. A thrill he surely sought.

Elsewhere upon the night, the Outlaw rode into Dodge Town, a place which is familiar to Silver City's aesthetics, although a place where most of the criminals seek to dwell. A town not fit for those who desire a life of peace and happiness in the smallest of matters. As the Outlaw rode into the town, the criminals who sat outside smoking and drinking saw his arrival and quickly ran inside. The Outlaw did not chuckle nor nod toward their responses, he continued moving. Riding toward the front of a hardware store, the Outlaw stepped from his horse and approached the entrance. Upon entering, a sharp kick bolted from the entrance. Knocking the Outlaw back and down the steps into the mud. Rising up without fail, the Outlaw looked up toward the entrance, seeing a man standing with a smirk.

"And you are?" The Outlaw questioned, standing on his feet.

"I've been looking for you. Lieutenant Cullen has promised me something of value if I found you."

CLOSE ENCOUNTERS

Who the Outlaw was staring at was Longshot. Through some trial and errors, he had finally found the famed Lone Outlaw. Grinning as he stared him down, the Outlaw lowered his hand, reaching for his revolver and Longshot began doing the same. Their eyes locked onto one another as they reached for their weapons.

"You think you can draw quicker than me?" Longshot grinned.

"You'll find out soon." The Outlaw replied with a grim face.

Both their hands on the hilts. Their eyes locked. One with a coldness of focus and the other grinning with patience. Before they could raise up their weapons, a woman exited the store, stopping Longshot out of his focus.

"No need to kill him. I heard we might need him. He's valuable."

"And who told you he was valuable alive? Better that he's dead. That way he won't gain an upper-hand on us."

The woman's ruby dress had glistened with the moonlight as she ceased Longshot and faced toward the Outlaw. Unimpressed, he removed his hand from his side and stepped forward to face the woman as Longshot crossed his arms, leaning against the store wall with his eyes solely focused on the Outlaw's hands.

"And who are you?" The Outlaw questioned.

"My name is Ada. Ada Red. I was warned about you."

"And who warned you of me?"

"A good friend I call Weldon. You see, after you paid your visit to him at his place, he sent word to me."

"He sent you to kill me? Why? Couldn't have done it himself?"

"Don't take my lean presence for weakness. He called me because I am one of the most skilled assassins in all the Northern West."

"I've never heard of you. I would have if you claimed yourself to be."

"Because we haven't met and had no reason to meet. Until this night."

"And what will you do now that we've met? Will you seek to kill me like your colleague over there or are you willing to bring me back to Weldon alive? If you even can."

Ada chuckled as she waved her dress, showing the Outlaw her own revolver strapped to her leg. He nodded with impression, yet he's seen such before in his travels. Longshot sighed, pressing against the wall and stepping forward.

"Let's just kill this bastard and be done with it. I want to get paid."

"You will be paid." Ada replied with a smile. "Just have some extra patience."

The sound of a galloping horse began to sound in the distance, gaining the Outlaw's attention. Longshot steadied himself near the steps with his hand on his revolver and Ada done the same. Both ducked down as the Outlaw went to face the coming rider. Seeing nothing but a silhouette through the low-lit darkness, the horse appeared before him and riding into Dodge Town was Thaine. The Outlaw sighed as Thaine saw him. Only responding with a laugh.

"Well, I'll be dammed." Thaine laughed. "The hell are you doing here, Winston?"

"On business. And you're here because?"

"I have my reasons. Besides being hunted down by Cullen's soldiers. Whom I might add are on their way here."

"For what purpose would they come into Dodge Town?"

"I've started some shenanigans and there's no way out of it without a shootout."

"And you've brought the shootout to this place? Yet, not in the wilderness nor the open desert?"

"You know me? Where's there's buildings, there's diversion."

"Every time with you, Tucker. Every damn time."

Thaine looked toward the store, seeing Longshot and Ada standing there with a stare. He nodded before catching a better look at Ada's features. He grinned.

"You didn't tell me you were speaking with such a beautiful woman."

"I'm not here for that."

"Damn shame."

Thane approached the steps before Longshot took out his revolver, aimed toward Thaine's forehead. Thaine's hands raised up with a grin on his face. Ada could only watch as she showed no emotion. Although, she was intrigued by Thaine's characteristics. She saw no fear in him and he saw no fear in her.

"Milady, I would love to know your name."

"Ada Red."

"I see. The dress. It does give off your name. I guess Ada Ruby wasn't working out."

"Red has a better strength to it."

"Alright." Longshot butted in. "Enough, you're Thaine Tucker?"

"I am. Who might you be, boy?"

"Folks call me Longshot. And I'm not your boy."

"Never said you were."

Voices echoed from the nearby woods. Dozens of them. Thaine turned toward the Outlaw and winked. He knew they were Cullen's soldiers and they had arrived into Dodge Town. The Outlaw began to move through the town, warning anyone who remained to either prepare for battle or flee. Most chose to flee out of the fear of facing Cullen's soldiers as their reputation had spread across the Northern West after the news had spread regarding their input into the American Civil War. Winston approached Thaine as the voices inched closer with their footsteps beginning to sound.

"This is your doing. You're not going anywhere."

"Never said I was. This is what I wanted all along. Someone has to show Cullen's who's boss around this land."

He glared up toward Longshot and Ada. Asking if they would join in the fight. Longshot declined and warned him if he would survive the coming shootout they'll meet again. The Outlaw agreed to it as Longshot fled. Ada looked out, seeing the lamps in the trees. She gave Winston and Thaine a wink before taking her leave. Now, only the Outlaw and Thaine remained for the fight as the soldiers began stepping out from the woods and into the town road.

"You're ready for this?" Thaine asked with a grin on his face.

"I am." The Outlaw said coldly.

WAR OF THE WEST

Without fail, the Outlaw rose up his revolvers alongside Thaine as the soldiers stepped forward out of the woods. Walking in front of them was Jack to Thaine's displeasure. He wanted Cullen to have led them. The fact of him not being present drew a sore pain into Thaine's ego. Cullen had other matters to attend to which were bigger than his recent attacks throughout the towns.

"Listen," Jack said. "There's no reason for this to be a shootout. Just hear me out."

"Where is Cullen?!" Thaine screamed. "Where the fuck is he?!"

"He has other business ventures. Your recent actions in certain towns has proven to be of little value for his attention. He sent us to come here for those reasons."

"I'm not listening to some young whippersnapper to tell me what to do!"

"Don't be rash." Winston said. "Let's hear him out before we start shooting."

Thaine sighed.

"Shit. Might as well."

Jack commanded the soldiers behind him to lower their weapons. While they lowered them, Thaine reached for his own revolvers, only to be stopped by Winston. With a shrug, Thaine removed his hands and crossed his arms. Staring a hole through Jack while gazing the soldiers around him.

"Here's the deal." Jack said, stepping forward. "Lieutenant Cullen has a warrant out for the both of you. But, he's given an offer for you both.

Something which will have you to avoid some prison time."

"And what's the pay?" Thaine questioned.

"I'm sorry."

"The pay? What is Cullen going to pay us? He didn't think we'll turn ourselves over for something cheap."

"He's not going to pay you anything. Only give you a free pass."

"Bullshit. I'm only accepting gold. Hell, give me some silver if you have it and I know a man of Cullen's status has some silver laying around."

"He's not going to pay you, Tucker. Never even spoken a word concerning it. Lieutenant Cullen only wants to give you a free pass and that's it."

Thaine chuckled and turned his back toward Jack and the soldiers. The Outlaw kept his eye on Thaine as he was shaking his head and his fingers began to twitch. Thaine began to chuckle and Winston knew what was about to happen. Turning over to look at him, Thaine grinned.

"Get ready."

"Thaine, no."

Tossing back his duster, Thaine turned toward Jack and the soldiers with his revolvers in hand. Jack caught the glisten of the guns in his gaze and quickly dove out of the way as the guns began firing at the soldiers. The soldiers quickly spread themselves around the area as Winston took out his revolvers and fired alongside Thaine as they stepped back before the soldiers could regroup and return fire.

"All you had to do what wait it out!" The Outlaw yelled.

"You know me too well, Winston. I never give in to these fools."

Backing away as they fired, two of the soldiers arose and returned fire with their rifles. Ducking around the stacked logs, Thaine fired back, hitting two soldiers in the chests as Winston fired, taking down several soldiers. As more soldiers fell, others came out of the woods like they were respawning. Jack sat back against the store as he watched the shootout. Taking a way to escape from the firefight, the Outlaw ran toward him and held him against the store wall.

"Don't kill me." Jack said shivering.

"I'm not going to kill you. Only that you send Cullen a message."

"Ok. What is it?"

"Tell him to leave me alone. Otherwise, I'll be coming for his head. I can't speak for Thaine, of course. He's already on that path. Best you warn your lieutenant before Thaine finds him."

The Outlaw tossed Jack to the ground. Backing away, Jack stood up and ran away back into the woods. Sighing as Jack vanished into the trees, Thaine approached him from behind, warning him of the soldiers entering the town as the shooting continued. Thaine pointed toward the woods.

"We have no choice."

"You're right." Winston replied. "Let's hide before they find us."

While seeking to make their way toward another section of the woods, the soldiers entered fully into Dodge Town. Some carried dynamite in their hands and laid it around the buildings. The soldiers didn't care for the town, they already were aware of it being a town for thieves and bandits. To their concern, the destruction of the town would be better as the criminals could no longer hide. Thaine looked back and saw the dynamite, his eyes widen.

"Shit."

"What now?"

"They've got dynamite. We need to go now!"

The dynamite was lit up with the flames as the two gunslingers ran toward the trees, the town exploded behind them. The blast even had enough pressure to toss them both through the trees and into the woods. Laying on the ground and groaning, up in the air was debris of wood falling down like heavy rain. Smoke consumed the air in the distance as they stood up into the silence of the air.

"Dodge Town is gone." Thaine said, looking back through the trees.

"Good riddance." Winston replied. "Thieves deserve no place of refuge."

"What now?"

"We find our way back to Silver City."

"Silver City?" Thaine jumped. "The hell for? Why now Maverick Town?"

"You have something there of value?"

"I have value in every place I go."

The Outlaw grunted with a nod.

Walking into the woods to avoid the soldiers' search party. They found themselves nearing the open road. Thaine sighed as he jumped out onto the road, finding themselves surrounded by the woods behind them and the open desert on the opposite. Hearing hooves nearby, Thaine turned to see Winston standing beside his horse.

"How the hell did you get the horse over here?"

"I sent him off as soon as I met Longshot."

"Damn."

Hearing more sound coming from the woods behind them, Thaine raised up his revolvers as Winston did the same. Waiting to see who was coming out, they paused with their fingers on the triggers. Waiting patiently to see who's approaching them. As they inched closer, Winston sighed, lowering his guns.

"You know them?" Thaine asked.

"I do."

The Outlaw watched as the Vigilantress and the Lone Kid came out of the woods. They greeted each other to Thaine's confusion.

"Why are you both out here?"

"We heard the explosion and wanted to see what happened?" The Kid said.

"I heard word you were heading out to Dodge Town." The Vigilantress replied. "Figured I would come by in case you needed an extra hand."

"We need to get going." Thaine said. "Did either of you bring any extra horses?"

"They did." The Kid said, pointing behind them.

Turning back around to the open desert, they found themselves confronted by a tribe of Natives. All on horseback. Three horses were left to the side for Thaine, the Kid, and the Vigilantress. The Outlaw stared at their leader and he recognized him. The leader nodded toward him and he nodded back.

"*Thunderstroke.*" The Outlaw uttered.

"Lone Outlaw." Thunderstroke spoke, approaching him. "We have matters to discuss."

NOLDAR'S TRICKERY

I

Eragard, the first of the fifteen-dimensional realms to the Millennium Gods, ruled over by their all-father, Eden. Theus, the Millennium God of Thunder and the Son of Eden is the Prince of Eragard and the military commander, leading the Eragardian armies into battle while preparing himself to one day become the King of Eragard when the appointed time comes.

Theus, leading Lady Soya, the Millennium Goddess of War and the Mighty Trio, combined of Aslan, the Millennium God of Nature, Ornod, the Millennium God of the Brave and Bold, and Vanor, the Millennium God of Warfare and Violence made their way toward one of Eragard's open fields, primarily used for warfare. They approach, already having the knowledge of a battle, currently taking place between the Light Elves and the Dark Elves. Both sides have been warned about having their war on the fields of Eragard countless times in their history. Theus, approaching the commanding generals of both armies to get their situation straight. Theus, looked onward, seeing the elves in battle. Clashing each other with clubs and war hammers. Theus flies over toward them.

The elves continued their battle and gaze upward, seeing Theus hovering above them as his silver helmet shines and his dark blue cape flows with the wind. Erianor, the general of the Dark Elves pushed the elves aside to get in the center near Theus.

"Theus, Son of Eden!" Erianor yelled. "Why have you come and have chosen to interfere in our war against the Light Elves?"

"Take your warfare onto another realm's land, dark elf." Theus said. "This is Eragardian soil you're spilling elvish blood upon. We do not take it lightly."

Erianor waved his hand in a negative gesture toward Theus, mocking him and his words.

"Go back to your castle, Prince of Eragard and leave this battle to us to finish."

Erianor walked away as Theus stared at him. Theus' eyes slowly glow a thunderous blue with small fragments of lightning sparked from them.

"You did not heed my words, dark elf. I said leave!" Theus declared as he charged up a thunderbolt in his hand. Throwing it at Erianor, hitting him in his back. The bolt knocked Erianor forwards, falling to the ground after flying through the air by the strength of Theus' thunderbolt.

"You dare to assault me! A dark elf! How dare you, Son of Eragard!" Erianor said with anger. "You have made a big mistake for yourself, boy!"

Erianor and the remaining dark elves vanished into thick black smoke. Leaving only the light elves and their general, Eriador. Theus came down and approached Eriador.

"Seems you have more of a brain than your twin brother."

"Appears to be the case, Son of Eden. I will take my remaining brethren and we will leave your field at once."

"I thank you for your honesty and respect, General of the Light Elves."

Eriador created a portal made of elvish crystals. He and the light elves entered, returning to their realm in a flash of light. Leaving the realm of Eragard. The portal closed and Theus turned away, seeing Lady Soya walking toward him.

"What is it now, my Lady Soya?"

"You know the dark elves will return and Emperor Voldor might come alongside them this time."

"Then let him and his army come. We will deal with them ourselves. Maybe that's what the dark elves need. Some Millennium Gods to settle their score once and for all."

Theus flies into the air, returning to the city of Eragard and its palace.

In the wilderness outskirts of Eragard stood an abandoned castle. Aged and broken down. Within the castle sat Noldar, the Millennium God of Guile with his enchantress, Illianna, known as the Millennium Goddess of Sorcery. Noldar had remained quietly in the middle of the trodden down castle that once belonged to an ancient sorcerer. When Illianna walked by his side, gazing her eyes into the portal Noldar had been staring into. Moving her dark and wavy hair to the side behind her shoulder.

"What are you gazing at now, Noldar?"

"I am preparing to open the portal to release my army upon Eragard. Theus and his lackeys have already dealt with the elf war. Now they'll have to contend with the wrath of Jontheim's finest arsenal. Frost Giants."

"Will Aurgelmir be attending this little get together party?"

"Aurgelmir is the one who gave me the opportunity to control his army and lead them into Eragard. So that they may destroy all who live therein and take some spoils back to their realm with them."

"When are they coming through the portal?"

"Right after the moonlight hits the top of Eden's golden palace."

In the portal Noldar and Illianna are staring into, they saw the army of frost giants, wielding frozen axes, hammers, and swords. Prepared and ready for Noldar's portal to open.

During the sundown in Eragard, Theus, Lady Soya, and the Mighty Trio entered the throne room where Eden and his wife, Meredith, the Mother of Theus and Queen of Eragard are sitting. They welcomed them into the throne room. They bowed before the king and queen of Eragard. Both wore their traditional royal garbs, paying honor and respect to the ancient Eragardians of old.

"Theus, our son." Eden said. "What is the news of the elves? Have they taken heed to the warning and left our borders as commanded?"

"The light elves did according to what we asked. But, the dark elves put up a fight. In truth, it was their general, Erianor. I took the small matter into my own hand and knocked him on the ground. Needed to make a statement. He didn't take kindly to it and said that he would return again to do battle with us or the light elves."

"Erianor has always been the stubborn, hotheaded creature of magic. Unlike his brother, Eriador, who has always shown respect toward us and any entities in the fifteen realms. Make sure that the dark elves to not return. Even if their emperor comes along with them."

Eden suddenly stares into space. For a moment, they question what he is seeing and after a while, Eden gets his focus back onto Theus and the others.

"Father, what is it?"

"Frost Giants are on their way! Make ready for war!"

Eden slammed his spear into the ground, trembling the castle and the surrounding areas of Eragard, awakening the people and the Eragardian soldiers. They made ready and stood outside of the palace, waiting for Eden to appear. Theus walked alongside his father as did Soya and the Trio.

"Frost Giants? How could they come here without anyone's notice?"

"Vindhler seen them coming through a portal. A portal made of dark magic and he sensed it toward me and gave me the warning. When you become King of Eragard, you will also have this power. As you have little of it now. You just don't know how to use it yet."

They moved outside the palace and could see the dozens of Eragardian soldiers, standing and prepared for battle. Eden turned to Theus, directing him to the soldiers.

"Take these soldiers and lead them into the battle with the frost giants. I know for certain that with you leading the way, they will be unstoppable."

"I will father."

Theus raised up his Warhammer, known as the mystical weapon called *Mithrandir*. He held it up above his head.

"For the Realm of Eragard!"

The soldiers yelled the battle cry with Theus before heading off toward the portal in the distance fields of Eragard. Eden and Meredith watched Theus and the army march from the palace walls, entering the open fields.

"They've got this under control, Meredith. No need to concern yourself of this matter."

Theus and the Eragardian soldiers entered the open fields. Finding nothing in sight, Soya walked over to Theus as the Trio look around the fields.

"Where are the frost giants?"

"They're on their way. Just have to keep our eyes open."

"Who would allow them into our realm?" Soya asked.

"Our enemies. One crosses my mind."

A low thump echoed through the air as one of the soldiers screamed after being attacked and slammed by a frost giant's battle club. The portal revealed itself, with the frost giants stomping out in mass. All yelling and holding up their frozen weapons of war. Theus turned toward them as does the soldiers.

"Let's clean this field."

He flew toward the frost giants, diving right through them with the hammer in front. Going straight through the frost giants, cutting off limbs and ramming through the abdomens of a few. Lady Soya fought the frost giants with her sword called the Stormslasher. The trio battled the front giants in their fashionable pairs of three. Aslan killed them with his battle sword, Ornod used his battle club, knocking off their heads as he encountered, and Vanor with his battle sword, slaughtering the frost giants, leaving only their limbs remaining on the ground, melting away without a hint of heat.

Theus hovered in the sky and stretched out his arms, conjuring a miniature thunderstorm above the battlefield. Only a little moonlight was able to shine upon the battlefield. The lightning intensified as Theus directed the lightning against the frost giants. Lightning struck down upon the frost giants, who roared in pain. Their bodies in an intense burning sensation.

"Now, you will understand why I am called the Millennium God of Thunder!" Theus declared. "Now, feel the power of the storm!"

Heavy rain poured down from the clouds as the lightning struck many of the frost giants. Most made the attempt to run away, but are captured and killed by the Eragardian soldiers. Soya and the Trio finished off the remaining giants with Theus throwing his hammer at the last one, knocking its head off its shoulders. The hammer returned to Theus as the storm ceased and the moonlight shined upon the melting corpses of the frost giants.

In the distance of the field stood Noldar and Illianna. Noldar, holding his Guilespear, yelled in anger as he witnessed the frost giants' defeat by Theus and the Eragardians. Illianna could only stare at the field, seeing the giants' bodies turning into liquid and melting away into the blood-coated field.

"There will be another time for battle, my lover." Illianna said. "Just be patient with this."

"How can I be patient when the first order of business has failed! Never mind. I will speak to Hadi about this and what is possible."

"You're going to Abaddon?"

"Yes. Where else can I speak with Millennium Goddess of Death?"

Noldar vanished into a portal, going straight for Abaddon. Illianna took one last look at the field, seeing nothing but liquid. She waved her hands and disappeared into a thick green mist. Nowhere to be seen.

Noldar entered Abaddon, the realm of the dead, who are neither honored nor dishonored. He walked through the dark, heated caverns of Abaddon calmly. Aware of the souls that are trapped to endure Abaddon for eternity. He approached the throne room and saw Hadi sitting. He made his way toward her, her two Death-Hounds growled toward him. Standing his guard. Hadi saw Noldar, commanding the hounds to stay down as she stood before him. Her tall presence and beautiful features brought a chill down Noldar's spine.

"So, this is Noldar." Hadi said. "The Millennium God of Guile."

"Yes, it is I. I am here to receive an audience with you concerning a troubling matter of my own accord."

"What does this matter of yours have to do with I, Guile God?"

"I need some assistance with eliminating Theus."

"The Millennium God of Thunder. He's your problem?"

"Aye. I need great assistance with defeating him so that I can rule over the land of Eragard."

"For this cause of yours, I surely hope you don't intend of making a mockery of me."

"I surely do not."

"I'll help you this once." Hadi said, as she waves her hands toward Noldar. Releasing an aura that surrounds him and enters his body.

"What just happened?" Noldar asked, looking around his body, feeling the odd energy.

"When you return to the land of the living, contact Lordi and Arnos. They will be your assistance in defeating Theus and conquering Eragard."

"Oh. Thank you, my death goddess." Noldar said.

He proceeded to walk away, but Hadi stopped him. Turning back to face her, she continued to stare at him with her dark red eyes, covered with the shadow of death.

"Do your work wisely, Guile God. Because if you do not take heed to your own words, you will end up here with me for eternity."

"I will not disobey."

Noldar left Abaddon through a conjured portal. Hadi sat in her throne. The death-hounds growled as she petted them.

Back at Eragard, Theus traveled to the Asbru, the one-dimensional portal between the fifteen realms. The gatekeeper, Vindhler could hear Theus approaching from behind.

"What brings you here?"

"Just to check on the sources of any other portals popping up around the fields."

"No. No portals so far. But there are some strange occurrences taking place in Eldigard."

"Such as?"

"Gods and heroes of their own. Showing up from the sky before the realm of Man. They're worshipping them as their new gods."

"Should I go down there to check things out?"

"In a matter of time, you will. Just not right now."

Theus nodded. Taking in Vindhler's words closely.

"Well, thanks for your trust and watchfulness, Vindhler."

Theus left the Asbru as Vindhler continued to keep a lookout into the fifteen realms of Eragard.

II

Noldar returned to his trodden down castle, using the power Hadi had given him to communicate with Lordi and Arnos. He used his portal device to contact them. Letting the power soar through the castle. Illianna entered, seeing Noldar. She ran toward him curiously.

"You're back." Illianna said. "What happened in Abaddon with Hadi?"

"She is willing to aid us in our mission to eliminate Eragard. She gave me this source of power to contact Lordi and Arnos to aid us."

"Very well. After you speak with the two, when do you plan to strike Eragard?"

"Right after I speak with Lordi and Arnos. Immediately after."

Noldar grinned. "No more waiting this time."

A small festival was held at the Eragard Palace with the celebration of the defeat of the frost giants. The people drank and partied as Eden and Meredith discussed plans concerning the realm and what can be done to protect it.

"In time, we will achieve peace in all the fifteen realms." Eden declared.

Theus entered through the scene, walking to his father's throne room. He opened the door seeing Eden inside.

"Father, can I have a word with you?"

"Yes, my son. Of course."

Theus entered the room, facing his father and mother.

"What is it?" Eden said.

"We haven't traced down the source that allowed the frost giants into our realm. We're still looking."

"The enemy will come when he or she decides its necessary. If it is a traitor in our midst, kill them when they present themselves. If it's an outsider, lock them up in the dungeon for future interrogation and judgment."

"I will see to that, father."

The doors shut behind Theus as he left. Walking outside, Soya approached him. He smiled at her presence. Relieved and calm.

"What is it now?"

"We have to find the one responsible for allowing the frost giants here. I sense we know who it is but I can't direct a finger toward him."

"So, it's a "he" that brought the giants in?"

"Yeah. I believe he's closer to us than what we intend to know ourselves. He knows all of us because he's been with us."

Theus began to sense something in the air. It's a heavy feeling. One of great weight. Becoming weary from the sense. Soya noticed him stumbling, as he attempted to stay standing.

"What is it?"

Theus slowly returned to normal. Taking in a breath and wiping the sweat from his forehead.

"A breach has been opened. Lordi and Arnos have been released from their imprisonment."

"Should I get the Trio prepared?!"

"Yes!"

Theus flew back toward the palace. Entering, he returned to the throne room to Eden and Meredith. Opening the doors and standing before them once again.

"You felt it too didn't you?" Eden said. "The tense air entering your body."

"I did. Lordi and Arnos's prison has been breached. They've escaped."

An explosion appeared from the city entrance. At the entrance is Noldar, wearing his dark green and brown armor with his ram-horned helmet. Illianna stood beside him and behind them is Lordi and Arnos. All four prepped and battle-ready. Theus gazed toward the entrance from the palace, seeing them. Soya and the Trio also see them. Theus moved with haste as Soya and the Trio followed him.

"Noldar!"

"What do you need us to do, Theus?" Ornod asked.

"We head straight for them and finish this mess."

Theus flew up into the sky toward the entrance with Soya and the Trio following him from behind as Eden watches onward with Meredith at his side.

They left the palace, heading toward the city entrance. Meanwhile, Noldar, Illianna, Lordi, and Arnos entered the city of Eragard and began slaughtering the those around. Screaming in horror as they're being destroyed. Arnos sliced them with his battle axe as Lordi injected them with a drug, causing them to have deceptive hallucinations and making them believe he's come to protect them. They walked toward him in deception, he snapped their necks one by one.

"Tis' good to be back in the land of Eragard." Lordi gestured. "Wouldn't you agree, Arnos?"

"I do. We can do so much out here to make a statement to all the fifteen realms."

Noldar smiled as he witnessed the carnage unfolded. He turned to Illianna with a bright smile.

"This is the beginning of our salvation, my love! Eragard is ours!"

Thunder roared above them, gaining their focus. Noldar reluctantly glanced up in the air, seeing Theus, Lady Soya, and the Mighty Trio. Illianna looked upward and stared. As did Lordi and Arnos with anger in their eyes. Fire engulfed their insides.

"He's finally come." Noldar said. "The great Theus Edenson!"

"He brought his whore alongside him, my love." Illianna said, gesturing toward Soya. "I'll deal with her."

"Noldar!" Theus said. "I should've known you were behind all of the troubles we've been experiencing."

"Of course, Edenson! Who else could derive such a plan that would send you and your friends into utter chaos? Only I, Noldar, the

Millennium God of Guile could do such a thing and all of you know it!"

"End this now, Noldar. Before the consequences before worse."

Noldar grinned. Loving how his plan is working.

"It will end, Theus. Just not the way you're expecting it to end."

Lordi and Arnos flew into the air to combat Theus. Arnos raised his axe, smashing it into Theus, knocking him down toward the ground. Soya flew toward Illianna and they engage in combat. Noldar stared at the Trio as they land on the ground in front of him. Three against one. Noldar loved those odds.

"Which of you will fall by my hand first?" Noldar said.

"I'll take the first hit!" Ornod said. "Get ready to fall, God of Guile!"

Ornod went for the swipe with his battle club toward Noldar, who made his body transparent, the club swung through his body. Noldar hardened himself together and raise his Guilespear, swiping it in the back of Ornod's head. Knocking him out. He faces the remaining two, Aslan and Vanor, smiling at them.

"Next?" Noldar asked with a big, sinister and happy grin.

On the other side of the city, Illianna and Soya fought, slamming each other into structures. Illianna flew toward Soya, yet, is struck with a right heel, knocking her into a wall.

"You always used your legs for everything." Illianna muttered. "Shame."

"And yet, you're the one who's lying on the ground." Soya said. "Stand up and face me like a woman, witch!"

"With pleasure, whore."

Illianna stood up, snatching Soya by her cape, punching her and threw her into a building. Illianna later controlled some of the nearby people, making them attack Soya. She fought them, but she refused to kill them before she was kicked in the back by Illianna.

Theus is double-teamed by Lordi and Arnos. Using their abilities to pummel him into the ground. They jeered as they proceeded to beat

Theus into the ground, deepening him into the ground. A proper burial place.

"You thought we could be kept in a prison?!" Lordi gestured. "You fool!"

"We're Millennium Gods just like you!" Arnos said. "We have power beyond what many comprehend!"

"Yet. You have no trait of intellect nor instinct." Theus said. "Allow me to show you what it truly means to be a Millennium God."

Theus charged up his power within his hands and shoved Lordi and Arnos from him. Through the flying dirt, Theus stood with Mithrandir in hand. He lunged toward Arnos, slamming him with Mithrandir into the ground. Making a quick right turn to swipe Lordi across the city. Theus hovered into the air and released crashing thunderbolts, striking Lordi and Arnos.

"Feel the power of the thunder!" Theus yelled as he released a stronger lightning bolt from Mithrandir, striking Lordi and Arnos.

Noldar began to face Aslan after defeating Vanor with an illusionary attack. While fighting Aslan, Noldar notices Lordi and Arnos have been defeated by Theus. Due to the lightning in the sky.

"No!" Noldar said. "Where's Illianna?! My love, where are you?!"

Upset, he searched for Illianna and saw Soya walking toward him. He can see she's dragging something with her. He looked closer, Soya is dragging an unconscious Illianna. Knowing his plan is failing, Noldar tried to run, but is cornered by a revived Ornod and Vanor. Surrounded by the Trio and Soya, the spark of thunder sounded from above him. He glared up as Theus came down from the sky.

"You got me this time, Edenson." Noldar said somberly.

"You're coming with us. For judgment."

Theus grabbed him, returning to the palace.

Within days, Noldar's judgment took place. Eden had placed Lordi and Arnos into a deeper state of imprisonment. To where neither Millennium God nor gods of any kind could break them out. Illianna had been thrown into a dungeon for a period of a year in the sight of the gods. Eden commanded Noldar be brought up before the Eragardian council.

"By the laws of Eragard, you, Noldar Thanatoson, Millennium God of Mischief and Guile, will be placed into the dungeons of Eragard until the necessary time for your release." Eden said.

The guards entered, snatching Noldar by his arms, pulling him out of the council's sight and to the dungeons. While walking down the alleyway of the dungeon, Noldar looked over at the cells, spotting those who are imprisoned, from trolls to demons to cyclopes to aliens and to Illianna herself.

"We will get out of here, my love." Noldar said. "I promise you!"

He made the attempt to approach her cell and the guards snatched him away from Illianna.

"Keep walking, Guile one."

The guards placed Noldar into his cell and shut the door. Locking it. They walked away as Noldar stared down the alleyway. He hung his head while standing in the middle of the cell. A split second after the guards left the dungeon corners, Noldar smiled.

"I'm inside." Noldar said. "Just as we agreed."

WAR OF THE THUNDER GODS

CHAPTER ONE: THE SHOWCASE OF POWERS

Within the starry skies of Eragardia, the fifteen realms seemed to be at peace. Peace however was not commonly seen amongst the living in these days as the ongoing war of the elves continued to be in flux across Elfheim, ream of the Light Elves and ruled by Emperor Aeden and Svartheim, realm of the Dark Elves, dominated by Emperor Voldor. The war had concluded with the elves seeking a truce to never step beyond the boundaries of their respective realms and into the others unless of a dire circumstance. One that may be of the end of all things.

Now, the Millennium God of Thunder, Theus had traveled across all the fifteen realms to keep them in balance as many sought to eliminate his power to invade Eragardia itself. Theus aided the Light Elves in their fight against the Dark Elves. After the Elves' War was complete, Theus entered Eldigard, known as Earth and met the risen heroes who dwell within. Joining them to form the unit called The Resistance, Theus continues to return to Earth and aid them in matters which deem more fit for a godly battle than a human's war. Helping the heroes take down his primary adversary, Noldar the Millennium God of Guile with Death, Kex Kendrick, King Stroh The Conqueror, Octagon, and the Blacholian force of Oranos. Theus bid the heroes farewell as he returned to his own realm.

A prepare for war was made after an unseemly warning erupted from the realm of Bidavellir as Ukko, one of the mighty trolls who dwells within the realm has sought out the challenge of facing the Eragardians in battle. His army was set and ready for the arrival of Theus and his comrades. Within days, Ukko waited. His patience growing thin as the moon and sun above him continued to set day by night with no sign of the Eragardians nor the spark of their coming power. Ukko began to grow tired. Walking out into the open lands and screaming into the air for the arrival of the Eragardians. He began to shout their names and curse them under the sun.

Yet, seven days later, a loud boom screeched thought eh clouds above Bidavellir, calling out Ukko from his home. His mighty war-hammer in hand as he gazed toward the sky and saw several streaks of light. Unsure as to what they could be, he knew they came from Eragard and he was proud as a grin formed on his large face. Rallying his army as they smashed their hammers against their shields, seeing the lights coming closer toward the ground. Ukko stood in front of the army, sealed in his burnt silver armored from his neck down. The lights inched closer, nearly bright enough for the army to cover their eyes. Ukko was not afraid as he let the light shine.

"Come Eragardians!" Ukko screamed. "This day, the land of Bidavellir shall relish in the taste of your blood!"

The light brightened and crashed into the dirt, forming a crater before the sight of Ukko and his army of trolls. The air around them was shrouded in flying dirt and debris as it cleared, unveiling Theus, Lady Soya, and the Mighty Trio of Aslan, Ornod, and Vanor before the sights of the trolls and Ukko. Theus arose from his knees and faced Ukko with lightning sparking from his hands and eyes.

"The Millennium God of Thunder." Ukko spoke. "You've accepted my proposal."

"You curse our names toward the sky. Continued to beg for our arrival and for what cause? So, that you would be defeated by the hands of Eragardia's finest?"

"No! I will not fall this day! I, Ukko, Maser of Bidavellir summoned the might of Eragardia to prove you're no longer required to be the protectors of the realms."

"And you're seeking to place yourself above all others?" Lady Soya asked. "Without any forms of test? No trials?"

"I need no tests nor trials to prove my worth! The weapons I've formed are a perfect match for anyone who opposes me. You will learn how this day."

Theus reached toward his back and raised up his hammer simply known as Mithrandir. The hammer sparked with lightning as it surged from Theus' hands and to the head of the war-hammer. Ukko gripped his hammer and slammed it into the dirt.

"Ready when you are." Soya said to Theus with a smile.

Theus grinned, leaping up into the air and causing the thunder to crack as rain began to fall upon the field. Ukko grunted with a stomp as he commanded his army of trolls to attack Soya and the Trio. The four Eragardians savored the notion of the incoming army and ran into battle. Clashing their blades against eh shields of the trolls. Over on the other end, Theus crashed down several feet in front of Ukko as the mighty troll swung his hammer into Theus' own.

"No godly powers will defeat me."

"I've dealt with you once before, Ukko. His time will not be any different."

Theus shoved the weight of Ukko from his hammer and jumped into the air, crashing the hammer down upon Ukko's own as the shockwave of lightning spun out across the battlefield with streaks of lightning crashing down upon the grounds. On the other end, Lady Soya relished the moments of slaughtering the trolls with her blade. A delicate moment. The Trio did the same with each of their skill sets proving useful in the fight against a mass of trolls. No different than the dark elves in battle, only much larger.

"These things never learn!" Ornod screamed in battle.

Theus moved swiftly with the lightning which he expelled toward Ukko. Flowing through the mid-air, gilding in a sort. Ukko screeched as he hurled his hammer toward the Millennium God, only for the hammer to return to him in force. Smashing him against the wall of the mountain. With Ukko on the ground, Theus lowered himself as he approached the downed troll. Walking closer, the crack of thunder in the air alarmed everyone on the battlefield, even Theus himself.

"Was that you?" Soya asked Theus.

"No. It was not me."

The thunder cracked once more as two beams of light entered the atmosphere, heading towards the battlefield. The Trio moved from the path as did the army of trolls. Ukko stood up and faced the beaming lights as did Theus.

"More of your forces?" Ukko questioned.

"Not mine." Theus replied. "Yours?"

"Hmph. No."

The lights had reached the ground and crashed, bringing up the dirt and the smoke around them. Blinding their sights. However, Theus raised up his opened hand and sparked a huge beam of lightning around the field, blowing away the dirt and smoke. With the scenery clear, what everyone saw standing in the midst of the field were two figures. Each one wielding a weapon of their own. The first was burly in size, holding a hammer of great strength. His beard and hair flowed with his gleaming armor. The second was leaner in stature, yet stern. Unlike Zhor, this one wasn't fully clad in armor. He wore the garments of a hunter. Skins and fur were his attire and they suited him well. Holding a axe/hammer hybrid in his right hand, holding it over his shoulder. Both their eyes were centered upon Theus and him only. Not even a turn or glance toward Ukko, Soya, the Trio, or the trolls.

"Who are they?" Aslan wondered.

Theus moved forward, facing them. His hammer set on his side.

"State your names."

The burly one took a step forward, placing his hammer on the ground to a sudden quake. His eyes locked with Theus.

"I am Zhor! The God of Thunder!"

Theus stepped back hearing the words which had come from this Zhor. A god of thunder? Soya went to press forward, yet was held back by the Trio in case of a coming battle. As they are aware of what happens when gods of the same stature collide in combat. A sight not even the humans have yet to witness.

"And what about you?" Theus asked the second one.

"I am Taraino. The God of Thunder."

Theus gave them a nod of confusion.

"I believe the both of you are mistaken. I am Theus, the Millennium God of Thunder. The powers of the heavens are mine to control. No one else's."

"You dare deny us our heritage?!" Zhor pressed himself. "We are thunder gods! It is why we are here!"

"Then, we shall take this matter of Eragardia. Let us see what my father Eden has to say concerning your heritages."

Zhor took a moment to pause himself and think. Taraino had already agreed to Theus' suggestion. Zhor stared and later gave a nod. Theus nodded back as he turned to Ukko and warned him to get control of his army and resist not causing another disturbance. Ukko agreed to the truce due to the interference of the foreign gods. From there, Theus and the two gods alongside Soya and the Trio left for Eragardia.

CHAPTER TWO: A HERETIC ENDEAVOR

Moving through the Asbru before touching the skies of their homeworld, Theus made his return to Eragardia alongside the two mysterious thunderers. Making their way toward the palace where Eden himself awaited Theus' return. His eyes keen on the two other figures. Upon their landing at the palace steps, Eden hugged Theus and greeted Soya and the Trio. Once Eden arose from embracing his son, he stood firm and focused his gaze toward the two foreign gods.

"Who are these men?" Eden questioned. "I sense a strange power from them."

"Father, they came from the skies during our battle with Ukko. They claim to be thunder gods themselves."

"Thunder gods? From where?"

"I understand this may all seem a bit difficult for all of you to comprehend." Taraino spoke.

"I will not allow you to utter a word until we are inside." Eden commanded. "As long as you're out here amongst the ears of my people, I will not tolerate a foreigner speaking their ideals."

Taraino stepped back and nodded. Eden took the response as a show of respect. From there, he proceeded to allow the two gods into the palace to speak their peace regarding their sudden appearance. Soya and the Trio were commanded to head to the other ends of Eragardia to prepare for a possible war against a foreign entity that may be related to the two gods. Theus, on the other hand spoke to Eden he would like to have a word with Noldar, the Millennium God of Guile who's still imprisoned after his bout with The Resistance and the Protectors on Eldigard.

Walking inside the palace, the sheer glow of gold was everywhere. The two gods wondered where such gold had originated from. For they have never seen so much in one place. Eden sat on his throne with Meredith by his side. His spear in hand as the two thunder gods faced him. Eden sighed as he measured them. Their weaponry and their countenance.

"Your names." Eden said. "Tell me of them."

"I am Zhor."

"Zhor?!" Eden responded. "And you're a thunder god?"

"I've been called the *Estranged God of Thunder*."

"Estranged? By what kinds have spoken of you in such a manner?"

"Those who do not understand my plight."

Eden nodded while glancing down on the golden floor toward Zhor's blundering hammer.

"And what of its name?"

"The hammer?"

"Yes."

"I've come to simply call it, the *Mallet*."

"Mallet. Huh. And why have you given it such a boastful name?"

Eden took a small liking to Zhor, although not as much as Zhor would perceive the King of Eragardia to give him. Eden turned his focus toward Taraino, who remained silent and still. His eyes and gaze centered upon Eden and not even a gaze nor turn toward Zhor. It was almost as if the two thunder gods appeared at the same time, were yet on opposite agendas and Eden knew this to be true.

"And your name?"

"My followers call me Taraino."

"Taraino." Eden nodded. "And you're a thunder god as well?"

"*The Primeval God of Thunder.*"

"Primeval?" Meredith paused.

"You're saying you've been around for eons. Ages of war you've fought?"

"I have."

Eden took another look at the two gods and nodded.

"Tell me, what brings the two of you here to Eragardia?"

"I was sent here for a great cause." Zhor spoke.

"A great cause?" Eden paused. "What kind of cause would send you to the dominion of Eragardia?"

"I was told there could be only one thunder god and I summoned enough power to transport myself to a place where the most dominate thunder god could be found."

"Ah. You speak of Theus. My son and the rightful thunder god."

"I've come to take him on in combat. Defeat him and claim the rightful title of God of Thunder."

"I see. You've come from a land I do not know to challenge a Millennium God for the right of his title?"

"Rightfully my title."

"I have to disagree." Taraino said. "I've been around much longer than this Zhor. If anyone is worthy of challenging the Millennium God of Thunder, it shall be I."

Zhor turned toward Taraino with anger kindling in his eyes. His hand twitching for the grip of his hammer. Taraino stood calm. No emotion. No expression. Eden watched on as the two foreign gods stood opposite of one another. The energy surging from them both gave Eden a great understanding to their purpose.

Elsewhere in Eragardia, Theus arrived inside the prison and approached the door in which Noldar stood behind. Knocking for the door's opening, Noldar stood against the dark walls of the cell as the door creaked opened, allowing Theus to enter with two Eragardian guards standing by the sides of the door. Noldar looked at Theus entered and greeted him with applause. Not of truth, but of mockery.

"Tell me, what brings the Prodigious Theus to my cell?"

"It appears we have visitors."

"Visitors? Of what kind are you referring to? Celd? Death? Kendrick?"

"No. Two individuals who proclaimed themselves to be gods of thunder."

Noldar's eyes had widen to the sound of the words.

"You're telling me you're not the only one? Aside from Zeus that is."

"There's something off about them and every time something like this occurs, it always has your hand upon it."

"That is true for a number of things. Although, this time it is not."

"That so?"

"I have no clue who these two thunder gods may be. Why would I consult in them when I already have a hard time dealing with you."

Theus grunted with annoyance in his breath to Noldar's own selfish amusement.

"You have nothing to do with this?"

"Nothing. I swear to Eden himself. I have nothing to do with these foreign gods you've met."

"Very well."

Theus went and took his leave. Stepping out of the hallway to make his exit, one of the guards approached him with haste. Theus recognized the motive from the guard as he's seen it in others before.

"Son of Eden, word is requested for you."

"Of what kind?"

"Emperor Voldor of Svartheim requests your presence in his realm."

"The Dark Elf seeks to have an audience with me?"

"Yes, my lord."

"Thank you for the message."

Theus went and returned to the palace to inform his father of the news. While reaching the palace, the guards standing at the entrance told Theus of Eden's current conversation with the two foreign gods. Seeing as he did not want to disturb the meeting, Theus went to the Asbru to make his preparation. Walking the Asbru center, Vindhler stood by and acknowledged Theus' presence.

"I see you received the message."

"Yes, Vindhler. I need to get to Svartheim. Emperor Voldor wishes to speak with me. Not sure why."

"He knows of the foreign ones."

"He does? How?"

"That is a question you will have to ask him yourself."

The Asbru glowed and brightened with a rainbow-hued light. The trail was open as Theus stepped through the light and onto the Asbru, instantly transporting him to Svartheim.

Seeing the realm covered in shadows of darkness with the humming sound of the dark elves marching on the fields preparing themselves for a coming battle. Theus kept himself to the skies to get a look across the realm. Seeing the palace in the distance, glowing in the glistening darkness of violet and grey, Theus flew toward it and arrived to the confrontational surprising from the dark elf guards.

"I have not come to fight. Your master has requested my presence."

The guards lowered their spears and stepped aside as Theus entered the palace, sensing the presence of Voldor. Following one of the maidservants into the throne room, Theus looked on, seeing other dark elves clothed in wealthy garbs. He's never seen dark elves with such notion of fashion. The throne room doors opened for the maidservant to lead Theus in and once inside, Emperor Voldor sat on the throne, glaring toward Theus.

"He has arrived, my lord."

"Thank you for bringing him in." Voldor replied. "Leave us. All of you."

The maidservant and the guards took their leave from the throne room as Theus stood center in the room while Voldor laid back in the chair. The doors closed to a gong. Theus kept his eyes on Voldor, seeing him dressed in his elvish armor. The gleaming light from above shined down upon him, brightening the armor's presence before him.

"You sent word for me." Theus said. "What do you have for me?"

"I know about those foreign gods who are currently within Eragardia.

I sense a grave danger from them both."

"Do you? And do you happen to know where they came from or anything related to their arrival?"

"I only know they're not from our worlds. None of the fifteen realms."

"None? Such a thing is not possible."

"I'm here to tell you, it is possible and it is true."

Theus nodded, taking in Voldor's words.

"Then, is that the reason you summoned me here? To tell me these foreign gods originate from a place I do not know?"

"Yes."

"If that's the case, there exists an alternative. A way to return them from where they came."

"There is."

"I take it you know the way." Theus spoke.

"Combat."

"Combat?"

"These foreign gods came here for one reason and one reason alone. To see who the definitive thunder god is. Between the two of them and yourself, a battle must take place. A winner must be chosen to end all of this."

"I do not understand any of this." Theus replied. "Zeus isn't here. If this was a battle between gods of thunder, he should've arrived as well. Not just these foreign gods and I."

"On that, I have nothing to add. Although, I am sure you have several allies from the Olympian realm. Perhaps, they can offer you some details to this growing war of the thunder gods."

Theus remained silent as his mind wandered. Within a few minutes, a thought entered his mind as he raised his eyes toward Voldor.

"I have someone in mind."

"Good of you to know. Now, I've told you all I know. Our conversation is complete. You may leave my palace and my realm now."

Theus took a pause. His right fist balled up as his hammer rested on his left side. Voldor stood up to the sound of his rattling armor.

"I do not wish to fight you, thunder god."

"Nor do I. Yet, you stand ready to battle."

"Only if you make a quick move of haste."

Theus grinned.

"Nothing from me. Thank you for the information, Voldor."

Theus exited the throne room as Voldor returned to the chair.

From there, Theus flew over the palace and saw most of Svartheim. Gazing up to the skies, Theus called out to Vindhler as the Asbru returned to him, transporting him back to Eragardia.

"Was Voldor's information enough for you?"

"Enough to a point. Vindhler, I need to make a quick stop to Eldigard. to speak with someone who has some information concerning the Olympian pantheon."

"I know who you're heading out to speak with."

"He knows a thing or two about them. I'll be back."

Vindhler gave Theus a smirk as the Asbru sent him to Eldigard. The sky beamed with light to Theus' arrival.

The light emitting from the Asbru was nearly brighter than the sun during the noon of the day. Hovering in the air, Theus looked ahead and saw the glowing fortress. Flying toward it, he arrived in time to find someone entering the fortress. Landing on the ground, Theus walked into the fortress and saw all the weaponry which sat inside. He recognized several of the blades, knowing them to have come from the armory on Mount Olympus. Approaching the weapons for a closer gaze, Theus is stopped by the sound of a voice.

"I wasn't expecting you to have come here. Let alone find this place."

"Ah. Taltus the Titagod. Good to see you once again."

Taltus and Theus greeted one another with a hug. A Millennium God to a Titagod.

"Seems you're doing well after our battle with Oranos."

"Doing best as possible." Taltus replied. "So, what brings you to my fortress?"

"There has been an unsettling turn of events back on Eragardia. Two gods. They proclaim to be gods of thunder."

"Zeus?" Talus asked without question.

"No. These gods call themselves Zhor and Taraino."

"I've never heard of them before."

"I need to know if you're aware of any other thunder gods within the Olympian pantheon. Or imposters of a kind."

"I know only one thunder god from Olympus. Only one."

"I see. Well, I'm not sure where they come from. But, what I do know is they cannot remain in Eragardia any longer. They want a battle from what I've been told."

"And will you? Battle them to the finish?"

"If necessary."

The ground began to quake, gaining their attention as they flew out of the fortress and gazed around the outside. Theus could hear the sound of mumbling voice from the sky, even Taltus could hear the voice.

"Theus!" The voice echoed through the sky, rumbling even the clouds.

"Vindhler?!" Theus said.

"Theus, you must return home with haste! Destruction has come!"

"What do you mean?!"

"The foreign gods! They're combating above the land! Eragardia needs you to stop them!"

"Open the Asbru!"

Theus turned to Taltus as the Asbru opened above them. Blowing away the clouds like dust.

"It's two gods against one." Theus said. "Would be nice if I could get some assistance."

Taltus grinned.

"After the battles we've been in together, you've helped my world. Now, I'll help your world."

Theus gave Taltus a nod as the Asbru fully opened and transported both Theus and Taltus from Earth to Eragardia.

CHAPTER THREE: WAR FORETELLS THE FUTURE

Beaming through the Asbru, Theus and Taltus arrived back in Eragardia to find the entire area seemly covered in dark clouds and lightning. Theus gazed ahead to the sound of thunder, seeing Zhor and Taraino clashing against each other with their weapons. Causing the rumble of the thunder. Below them were the people fleeing in fear from the collapsing buildings and lightning strikes.

"I take it those are the two gods you spoke of." Taltus said.

"Indeed. Aid me in stopping them from destroying my homeland."

Theus went and flew toward the thunder gods as Taltus followed. Inching closer to the foreign gods, a streak of dark lighting struck Taltus in the back, knocking him to the streets of Eragardia. Theus paused and looked down, seeing Taltus slowly standing up. Wondering what had happened, he noticed Taltus looking ahead to see the arrival of the dark elves, led by Voldor.

"Theus, deal with the gods. I'll take care of these invaders."

"Agreed."

Theus reached Taraino as he slammed his weapon across Zhor's back, causing him to collapse into the palace. Taraino turned to see Theus and raised up his weapon.

"Why are you two fighting?" Theus asked.

"There can be only one god of thunder and it is I."

"You do not want to do this." Theus replied, as his hands began sparking lightning.

"I must. It is my purpose."

Taraino went for a strike against Theus, yet with his hands, he stopped Taraino's attack and grabbed his hammer, smashing it against Taraino, tossing him across the sky. Theus went and followed Taraino through the clouds of darkness as lightning fell around them to the ground. Meanwhile, Taltus bolted through the hordes of dark elves to reach Voldor. Taltus hovered in the air and let out his lightning vision, striking the dark elves in his sight. Voldor was impressed by the attack and even applauded.

"You have a gift." Voldor said. "Truly."

"I do not know who you are, but I suggest you return home before more things happen."

Voldor held up his spear and aimed it toward Taltus. Seeing it as a open to attack, Taltus flew with his fist in front, going for an attack against Voldor. Yet, Voldor dodged the punch by ducking underneath the arm of Taltus and swiping him with the spear into the ground. Voldor chuckled, raising the spear for the impalement. Seeing the blade, Taltus moved with speed to avoid the spear's coming attack. Turning around, Taltus snatched Voldor by his throat and drug him across the grounds of Eragardia before hitting him with a right punch, knocking him into one of the stables to the horses' displeasure.

"What are you?" Voldor arose with an explosion of elvish magic.

"I'm the titagod." Taltus answered. "The one and only."

Still in the sky, Theus and Taraino fought with their weapons alongside the coming strikes of lightning. Theus went for a swipe with Mithrandir. Yet, Taraino deflected the blow before striking Theus in the chest with a palm strike. Theus stumbled in the air and while Taraino prepared for another strike, Zhor arose from behind him, moving through the dark clouds, smashing his hammer across Taraino's head. The blow knocked Taraino back onto the ground as he vanished from the air in their sights. Zhor gazed upward, seeing Theus.

"You cannot win this battle."

"I must. The two of you have brought nothing but tragedy to my home. After I offered you aid. You both claim there can be only one true god of thunder. Yet, I am a Millennium one."

Zhor let out a blood cry of a roar with his mallet in his hands, surging with lightning. Going in for a strike, Theus swiped him with Mithrandir, knocking Zhor back. stopping his movement in the air, Zhor stared toward Theus with only rage in his eyes. Seeking for another attack, he moved and was knocked from the sky by the returning Taraino. Theus flew toward them both and caused a great lightning storm which struck both thunder gods. Taraino and Zhor fell to the ground in front of the ongoing battle between Taltus and Voldor.

"These are the two gods?" Voldor questioned with disgust.

"They are." Theus said, hovering down from the sky. His eyes beaming with lightning. "Why are you here, Voldor?"

"You didn't think I would use this opportunity to take over your land? Poor Eragardian. Such ignorance like all the others."

Voldor let out a horn and blew, bringing forth more of his dark elf forces from the portal which opened around them. Theus saw the hordes coming through and there were dozens. Taltus stood up from the ground and flew into the sky to get a better look. Portals were opening across the streets of Eragardia.

"What's your plan?" Taltus asked Theus.

"You're outmatched, Millennium God of Thunder!" Voldor laughed.

"You know, I've always known your kind to be of traitors." Theus said. "Such is why I always had a contingency for your sudden arrival."

"Contingency?" Voldor questioned. "Of what nature?"

Theus raised his hand and struck he dark clouds with lightning. From them came forth rain, heavy rain. The rain poured upon them as Vindhler spoke to Theus from the distance. Stating they've arrived. Voldor stood boldly alongside his army. He wondered who Voldor spoke of and from the entrance of the city arrived the army of Wraith soldiers from Shadoheim and with them was their leader cloaked in piercing armored shadow from head to toe. The Wraith Knight. Voldor's dark eyes widen with anger and shock. He screamed as he saw Wraith Knight coming toward them. Both armies went for one another. Voldor rain past Theus and Taltus solely to reach the Wraith Knight.

"What of these two?" Taltus said, watching Zhor and Taraino return to their feet.

"I will deal with them. God to gods."

Theus stood ready as Taltus remained in case of backup. The three gods all prepared for another battle and the ground quaked. Catching them all by surprise as they each hovered above the ground. It cracked open, revealing Hadi. Theus clutched his fists to her arrival and Taltus stared. He remembered.

"I knew I felt the eerie presence of more than one thunder god."

"Why have you come here?!" Theus asked. "Do you wish for another battle?"

"No, Edenson. I came because this is off balance. The realms are shifting because of you three. Only one of you must remain."

"One of us?!" Zhor yelled. "Then it shall be I!"

"Not if I have anything to do about it." Taraino replied. "This day proves that I am indeed the true god of thunder. No matter the circumstance or cost."

Hadi stared at them. Sensing their power. She sighed.

"You two aren't from this realm nor this universe. You originate from a place I do not know."

"What are you saying?" Theus wondered.

"They're valuable. Very valuable. Therefore, I will take them."

The ground arose with dark spiked arms. Their hands snatched the legs of Zhor and Taraino from above and began to drag them into the glowing pit beneath them. The two gods struggled to get free from the hands as Theus, Taltus, and Hadi watched on. Zhor yelled with rage and smashed the arms with his hammer, causing them to let him loose as he rushed for Hadi. Quickly, she raised her right hand and froze Zhor in place before flicking him into the pit. Taraino continued to struggle after seeing Zhor fall into the ground. His eyes turned toward the three.

"This is not the end. I will find a way out and I will take my place as the definitive god of thunder. It is my destiny."

"No." Hadi replied. "It is not."

The arms collectively drug Taraino into the pit and it closed. Sealing shut as if it never opened.

"Where have you sent them?" Theus asked.

"They're being placed in my realm. In a chamber of silence. They will remain there under the end of days. When that time comes, they will be let loose, and they will fight again."

Hadi turned away as she vanished into a portal of her own making. Warning Theus their battle will come another day as she gave a sinister wink to Taltus.

"And is that all?" Taltus asked.

"For this day." Theus answered with a nod.

The two turned their attention toward the ongoing fight of the dark elves and the Shadoheimians. With the elves losing the fight and Voldor taking several strikes from the Wraith Knight, Voldor took the opportunity to escape as he saw Theus and Taltus arriving. Opening a portal, he rallied the remaining elves to make their exit and just as he entered the portal, Theus and Taltus landed on the ground in front of him. They didn't stop him from escaping.

"Next time you come here, it will be the end." Theus proclaimed.

"We shall see." Voldor answered, disappearing into the portal as it shut.

Wraith Knight approached Theus and they shook arms. Theus introduced the Knight to Taltus and they greeted one another as warriors to the common cause. Wraith Knight's armor and design reminded Taltus of Swordman's look. Seeing it was more universal than he originally thought. Theus returned to the palace and saw the Trio and Lady Soya helping the others. Within the throne room Eden and Meredith spoke to each other concerning the foreign gods as Theus entered.

"You've returned." Eden said.

"I did and at the right time."

"Where are the two gods?" Meredith wondered. "Are they still here?"

"No. Hadi came and took them into her realm. She placed them in a trap until the end of days."

Eden nodded hearing the words.

"Very well. Such is good to hear."

Theus and Taltus aided the city with repairing and helping those who were caught in the crossfire of the battles. Seeing his time to return to Earth, Taltus left Eragardia. He greeted Theus before taking his leave.

Meanwhile, as the guards continue to clean up Eragardia, they learned a portion of the prison had collapsed and Noldar had escaped.

ACQUIRE THE OMNIBUSES OF THE DARK TITAN UNIVERSE!

ABOUT THE AUTHOR

Ty'Ron W. C. Robinson II is the author of several works of fiction. Including the *Dark Titan Universe Saga*, *The Haunted City Saga*, EverWar Universe, Symbolum Venatores, Frightened!, Instincts, and others. More information pertaining to the author and stories can be found at darktitanentertainment.com.

Twitter: @TyronRobinsonII

Twitter: @DarkTitan_
Instagram: @darktitanentertainment
Facebook: @DarkTitanEnt
Pinterest: @darktitanentertainment
YouTube: Dark Titan Entertainment

www.ingramcontent.com/pod-product-compliance
Lightning Source LLC
LaVergne TN
LVHW091626070526
838199LV00044B/958